VICIOUS SECRET

Also by Morgan Bridges

Possessing Her
Once You're Mine
Now You're Mine

The Obsidian Order
Vicious Society

Dark & Dirty Vows
A Match Made in Hate
I Thee Lust
To Have & to Hurt

VICIOUS SECRET

MORGAN BRIDGES

Cover design by Dark Imaginarium Design

ISBN: 979-8-3470-2985-3

Published in 2026 by Podium Publishing
www.podiumentertainment.com

If you see the villain and think his red flags look like Six Flags, enjoy the ride.

CONTENT WARNING

Vicious Secret is a dark stalker romance that contains graphic scenes of a sexual nature and explicit violence. It features a morally gray MMC and dubious consent. Additional themes that some reader may find triggering include on-page murder, stalking, dubious consent, knife play, breath play, and mentions of domestic abuse and drug addiction.

VICIOUS SECRET

CHAPTER 1

XAVIER

Three Years Ago . . .

Who is she?

I squint at the grainy black-and-white screen, wanting to see the young woman better. Her brows snap together right before she walks up to my target, Benjamin McKenzie, and pokes him in the chest. Despite the fact that I was sent to watch him, my gaze narrows on her.

"You're not giving up this opportunity for me." She jabs her finger at his sternum one more time with him towering over her. Then the girl plants her hands on her jean-clad hips and glares up at him. Feisty little thing. "This scholarship is too important to throw away. I mean it."

He reaches out to cup her cheek. "I don't know what I'd do if anything happened to you," he whispers. "You're everything to me, Lilah."

Benjamin has a weakness. This girl could get him killed.

If the Obsidian Order ever found out about her . . .

I exhale, and the noise is lost in the stillness of the empty room. Soon this part of his life—and this girl—will be gone and forgotten, similar to the abandoned house I'm in. The dingy, off-white paint is peeling in places, and the glass has cracks throughout, like a spider's web. A death trap.

I've lived in one my entire life, except mine was opulent.

Although the girl rolls her eyes, her face softens. "Nothing's going to happen to me. You're the one who taught me to defend myself. Remember?"

Benjamin shakes his head. "It's not enough. Come with me. I'll find a way to—"

"To what, Ben? To hide me in your dorm room for the next couple of years? Listen, I know you're good with computers and all, but even that's a stretch for you." She pauses and her expression hardens with resolution. "You know I can't leave the littles."

My target goes rigid, the tautness of his muscles visible even through the tiny camera lens. "I know," he whispers.

She pulls away from him with a wry smile and smooths out her faded blue tank top. "If that jerk downstairs tries anything, I'll kick his ass. End of story."

I run my gaze over her body. She's petite with slightly rounded hips, little muscle tone, and barely over five feet in height. If she's a threat, then I'm the fucking Tooth Fairy.

Benjamin grabs her shoulders and lightly shakes her. Her shocked expression quickly morphs into one of wariness, but it's nothing compared to the desperate energy rolling off of him.

"Listen to me," he says. "Frank is stupid, but he's stronger than you."

She jerks from his hold, causing her long hair to sway along her back. "Then I'll be faster."

"Damn it, Delilah!"

His shout is so loud I swear I hear it from across the street, as well as through the speakers of my laptop. He mutters to himself, and I catch him repeating her name. A frown tugs at my mouth.

I hope that's not her real name. If so, Benjamin really should leave her behind.

He rakes a hand through his hair. "Don't be so naive. You know what Frank's going to do to you the second I walk out that door tomorrow morning."

"I won't let it happen." Her nostrils flare with disgust before her gaze narrows. I wish I knew what color her eyes are. "No one's going to hurt me or the girls."

"There's no way you can avoid him for the next three years," Benjamin says. "Don't be stupid."

Her bottom lip trembles, bringing my attention to her lush mouth. She can't be more than fifteen, maybe sixteen, yet she looks like a full-grown woman. It's easy to see why she'd attract attention, unwanted or not.

"Don't talk to me like that," Delilah says, her voice steady, in spite of the heated exchange. "If Frank touches me or Emily or Sandra, I'll kill him."

Benjamin folds his arms. "*I* should kill him. Then I wouldn't have to worry about you guys."

That's what I *would do, but I've been trained for this. You'll learn soon enough, recruit.*

Delilah sighs. "No, Ben. It has to be self-defense, or you'll end up in prison. Now who's being stupid?" She lifts her chin. "I'm not arguing with you anymore. When you're done being pissed at me, come and say goodbye."

My target flinches when she slams the door behind her. I scoff. Whoever this girl is, she has Benjamin by the balls.

I switch to the camera located in Delilah's room. It's the same layout as Benjamin's, with only a bed, a nightstand, and very few personal effects or decorations anywhere.

If you ignore her beauty.

I've grown up around money and women who know how to use it to their advantage. Clothes, cosmetics, and medical enhancements. If it can be bought, I've seen it done. Delilah's attractiveness doesn't faze me.

The fact that she's important to my target is the only reason I allow myself to watch her for a few minutes. She walks over to the bed and sinks onto a mattress covered with a threadbare blanket. Then she grabs a snow globe with a castle inside, running her fingers over the smooth glass.

Her brow furrows as she stares at the object, and she purses her lips. I watch her face, intrigued by how expressive it is. She doesn't try to hide her emotions from showing. Such a liability.

I click the button to shift back to Benjamin's room. When the screen displays no one in the room, I quickly run through the different cameras to locate him. The hallway, stairwell, and the living room show no signs of my target.

My lips thin at his sudden disappearance, but the second my laptop brings up the feed from the kitchen, my pulse kick-starts. Benjamin is standing in the doorway with his hands fisted at his sides. Frank Goldstein, his foster parent, reaches into the refrigerator for a beer and straightens, twisting off the bottle cap and taking a long drink.

"What the hell do you want?" he asks, his words slurred.

Benjamin steps further into the kitchen and over the debris scattered across the uneven linoleum floor. The countertops are littered with empty beer cans and crumpled snack bags, and the cabinet doors hang at an angle, about to fall off. My disgust is nothing more than a passing thought as my target's voice fills my ears. There's a resolute thread to his tone that shoots adrenaline into my blood.

"You know why I'm here," he says.

Frank waves a hand. "Your little girlfriend?" When Benjamin nods, the older man grins. "What about her?"

"Stay away from her and the others."

The middle-aged man snorts. "Or what?"

Benjamin takes a menacing step forward, and I jump to my feet. Although my orders were only to watch the bastard son of the late Harold McKenzie, I'm pretty fucking sure the founding families don't want him to die.

He won't on my watch.

If he dies, I'll have signed my own death warrant.

I pull up my hoodie to obscure my features before I race down the rickety stairwell, out the back door, and across the street toward the house I've been surveilling for the past few days. The soles of my boots pound against the pavement before the noise is muffled by the overgrown grass covering the backyard. Thoughts swirl in my mind with all the possible outcomes of this confrontation and none of them are ideal.

The firearm in my waistband calms my thundering pulse. However, stealth is necessary in this situation. Not that a gunshot would be surprising in this shitty part of the city.

I reach for the knife in my boot, my fingers curving around the handle with a familiarity that's a result of the terrors still haunting me.

Tonight, I'll be someone else's nightmare.

A masculine roar is followed by a crash as I rush up to the back door that leads into the kitchen. Through the window, I scan the shit show that could get me in trouble with the Order—and more importantly, my father.

Frank has Benjamin pinned against the refrigerator. Every time he punches the young man, the bottles inside rattle from the strength of the impact. My target gets in a solid hit, but it's not enough. If I don't intervene, he'll be dead in minutes.

I grip the doorknob just as a streak of blonde fills my gaze. Delilah rushes into the room, her hair whipping out behind her, jade eyes wide and shimmering with rage.

In one fluid motion, she grabs a cutting knife off the counter before sinking it into Frank's back. He throws his head backward and bellows like a wounded bear. The young woman rips out the blade with a grunt and stabs him a second time.

The savage beauty of her stuns me.

My lips part as I suck in a breath, ignoring the shouts of pain from Frank and the warnings Benjamin gives through labored pants. Delilah darts in front of my target and takes up a defensive stance while facing her foster parent. Tiny drops of crimson splatter onto the floor, and another rivulet of blood snakes its way down her raised forearm, painting her skin with violence.

She's fucking magnificent.

"If you touch him, I'll kill you," she says. Her voice is so quiet I can barely make it out, but the fire underneath is scorching. "I mean it, Frank."

Delilah was a woman in the Bible who betrayed the man she was supposed to have loved. This girl, like all the other women I've ever met, should live up to her namesake. Except she doesn't.

I was wrong. She *is* a threat. And not just to Benjamin.

If this is who has my target snared like an animal in a trap waiting to die, then I fully understand. And I envy him. So fucking much.

A surge of want rises in me. It's so sudden and strong, it causes me to stumble back and loosen my grip on the knife. Delilah is an anomaly, a type of woman I didn't know existed. One who's willing to put herself in danger for someone, even if it means she'll die. That deep, unshakeable loyalty . . .

I want that.

I need it.

I *need* her.

I don't give a shit what the girl's name symbolizes. Delilah is mine.

CHAPTER 2

DELILAH

"Sweet mother of fuck."

I lean against the bedroom door with a loud sigh. Ben chuckles at my outburst and then grimaces, clutching his ribs. "Don't make me laugh."

I throw up my arms in exasperation, probably resembling an inflatable tube man. "I'm not trying to be funny." I glare at him. "Seriously? What in the world were you thinking to threaten Frank like that?"

"Me?" My foster brother shoots me an incredulous look. "I'm not the one who stabbed him. You're one to talk."

"That's fair." I give him a gentle shove toward the bed. Once he's lying down, I hand him a bag of frozen mixed vegetables. "Don't give me that look," I say, shoving the bag in his face. "It's not like we have fancy ice packs in this dump."

Ben takes the bag and presses it to his side with a hiss. A frown pulls at my lips, but I'm quick to smooth out my features. If there's one thing my foster brother hates, it's to see me upset.

Considering I just stabbed someone, I'm pretty freaked out. On the positive side, at least I didn't kill Frank. That shitbag better not bleed to death, or I'll be screwed.

"Sit with me, Lilah."

The nickname melts some of the tension still gripping my body. I smile at Ben and plop onto the bed next to him. My movements jostle him a little, and my grimace returns.

"Sorry."

He shakes his head. "I could've died if you hadn't interfered."

"There's no way I would've let that happen." I take his hand in mine and give it a squeeze. "We're family."

His gaze sweeps over me with agonizing slowness. "Right. Family."

A flush works its way up my neck at his intense stare, and I retract my hand to avoid any awkwardness. There shouldn't be any between us. Ben is the one who took me to buy training bras and pads when I was twelve and he was fifteen. He's the person who listened to me cry over a piece-of-shit mother who abandoned me.

But things have changed recently.

Maybe it's because Ben's a legal adult and I'm fifteen, still a kid to him. Or it could be because he's leaving, and now he's pushing me away to avoid missing me. I know I'm going to lose my mind without him around.

The one person who can keep me safe will be gone in the morning. That leaves everything on my shoulders. At least I still have that knife.

"So, now what?" I ask. "Are you done being mad at me?"

He blows out a breath, looking up at the ceiling. "I've never been able to stay mad at you for very long. You know that."

"Yeah, but this is different. Either Frank will get the hint that I'm not messing around with him, or he'll be more pissed off than before. Regardless, I won't leave the girls alone. I need you to understand that."

Ben flicks his gaze to me. "I do understand. I just hate the idea of not being here when you need me."

"You act like we're never going to see each other again." I make a serious face. "Don't make me stab you. I'm pretty good at it."

"Lilah . . ."

"I'm going to get a job and save up for a cell phone, and then we'll text and call all the time. You just watch." I lightly punch him in the shoulder. "Then I'm going to study my ass off to get into that fancy college too. I mean, there has to be a scholarship for people who are smart but poor as fuck, right?"

My foster brother rolls his eyes at me. "How do you think I got in?"

"See?"

"True."

"What's that place called again? South Harbor Institute of Technology?" I grin at him, showing my teeth. "I hope so 'cause the acronym is SHIT."

His lips twitch. "You know that's not the name. It's called South Harbor University."

I hang my head. "Yeah, well, Boston is two hours away, which isn't walkable."

Ben lifts his hand to run his fingers down my cheek.

I go completely still. It's not that he's never touched me before. When he taught me how to throw a punch there was definitely some contact, but that was platonic.

This is . . . intimate.

"Lilah, I'll come see you every chance I get, okay?"

I nod and he drops his hand. "I better go check on the girls," I say. "Are you good? Do you need another ice pack? And by ice pack, I mean frozen corn this time."

He shakes his head with a thin smile. "I'm fine. It's just some bruising. You should see the other guy."

I wink at him. "Right? I hope you sleep okay. If you need anything, let me know."

"Thank you," he says, his voice threaded with emotion. "I mean it."

"Always. You'd do the same for me."

"Always."

After getting to my feet, I head toward the door, keeping my steps even. Nerves skitter along my arms and legs, and it takes everything I have not to run once I'm in the hallway. It's not just because of my need to check on the girls again. There's something heavy in the atmosphere. When you're under a constant threat of danger, you learn to trust your instincts more.

And people less.

The house—that's more of a two-story shack—takes on a life of its own at night. The warped floorboards groan as I make my way down the narrow hallway to the girls' room. I strain to pick up on any unusual sounds that could indicate Frank's intent on revenge, but there's nothing except my light footsteps and the hum of distant traffic.

I grab the doorknob and slowly twist it. Opening the door a crack, I peer inside, my gaze landing on the single twin mattress that takes up most of the tiny room. Emily and Sandra are curled up together like a pair of kittens. Their adorable faces are at ease, despite the monsters lurking in the night.

Specifically, the one downstairs.

Relief at finding them peacefully asleep loosens the tightness in my chest. Neither of them have shared whatever horrors they experienced before coming to live with me in this foster home, but at eleven and nine years old, they carry a worldliness about them that breaks my heart. Even so, they've blossomed under my and Ben's protection and love.

"I'll keep you safe," I whisper, more to myself than them. It's a promise that I've dedicated my life to. In the next three years, I might end up sacrificing it, but I'm okay with the idea of dying for the girls.

I've never had anyone besides Ben willing to do that for me, and I've made my peace with it. Getting lucky enough to have him as my foster brother almost makes all the bad things in my life worth it. He's replaced years of abandonment with a platonic love.

I've given up on the dream of a romantic one.

After picking up a doll bed, one of the girls' few toys, I close the door and head toward my room. The knife that I stabbed Frank with lies on my nightstand. Even in the darkness, I can make out the red stain coating the blade. I wonder if it's had enough time to dry . . .

The sight of it turns my stomach. But not with regret. Never.

I draw in a deep breath and release it slowly before picking up the weapon and wiping it off. There's another cutting knife taped under my bed frame, but it's not as long or as sharp. I brought the other one with me from the previous home I stayed in. No, that's not right. It was a house, not a *home*.

I've never had one of those.

The closest I've gotten was finding Ben and the girls, but I know deep down that's not the true definition. A home is where you feel loved *and* safe.

I creep back toward the stairwell with my items, the hilt of the worn blade fitting comfortably in my palm. My forehead wrinkles with concentration as I carefully count the stairs and place the doll bed on the sixth one from the top, far left when facing the stairwell.

Task complete, I climb back up to the landing and drop to the floor into a sitting position with my back against the wall. I've appointed myself as my found-family's guardian for tonight. And every night.

If Frank comes up to the second floor, he'll regret it.

CHAPTER 3

DELILAH

The seconds crawl by, slowly turning into minutes that become hours. My muscles relax, but not enough for me to fall into a deep sleep. Years of vigilance have sharpened my senses to the point I wonder if I'll ever sleep peacefully again.

I guess I'll rest when I'm dead.

As if conjured by my thoughts, a dark energy permeates the atmosphere like a cold wind, making my skin prickle and my eyes fly open. I shift into a crouch while my heart gallops in my chest, urging me to run with every beat. I grip my knife more tightly instead.

If it's flight or fight, I choose violence.

Cloaked in darkness, the intruder makes their way up the stairs, coming closer with every second. Their movement carries an air of stealth and purpose that's too focused and refined to be Frank. It's not that I can hear or see this person clearly from my position. I can *feel* them.

Their presence is confirmed the instant their shadow slides up the wall and when they step on the stair with the toy. A loud creak breaks the silence like a mirror being struck with a hammer. The noise is my signal to act.

Hesitation could get me killed.

My instincts have me lunging forward with my knife raised. The blade sinks into flesh before my eyes fully take in the figure directly in front of me. A masculine grunt sweeps past my ears as I jerk back my arm, ready to strike again.

The assailant moves with lightning speed. He blocks my attack by grabbing my wrist, the sudden jolt sending a tremor through my body. Before I can regroup, he squeezes my wrist, his fingers digging into my skin with a merciless pressure. The knife falls from my hand and hits the carpet with a thud. It's the clang foretelling my impending death.

The tenor of his voice eclipses all other sound—low, smooth, and tinged with a quiet amusement that confuses me.

"Not bad," he says, jutting his chin at the stab wound in his shoulder, "but not good enough."

My wrist tingles under his punishing grip, but it's nothing compared to the hold he has on my senses. I peer up at him, struggling to make out his features still concealed by the black hood covering his head.

Whoever he is, he's not a squatter or junkie like I first assumed. This man's speech pattern is articulate, full of decorum and education. I'd bet my left tit this guy comes from money. So what in the hell brings him to this side of town?

"Who are you?" I ask.

His response is to shove me backward, sending me crashing into the wall behind me. The impact steals my breath, and I stare at him, our gazes level. He remains on the stairs, and I stay on the landing. He has to be over six feet tall, very intimidating to my five-foot-five self.

I straighten my upper body, keeping my knees bent in preparation to fight. "Who the hell are you?"

"You first, little raptor."

"I'm not a fucking dinosaur."

"No, but you are a clever girl. You put that toy on the stairs so I'd step around it and the wood would creak, letting you know someone was coming. Right?"

I nod while wondering at the asinine turn the conversation has taken. "Listen, if you don't get out of here, I'm going to scream."

"Ah, ah," he says, clicking his tongue in admonishment. "Benjamin is still recovering from getting his ass beaten, so he can't help you. Besides, you wouldn't want to wake up the girls, would you?"

I don't know how this guy knows all of this information, but he can go fuck himself. *Hard.*

"What do you want?" I snap.

Although I can't see his eyes, I can feel the heat of his gaze as it sweeps over me from head to foot, returning to my face. I scrutinize him in return, wishing I could kill him with a single glance.

"What I *want* and what I intend to do are two separate things," he says. The unknown meaning behind his words both piques my curiosity and terrifies me. "All you need to know is that you're safe."

A harsh laugh bursts from me. "Really?" I give him a pointed look. "I don't believe that shit for a second."

He nods. The moonlight streaming through the window glides over the lower half of his face, revealing sculpted lips twisted in a smirk, a nearly straight nose, and a square chin. The youthfulness of his features contrasts heavily with the aura of danger surrounding him. He can't be much older than Ben, yet he commands the room, as if bearing the experience of a man a decade older.

I glance at the knife on the floor, silently calculating the seconds it would take for me to grab it and stab this guy. Again. Only this time, I wouldn't have the element of surprise.

"Don't even think about it," he says.

"I thought I was safe."

"You're safe from the world, but not from me."

Fear streaks through my veins, making my heart beat dangerously fast. I fist my hands at my sides to curb my impulse to reach for the fallen weapon. "What does that even mean?"

"Listen carefully, little raptor." I bristle at the stupid nickname but remain silent when he continues speaking. "Frank won't ever threaten you or anyone else ever again. I promise you, Delilah."

I don't know what shocks me more: the idea of my foster parent no longer being a danger to me, or the fact that this stranger said my name like he *knows* me. My legs threaten to buckle at the renewed adrenaline rush flooding my system. I glare at the man while reining in my body's need for action.

"What do you mean? Is Frank gone? You're not making any sense."

"Aren't I?" He tilts his head. "Let me be clear: I killed him . . . but not before torturing an apology from him on your behalf. Once your name crossed his lips, I removed his tongue for saying it in the first place. Now do you understand?"

The air thickens with malevolence. It seeps into my body, clogging my lungs and making it difficult to breathe. My breaths come out in tiny pants as his words fully penetrate my mind.

The stranger makes his way up the stairs with a lethal grace that I admire, although I'd never admit it. He might be young, but his every move speaks of power and authority. That's as much a part of him as his skin.

I throw out my hands and press my spine against the wall. "Stay back." My high-pitched voice has me mentally cringing at the show of weakness. My warning holds no more power than I do at this moment.

He stops. Stunned, I can only stare helplessly. With him being on the same level, he towers over me, looming like a demon he slowly folds his arms across his chest although proclaiming to be my guardian angel.

"Why?" My whispered question is the only sound in the night. As I wait for his response, I swear my heart is going to burst out of my chest.

"Why?" he repeats softly. "Because *no one* touches what's mine."

Despite this man breaking into the house and admitting to murder, I can't stifle the righteous indignation that surges through my body. I lift my chin in defiance. "I'm not yours."

"Not yet."

I part my lips to say something appropriate to that ridiculous statement, like a "fuck you" or "kiss my ass," but he turns around and descends the steps without another word.

My head spins until I grow dizzy and sit down on the carpet to avoid fainting.

What—and I can't stress this enough—the fuck just happened?

CHAPTER 4

XAVIER

The crisp morning air brushes past my body, tugging at my clothing like a needy girlfriend. My motorcycle hums louder when I twist the throttle. I rush down the freeway going faster than is advised, not giving a fuck. This is one of the few times I'm in complete control of my life.

Too soon, the large gates of my father's mansion come into view, forcing me to slow down. And shift my mind back to reality. The wrought-iron gate slowly swings open, and I ride through, dreading this encounter.

My father summoned me, and I have no choice but to answer if I want to keep breathing. Some of the founding families see their sons as a means to a legacy, a continuation of a powerful dynasty. Edward Donovan only cares about his empire.

Unfortunately, that makes me a soldier in his fucked-up army.

I park my motorcycle in the courtyard and cut the engine. It dies, like I wish my father would.

After removing my helmet and setting it on the seat, I run my fingers through my dark hair and take a deep breath. Fortifying myself.

Speaking with my father is like entering a battlefield; I have to be armed.

The mansion looms, growing more imposing the closer I get. I walk through the front doors, the marble underneath my boots and the grand ceiling overhead familiar. I've walked these halls all my life, but this will never be my home.

I make my way through the hallways, passing the portraits of ancestors dating back to before the Revolutionary War. People who have long since passed but had a hand in creating this country. And the Obsidian Order.

Another army I'm going to be a part of. Like with my father's, I'm being drafted.

In this place, behind enemy lines, my senses are heightened. I can't remember a time when I wasn't aware of my surroundings and the people inside them. If that type of vulnerability ever existed in me, it was erased the moment my father hit me. Or when my mother stood there and watched.

I turn the corner and she stands there, as if conjured by my thoughts. My mother paints an elegant picture, beautiful and stately, like an expensive piece of art only to be admired from afar. Or a statue, hard and cold, unable to show affection.

Or offer protection.

"Xavier," she says with a small incline of her head.

I come to a halt, keeping my expression blank. "Mother."

Her icy blue gaze probes mine before drifting away. I'd suspect it was guilt that keeps her from looking at me for very long if I thought she cared about me in any capacity. But I know better.

"How are you?" she asks, her voice carrying a practiced formality.

"I'm fine."

I don't bother to ask how she's doing. Unlike her, I don't waste my time with pleasantries that mean nothing. There was a time when I would've begged for a kind word from my mother, but her allegiance lies with my father. It always has, and it always will.

However, it's a devotion born from fear and danger, not love and respect. Not the way Delilah is loyal to Benjamin. I'd do fucking *anything* to have her feel that way about me.

My mother delicately clears her throat. "Your father is expecting you."

This statement defines our relationship. If you can even call it that. She maintains an air of detachment like a cloak, draping herself in it to remain emotionally hidden and unscathed.

From my father? Certainly.

From me? Possibly.

"I know," I say.

"Very well."

I give her a curt nod and start walking. No other words need to be said. The opportunity for real conversation died the day she abandoned me.

I reach the espresso-colored doors of my father's study and stop. A quick knock grants me permission to enter, and I step into hell.

Also known as my father's sanctum.

Closing the doors behind me, I fully enter the room. The grandeur of this place rivals a king's court. The air is thick with the scent of aged leather, polished wood, and cigars. My father sits behind a massive oak desk, surrounded by shelves filled with books.

"Xavier." He sets down the papers in his hands and flicks his gaze to me. "I trust that you have something to report about the McKenzie boy?"

Benjamin and I are both eighteen, but this is how my father views me—as a child to be controlled without rebellion.

"He left for South Harbor this morning and should be there by now."

My father studies me for a moment, his gray eyes scrutinizing. We share the same eye color, but there's also a coldness, a hardness in his that we both possess. "Getting McKenzie there is only half the battle," he says. "Keeping him there is going to be more of a problem."

I remain silent. Every sentence, every word is a strategic move in a game of chess I've been forced to play. One wrong choice leads to more than a lost pawn.

"Does he have anything we can use to persuade him to fall in line?" he asks.

Delilah.

Her face appears in my mind, her green eyes sparkling with emotion and her lips tilted in a smile. For an instant, I forget myself and my surroundings, and the threat directly in front of me.

The very thought of her ruins me.

My chest tightens, and I steel my facial expression, keeping it impassive. I force myself to erase all memory of Delilah in this moment with practiced mental discipline learned from years of self-preservation. Anything good in my life is considered a threat to my father. And he'll eliminate it.

Or worse, force me to do so.

"Keeping him in line won't be a problem," I say, choosing my words with care. "He has nothing holding him back."

"So no girlfriend?"

I don't know if they're together, but it doesn't matter. They won't stay that way. I may not be able to kill Benjamin to keep him from Delilah. However, there are other ways to accomplish that.

As far as any other man . . . I have no restrictions.

When my father forced me to learn various forms of self-defense along with fighting techniques, I'm certain he didn't think I'd use them for a girl. To be fair, neither did I. Delilah is the one thing in my life I didn't see coming.

But I can't unsee her.

And I don't want to.

"After having watched him for several days, I didn't see any evidence of a relationship," I say.

"Hmm." My father strokes his chin in thought. "It doesn't matter. There are other ways to keep people in line. Stay close to him and figure out what his weaknesses are and how to exploit them. Obtaining leverage on the McKenzie heir is your sole purpose now."

I nod. "I understand."

"I hope so."

"Anything else?" I ask, ignoring the insult. "I have to be on campus for the pledging ceremony."

My father leans back in his chair. "That's just for show. The real initiation will begin soon, *recruit*."

I'm no longer talking to Edward Donovan. Before me sits one of the three council members of the Obsidian Order. A guild of assassins.

"The Order."

"The Order," he repeats with emphasis. "We're sworn to secrecy, but I have prepared you for this moment your entire life."

His words echo with a history of family traditions, a legacy built on manipulation, violence, and power. I stare at the man I closely resemble, unable to escape my destiny any more than I can change my DNA. My birth was for this very purpose: to serve a secret society that I know almost nothing about but must dedicate my life to.

Until death.

More binding than a marriage, and more demanding as well.

His gaze sharpens, the gray like honed steel. "*Don't* embarrass me, son."

I give him a curt nod. The gravity of an unknown situation, weighed down with expectations, wraps around my neck like a noose. The impending danger causes it to tighten, as does my father's silent warning.

"You're dismissed," he says. "But I'll be watching, Xavier. They all will."

Ten founding families. Hundreds of years of history. Thousands of members that have gone before me.

And one girl who makes my life worth living.

CHAPTER 5

XAVIER

A few weeks later . . .
Freshman Year at South Harbor University

Mors solum initium.

Death is only the beginning.

The ancient words resonate in my mind, in both languages. They dig into my psyche like an ax to wood, slowly chipping away at my calm demeanor. I knew this day would come, but it won't be my last on this earth.

It could be for a weaker man.

Someone rips off the hood covering my head, leaving me to blink away the darkness. My vision is slow to adjust, but my instincts are fired up, ready to push me into action. To kill.

I'd bet my inheritance that's why the league of assassins brought me here.

I'm quick to scan my surroundings, taking note of the others. My competitors. The men who will either be my brothers-in-arms or the ones who will attack me.

The setting for our initiation is a castle dungeon, a structure that's probably older than the Obsidian Order itself. The air is thick with the scents of dirt, stone, and fear. A flickering torch along the wall provides light for us to see, but the space is still dark enough to create an ominous atmosphere.

The cold, unforgiving floor underneath me slowly drains my body's warmth, just as the chains around my wrists and ankles clinking together siphon my patience. The sensation of being bound, of being another's prisoner, has memories clawing my mind, drawing metaphorical blood.

I'm more than ready to draw *actual* blood, if only to repress the dark images trying to emerge.

I run my gaze over the twelve other men sharing my predicament. All of them are like me, sons from one of the ten founding families. All of us were born for this purpose.

Except one.

The newcomer's brow is furrowed with the standard "what the fuck" expression. He doesn't bother to hide his shock or his frustration at being shackled. But he should. Giving anyone insight into your thoughts puts you at a disadvantage.

He'll learn soon enough . . . or he'll die.

A man stands in the middle of the room with his arms crossed, a pile of black hoods resting at his feet. If Mark Barnum could get away with it, he'd have a pile of corpses next to him instead. I don't know anyone more ruthless than him, someone willing to do whatever it takes to survive.

Except me.

"Listen up, recruits." Mark's voice rings out, instantly silencing the mutterings of those around him. I summon my inner fortitude, the one that has kept me alive through a lifetime of torture. Both physical and mental. There's nothing he can say that I can't handle.

Mark grins. "You assholes aren't getting out of here until someone dies."

This immediately goes from being a dungeon to an arena. Blood will be spilled. It just won't be mine.

From the corner of my eye, I watch the newcomer's reaction. The young man runs a hand through his blonde hair, rattling his chains, and bringing everyone's attention to him. Poor bastard just made himself a target.

The rest of us have been trained for this. Bred for this. Joining the Obsidian Order as an elite assassin is akin to serving our family. It's an honor.

One that's not allowed to be refused.

"To make things *interesting*," Mark says, drawing out the word, "I've provided an incentive." He removes three knives from the back pocket of his jeans and places them by his feet. "*Mors solum initium*, motherfuckers."

The second he walks away and locks the cell door behind him, there's a flurry of activity as everyone rushes to grab one of the weapons. The sound of chains colliding is only superseded by the shouts of profanity.

I keep my focus on the clusterfuck in the middle of the floor while slowly getting to my feet. Adrenaline unfurls inside me, familiar and potent, sweeping through my limbs and preparing me for battle.

I don't need a blade to kill someone.

A shout of pain echoes in the space as Eric Gage slashes someone with his newly acquired weapon.

Ryan Emerson clutches his stomach, pain etched into his features, a red stain creeping along the expensive material of his shirt. The metallic scent of blood mixes with the smell of dirt as it floats in the air.

"Is that all you've got, Eric?" Ryan spits on the ground. "Looks like you've spent more time getting high than learning to fight. It's fucked with your brain cells, and you didn't have many to start with."

"I'll show you fucked up." Eric smirks, but the flash of anger in his eyes undermines his taunt. "And when I'm done, I'll show your girlfriend too."

Eric slashes at Ryan in a downward arc, but he dodges the attack easily, using Eric's momentum to plant a heel behind his knee. Eric falters. He staggers back, nearly avoiding Ryan's follow-up strike. Even wounded, the heir to the Emerson fortune is a formidable challenger.

From the far end of the cell, I track their movements, as well as those around me. The attention of everyone present is centered on the fight. I'm sure most of them hope Ryan will take Eric's life and save them the risk of dying or the responsibility of having to kill someone.

At least for today.

The time will come for all of them.

When being inducted into an assassin's guild, murder is par for the course. Our fathers and uncles have all undergone this rite of passage, but with it being a secret society, its operations must remain hidden. That didn't stop my father from preparing me every day of my life. This isn't my first time in a cell.

Or being ordered to kill someone.

Out of everyone, Eric has always been the most volatile. Every child born to the founding families attended the same prestigious schools and elite social events, so his behavior isn't shocking to me. In fact, there are few things in my life that have ever surprised me.

The most memorable one is a girl with green eyes, honey-colored hair, and a knife in her hand. The last time someone pulled a weapon on me, it was her. I smile briefly at the image.

I'm quick to dismiss thoughts of Delilah. It's not an easy task, but with the threat of death a few feet away, my brain complies. For once. She's been on my mind since the moment I first saw her.

Eric rights himself, chest heaving and his blonde hair falling across his forehead. Even from across the room, I'm able to pinpoint the exact moment he calculates the odds of winning this fight with Ryan. There's an infinitesimal widening of his eyes that gives him away.

"At least I *have* a warm pussy waiting for me," Ryan says with a grin. He laughs harshly, though sweat dots his forehead and darkens the roots of his hair. "The only thing waiting for you is a syringe. Hard to fuck, but not impossible I guess."

Hushed laughter floats into the air, immediately stifled by coughs filled with unease.

A flush crawls up the sides of Eric's neck, his rage palpable. For a second, my mask of indifference slips at the idea of Eric being stupid enough to continue the fight with Ryan when he's clearly outmatched. However, Eric's arrogance finally comes to terms with what his instincts know to be true: He won't win.

"Fuck off," he snarls. "My father is one of three council members, and I'll take his place someday. My drug empire brings in more money and power than yours can ever dream of. You'll need that girlfriend of yours to suck your dick hard enough to make you forget that reality."

Eric whirls around, chains clinking, his hungry gaze scanning the room for another opponent. Correction—a victim.

My muscles tighten the second his attention lands on the newcomer, but I maintain my expression of boredom. No one knows about my orders, not even my target.

Benjamin McKenzie remains hunched in the corner, his eyes darting back and forth until they settle on Eric. Alarm flickers over his countenance and he takes up a defensive stance, balling his fists. Despite his ability to fight, it won't be enough. Even if he had one of the knives, his chances would be slim.

Eric's mouth tilts in a brutal smile as he makes his way toward the newcomer. "Where the fuck did you come from, pretty boy?" He stops a few feet from Benjamin, his gaze scrutinizing and critical. "You're not one of us, so how'd you get here?"

Benjamin remains silent. With the seconds ticking away, and his death imminent without my interference, I shift my gaze to Declan Kent. The heir to the medical dynasty catches my eye and lifts a brow in question. I jerk my chin at the knife in his hand.

It's a lot to ask for in this situation. If there was ever a time to test the trust between Declan and me, it's now. The only other person who carries a weapon is Simon Paine, and my chances of getting it from him without sustaining an injury are dicey at best.

Declan gives me a pointed look, and I return it, an understanding passing between us. I've never considered him a friend, but after today, I will. And I'll owe him.

He hands me the knife, his forehead wrinkled with resignation. I take it from him and hold the weapon by the tip of the blade. The weight of it is lighter than I'm used to wielding, and I adjust my grip accordingly.

"Any last words?" Eric lifts his arm, the firelight from the torch reflecting off the steel, gleaming menacingly. At Benjamin's continued silence, Eric rolls his eyes. "You can refuse to talk, but you won't be able to stop yourself from screaming."

Desperation and anticipation light up Benjamin's gaze and

amplify the tension lining his shoulders. And his inexperience. Eric, however, moves with a fluidity that speaks of training cultivated from years of practice. Some of it forced, but most of it for the pleasure of causing another's suffering.

He tosses the knife from one hand to the other, toying with his opponent. "This'll be fun."

Eric feints left and the newcomer scrambles back, further putting himself at a disadvantage with no room to escape.

I move before Eric does. With sharp precision and deadly force, I hurl the blade straight at Eric's exposed side. It strikes home with a gratifying impact, piercing flesh and tendon.

A scream fills the dungeon, but it's not Benjamin's.

Eric removes the blade with a low grunt and whirls in my direction, his knives carving through the air while he searches for his attacker. The copper scent of fresh blood blooms. His fury seeps from his body quicker than his blood.

"What the fuck, X?"

I shrug. "Just trying to keep things interesting."

In my peripheral vision, I catch Benjamin studying me, his hands shaking. My fighter's instincts chafe at having limited mobility because of the chains on my wrists. Fighting Eric without any weapons is going to be a challenge, but the McKenzie heir must live.

Eric starts walking in my direction, and Declan takes a step closer to me. The show of solidarity gives Eric pause. His surprise at Declan's loyalty is obliterated when Simon launches himself at Eric.

From a strategic perspective, I understand Simon's choice. Eric has no allies, and with him being wounded, he's vulnerable. But that doesn't mean he's weak.

Eric twists away from Simon's charge with a viper's swiftness and deflects the blow by drawing his blade across his body. The screech of steel has me clenching my teeth. The fighters are oblivious, the grating sound falling on deaf ears.

Circling his opponent, Simon grins maniacally as some of the spectators begin to toss out insults to both parties, encouraging the escalation of violence. Eric swipes at Simon's ribs, but the strike doesn't find its mark.

They trade attacks, each one getting more violent. And desperate. Simon's physical power contrasts with Eric's skill. Which one is more valuable?

Chests heaving from exertion, they clash again and again in a flurry of jabs and slashes until more blood is spilled. Simon drives Eric back step by step with sheer force, overwhelming his technical skill set. Their blades scrape violently as each tries to deliver a killing blow.

The room—and its occupants—hold their breath. Eric's determination to live isn't to be underestimated, but the chances of him outlasting his attacker's onslaught is nil.

With an enraged bellow, Simon throws his entire weight behind a powerful strike. Eric sidesteps at the last second and brings one of his knives upward in a vicious scything motion.

Simon gasps, the wet sound cut short as a red line appears on his throat like a red smile across his skin. Blood pours from the wound and lands onto the ground.

Right before his body does.

Declan dismisses him with a shrug, and I do the same. Death is a part of this life.

Benjamin stands with a watchful eye, having never moved to help or hinder Simon's death. Or Eric's. Throughout the fight, there was a ceaseless vigilance in the set of Benjamin's jaw and the stiffening of his spine. He'll need more of that.

I look from Simon's body and over to his cousin, Alaric Paine. "Looks like you just got promoted," I say.

Then there were twelve recruits.

—

Delilah: Dude, this new foster home is amazing! Emily and Sandra have their own rooms! Can you believe it? Sandra still crawls into Emily's bed every night. I think it makes the girls feel secure and I don't blame them. This is a whole new environment with new schools and everything.

Ben: That's great. I'll come down after my first exam to check things out.

Delilah: Can't wait to see you! How's that fancy college of yours? Everything you dreamed of?

Ben: Haha yeah.

Delilah: Cool. Well, I've got to run. Xoxo

Ben: Oxox

Delilah: Pigpig

Ben: You're so weird.

Delilah: Yup ☺

CHAPTER 6

XAVIER

Sophomore Year

The acrid smell of herbs and chemicals wafts under my nose as I walk into the classroom. Behind me are the other recruits, all of us a year older, a year deeper into the clutches of the Order.

The fluorescent lights above cast sinister shadows on the array of equipment set up on the lab tables that line the sides of the room. Traditional wooden desks take up the center and the majority of the space.

I slide into one in the back row. Declan sits next to me, followed by Benjamin on my right. Being flanked by the two of them is a little surprising, but not unwelcome. Although I prefer to work alone, allies are good to have in a den of vipers.

The professor watches all the students from behind his desk, facing us. Ames, ruler of the media empire, is renowned for his ruthlessness but also his brilliance. If you want to learn how to kill someone with the greatest stealth, leaving no trace behind, he's the one to go to.

"Hurry the fuck up and sit your asses down," he snaps. "You have a lot to learn, and my job is to make sure you don't kill yourselves in the process."

Though slight in build, Ames makes up for it in presence. It looms from where he stands, like an aura composed of darkness. From his charcoal three-piece suit—clearly custom fit—to the polished oxford shoes on his feet, this man screams wealth. Along with Ames's obvious refinement is his sharp gaze that pierces deeper than any blade, digging past pretenses to the vulnerability underneath.

Long story short: He's not to be fucked with.

Even his silence feels weaponized, similar to his words. "There are three things in life that can get you killed. What are they?"

Declan folds his arms. "Poison."

"Right." Ames nods. "Now, someone give me an answer that's not obvious."

"Power," Eric calls out. "Not mine, but someone else's."

"Wrong p-word," Ames says. "They are poison, pistols, and pussy."

Adam Shipley, heir to the real-estate empire, smirks. "Then I'll die happy."

"Get the fuck out." Ames tilts his head when the student remains still. "Are you deaf and stupid?"

"Come on, Professor," Adam says. "It was just a joke."

Ames walks from behind his desk and over to the door. After jerking it open, he gestures out to the hallway. "Don't come back until you're ready to listen without some smart-ass remark. This class is life or death, so the right attitude is a prerequisite."

Adam mumbles to himself as he makes his way out of the classroom with all our stares following him. Ames slams the door shut and resumes his place at the front of the room, leaning against his desk with his arms folded.

This man is used to commanding fear and respect. We have no choice but to give it to him if we want to gain the crucial but lethal knowledge locked behind his calculating eyes. After that, he won't hold any power over me.

Ames clears his throat. "If I'm to keep your young, ignorant asses alive, I need you to learn that what I say is to be taken seriously. Pussy has led to more deaths than you'll ever know. Women are the enemy just as much as anyone outside of the Order."

He begins to walk around the room, down the aisles, with his hands behind his back. "Imagine you just fucked the most beautiful woman to exist. She sucked your dick so well that you almost nutted on her face. Instead, by some miracle, you busted a nut inside her tight, warm pussy. So, you're lying there, limp and exhausted, and she whispers a single question. You know better than to answer, but you do because your guard is down."

He slams his fist on Eric's desk, making him flinch. I school my features to hide my amusement. Ames goes back to walking.

"That bitch will tell your secret because there's *always* someone willing to pay for classified information. And that divulgence will get you strung up by your balls," he says. "The Order doesn't care if you marry her or if you just like to fuck her. Secrets are meant to be kept secret."

He pauses, his gaze taking on a distant look. "Love is a poison of the heart. Remember that, and maybe you'll survive."

—

Delilah: Hey, where have you been? I haven't heard from you much these past weeks.

Ben: Yeah, the exams are brutal. Everything okay with you and the littles?

Delilah: Emily and Sandra have grown so much. I think they'll reach my height soon. When you come visit, you'll see for yourself.

Ben: I might not be able to come home for Christmas.

Delilah: What?!

Ben: Things at school are a lot. I just can't right now.

Delilah: Spring break then? That's a long time. ☹

Ben: I know. Tell me how you're doing.

Delilah: Fine.

Ben: Don't be like that. Come on, Lilah.

Delilah: I think something's wrong with me.

Ben: I've always known that. 😉

Delilah: No, I'm serious.

Ben: What do you mean?

Delilah: Well, I kissed this guy at school and things were going great, but now they're not.

Ben: I don't know if I want to hear this.

Delilah: I know all about the girls you slept with in high school, so don't be a hypocrite. Anyway, I thought this guy was going to ask me out, and now he won't even look at me. No, that's not true. He does, but it's like I'm the ugliest, most scary thing he's ever seen.

Ben: You're crazy.

Delilah: True, but that's why you love me. What am I supposed to do?

Ben: Did you have sex with him?

Delilah: No, but I thought about it. Good thing I didn't.

Ben: Guys are assholes. Save your virginity for someone who deserves it.

Delilah: It's not a big deal.

Ben: Value yourself enough to think it is. Don't let your biological mother giving you up be the lens in which you view your self-worth.

Delilah: Okay, Dr. Phil. Calm down.

Ben: I'm serious. You deserve someone who will respect you. Not just use your body.

Delilah: At this point, I'll die a virgin.

Ben: Don't be dramatic.

Delilah: Maybe I'll be a theater major when I go to your fancy college.

Ben: If that makes you happy.

Delilah: I'm just kidding. You know I want to be a psych major. Anyway, are you sure there's nothing wrong with me?

Ben: You're perfect.

Delilah: You're ridiculous. But thank you. Xoxo

Ben: Oxox

Delilah: Cowcow

Ben: Lol

CHAPTER 7

XAVIER

Junior Year

"The rules for this exercise are simple," the combat instructor says, his eyes gleaming with the promise of upcoming violence. "Fight until one of you taps out or loses consciousness. Injuries are expected, but don't cause your opponent permanent damage. Other than that, there are no restrictions. Donovan and Gage, you're up first."

I walk over to the mats in the center of the training facility and fold my arms, maintaining my bored expression. Eric, on the other hand, cranes his neck from side to side and stretches his arms above his head. I understand that we're primal at our core, ready to inflict pain at a moment's notice, but his show of prowess is unnecessary.

I'm going to beat the fuck out of him.

Eric sizes me up with a grin, his teeth bared, covering his face in a sadistic veil. It's not a secret that he looks for every opportunity to fight me since I threw that knife at him. As recruits of the Obsidian Order, we are under strict rules not to harm one another unless given permission. If it weren't for that, he would've already tried to kill me.

Tried being the operative word.

"Begin!"

Eric launches himself at me before the final syllable leaves the instructor's mouth. I use a hip toss to throw him onto the mats.

He hits the floor with a thud. The other recruits begin to mutter amongst themselves, and the sound of their whispers has Eric's eyes glittering with malice.

He's quick to recover, getting to his feet in the blink of an eye. I reluctantly admire his speed. That, along with his other skills, have only improved since our training began two years ago.

But so have mine.

His embarrassment at having been tossed on his ass has the sides of his neck reddening. I wait for him to charge again. It doesn't take long.

I catch him with a brutal hit to the forehead, my elbow splitting the skin above his eyebrow. Blood drips down his face. From my periphery, I catch the instructor nodding in approval. Too bad I don't need it.

Eric may not be the most intelligent guy in the room, but he doesn't lack tenacity. Again, he comes after me. We trade blows back and forth, our grunts and curses drowning out the jeering coming from our peers.

I sweep my leg out and knock him off his feet. Taking advantage of his position, I lunge at him, throwing all my weight onto his frame. We are both over six feet tall, our bodies toned with muscle from our unrelenting training. Subduing him won't be easy.

Eric thrashes wildly, his adrenaline and fury getting the best of him. Without his ability to think rationally, he puts himself right into my hands. I headbutt him directly on the cut already bleeding.

Blood gushes from his wound as he groans with pain. The wet, sticky texture of his blood coats my skin, but I ignore it in favor of ending this altercation. Pressing my forearm against his throat and keeping it there takes every ounce of energy I possess.

Eric's fist connects with my jaw. My head snaps back, but I maintain the pressure on his neck, straining to remain in control of the fight. His wild movements lessen in intensity until he's no longer moving.

"Release him, Donovan!" the instructor barks.

I retract my arm and get to my feet. The blow to my face has me blinking to correct my blurry vision. Damn, that fucker hit me hard. Only now am I feeling the effects of the strike.

After using the bottom of my black T-shirt to wipe away the blood on my face, I head over to the group of recruits. Declan is there with his brow arched in question. I nod, letting him know I'm good.

"Next time, make sure you don't get punched in the face," Benjamin says.

"Next time, shut the fuck up."

He grins at me, and I return it with a smirk.

The instructor walks up to Eric's body and kicks him in the leg. "Wake up, asshole."

Eric groans as consciousness returns. He squints before rolling onto his hands and knees. Once on his feet, he scans the room until he locates me. I meet his stare head-on with cool indifference.

His nostrils flare, eyes blazing with something beyond rage. He narrows his gaze until it's little more than slits. The look promises retribution.

I break eye contact by turning my head, a clear dismissal. Of his threats. And of him.

Eric Gage can go fuck himself. I have more important things to think about.

Viridian eyes that invade my dreams and tease me relentlessly come to mind. My obsession over Delilah didn't end the night she stabbed me. In fact, it's only gotten worse. Professor Ames is right: Emotion is a poison of the heart.

When it comes to Delilah, I'm terminal.

For the last two years, I've been watching over my girl. And keeping anyone else from having her. It hasn't been easy. Sneaking away to be near her without my father's suspicions following me is hard enough, but keeping other men from wanting her? Nearly impossible.

If Delilah thinks she's going to have a boyfriend, much less give him her virginity, she's got another fucking thing coming.

Her kiss is mine to taste.

Her body is mine to touch.

Her innocence is mine to own.

The instructor draws my attention by clapping sharply. "Donovan gave a textbook demonstration of MMA techniques combined with strength training. The rest of you losers should take notes." He shifts his focus to Eric. "Gage, go and get cleaned up. You're bleeding all over my floor."

"Sure thing," Eric says, spitting on the mats.

The other recruits part to let him pass. Eric strides through the group, shouldering a few of them before leaving the room. Good fucking riddance.

The instructor points to Benjamin and John Felton, heir to the finance and banking empire. The newcomer—who's not so new anymore—takes his spot on the mats with his knees bent and arms resting lightly by his sides.

At least this time I don't have to worry about him getting killed.

CHAPTER 8

DELILAH

Delilah: Can we FaceTime? The girls really want to see you since it's been a long time (hint hint)

Ben: I'm really busy studying.

Delilah: Come on! You never visit anymore, and you hardly call. I can handle you ignoring me, but the girls don't understand. They still need their older brother. I know I do. Gloria is nice and all, but it's not the same.

Ben: Give me a second.

I sink onto my bed and stare at the cell phone with my heart thrashing in my chest. Maybe I don't fully understand what it takes to be an honor student at South Harbor University, but Ben makes it seem like a black hole that sucks you in and kills your social life. If I have to make excuses to the girls on his behalf one more time, I think I'm going to go crazy.

Ben better call. That's all I'm saying.

My cell phone rings, and I immediately answer, setting it on a stand. Surrounded by shelves of books in a library, my foster brother comes into view.

Same blonde hair and blue eyes, but his smile isn't as light and carefree. There's also a tightness around his jaw that wasn't there before.

Along with a fist-sized bruise.

"Who's the fucking cockwaffle that hit you?!" My voice isn't exactly a screech, but it's close. I take a deep breath and try to speak more calmly. "I hope you kicked his ass."

Ben shakes his head with a small smile. "Hello to you too, Delilah. Some preppy asshole thinking we had a problem. And now we don't. How are you?"

"Currently, I'm pissed that you're hurt. I can't believe someone would do that. I thought those people had class."

"Money doesn't change what's inside a person. If anything, it exposes who they are. Why don't you tell me how you're doing?"

I shrug. "Same old, same old."

"In my experience, no news is good news."

"True. Things are calm here, which is wonderful." I pause, biting my lip while trying to gather my words. "The girls are going to be really sad if you don't come for the holidays again."

"I'll do my best, but I can't make any promises. My schedule is . . . uncertain right now."

I scrunch my forehead in confusion. "That doesn't make any sense. You know what classes you have and when."

"That's not what I mean. I don't know what'll be expected of me and how much time it'll take."

"Okay," I say, drawing out the word. "If you say so."

"Just drop it, all right?"

I fold my arms tightly, trying to ignore the hurt seeping into my chest. "Fine."

Ben sighs and rakes his fingers through his hair. The lights above him catch and reflect something shiny on the screen. I squint and get closer to my phone.

"What's that?" I ask.

"Huh?" He drops his arm, holding his hand in front of his face. "Oh, this is nothing."

"Nothing? That looks like a gold ring. Unless you're slowly turning into a rapper, I need to know where that bling came from."

Ben's lips twitch. "A rapper?"

"We're from the rough neighborhood. For all I know, you could be the next Eminem. Show it to me."

He pauses. It's slight, but in our relationship, his hesitation is like a bullhorn. I blink at the screen in disbelief.

"It's not a big deal." He lifts his hand, positioning the ring in the center of the screen. "See?"

I run my gaze over the golden object, my eyes widening. On the ring's oval face is a raised anchor with an M engraved above it. The arms of the anchor extend outward, completely surrounded by ornate filigree to add to the overall antique look. Not to mention the diamonds lining the entire thing.

"Are those real?" I ask.

Ben drops his hand and nods.

"And what is the 'M' for? Your last name is Johnson." I roll my eyes. "Oh, duh. It's for a fraternity, isn't it?"

His gaze darts to the side before meeting mine. "Yeah."

"Have you been hiding this for years?" My voice rises, along with my sense of betrayal. "Why didn't you want to tell me? I know we used to make fun of preppy people like that, but let's face it, we wished we were them. You're family, and I'd never judge you."

"I know. It's just that this group is intense. And like you said, we used to make fun of rich, privileged kids who wiped their asses with hundred-dollar bills. But when you hang out with them . . . I don't know. It's different."

I wave my hand in dismissal. "As long as you don't become a prick, I don't care what fraternity you're in. Hell, I might join a sorority when I go to college."

"Are you still thinking of coming here?"

"Of course." I narrow my gaze in suspicion. "Why wouldn't I?"

He shakes his head. "I just don't want you to get your hopes up. That's all."

"I'm not going to be valedictorian, but I will graduate with honors, Ben. I'm going to get into South Harbor. End of story."

"Okay, okay. Forget I said anything. Where are the girls? I need to go soon, and I don't want to miss seeing them."

I sigh. "Right. Before I go downstairs and get them, I want you to promise me something."

"What?"

"Don't let that fancy-schmancy college change you too much, okay? I want my Ben to still be there when you graduate."

He stares off into the distance, his gaze becoming unfocused. "Change isn't something we can stop, Lilah. We age, grow, learn, achieve. These experiences mold us, whether we want them to or not." He clears his throat and looks at me with a sad smile. "I'll always care about you. That will never change."

"Right back at you. Besides, everything will be great when we're together again. Only one more year."

"You're growing up faster than I can handle."

"You just wait until I'm a legal adult."

He shakes his head. "That's what I'm afraid of."

CHAPTER 9

XAVIER

Senior Year
The Present

"I have a favor to ask you," Benjamin says without looking at me.

He lowers his voice to barely above a whisper despite it being just the two of us in the room. When he flicks his gaze to me, there's something deep and intense in his eyes.

Something that can only be triggered by a girl.

"It's personal."

I shove him with a laugh, attempting to deflect. "No, you can't suck my dick. I thought I made that clear freshman year when I saved your ass in the dungeon."

His mouth thins. "I'm serious, X. This is important."

"I know." My stomach clenches with foreboding. "Something's been up with you for a while now."

Benjamin walks over to the window and folds his arms over his chest. "I don't know if I should ask you this, but I don't know who else I can trust."

He falls silent. I leave him to his internal debate. Benjamin will say what's on his mind if he's given a moment to think about how to say it correctly. The problem is that I don't want to fucking hear it.

With a quiet exhale, I drop into a chair and cross my ankle over my thigh. And wait. I run my gaze over the space, taking in the details to soothe my impatience.

The castle that houses the fraternity's members is a clash of present and ancient times. Sconces have been replaced with light fixtures and wiring. The towering ceiling, arched window, and hand-carved crown molding coexist with the modern upgrades found in the furniture and the en suite bathroom, but the space maintains its air of grandeur.

We, along with those that came before us, are the elite, and we live like it.

Above the massive fireplace is the crest of the Obsidian Order. At the center is a crow with its wings outstretched in mid-flight, symbolizing the guild's intelligence, its air of mystery, and—of course—its connection with death. Any recruit still standing at the end of the Trials will be called a crow instead of a recruit.

We're down to nine.

Finally, Benjamin takes a deep breath, as if gathering his courage. I force myself to remain still, although the subject is of great interest to me. Even after all these years together, Benjamin has never mentioned Delilah, but I've been anticipating this conversation for a while.

"There's a girl who's coming to the university this year," he says. "Delilah Scott."

I shrug, my nonchalance completely at odds with the way my blood heats at merely hearing her name. "And?"

"I've been *summoned*."

Benjamin takes up the chair across from me, resting his forearms on the table while clasping his hands. He stares at his fingers as though imagining blood on them. Considering he's going to kill someone soon, it's a distinct possibility.

"Your first time?" I ask.

He drops his gaze and nods. "Yeah. What about you?"

"I've been summoned several times."

"Damn."

"It's part of the oath we took." I tilt my head. "Speaking of, which part of 'celibacy for a year' did you not understand?"

Benjamin squeezes his hands until his skin blanches. "My relationship with her isn't like that."

"But you want it to be." It's a statement, not a question.

"I'm not going to break my oath."

"Good." I raise a brow. "The Order puts more importance on our final year than any other. It's the first time we're sent on missions and the reason we have to be celibate all senior year. They don't want us thinking with our dicks and fucking things up. If you know that, then why are you mentioning this girl?"

Benjamin jerks up his head and his gaze shoots to mine. "She's important. More than anything else in my life."

"Dangerous words." The very ones I've spoken to myself in the dark hours when it's just me and my thoughts of Delilah. "No one is worth the risk."

"She is."

I couldn't agree more.

"Why?" I ask.

"She's family."

"Your lineage can be traced back to the Mayflower, and she isn't part of it."

Benjamin shakes his head. "We're not related by blood, but she's . . ."

"Like a sister?"

He slowly nods, but his hesitation speaks of things he wants to deny. Or keep secret. It doesn't matter. She'll never be his.

I'll kill him first.

"Why are you telling me about her now?" I ask.

"You know every summons is different. I have no idea how long I'll be gone. It will be easier for me to concentrate if I know you're watching over her."

I've been watching over her for three fucking years. In a few days, she'll be the closest she's ever been, and I'll struggle to maintain my distance more than ever.

"Why me?" I ask.

"You're the only one I trust to look after Delilah while I'm gone."

The air becomes charged with unspoken thoughts. Her name holds a significance that neither of us is willing to admit out loud. Although a delicate thread, this woman binds us together.

"Will you help me?" he asks. His eyes reflect a mixture of desperation and pleading. "I have to know before I leave."

"Yeah, sure."

Benjamin exhales and runs his fingers through his hair. "Thank you, X. This means more than you know."

Yes, yes it does. It means I'll be around her, breathing in her scent and watching her from the shadows, doing my best not to touch her despite being willing to kill for the chance.

"Do you have a picture of her?" I ask, my lips lifting into a smirk. "It might help."

Benjamin releases a nervous laugh and retrieves his cell phone. After a few seconds, he hands me the object. I take it, and my breathing stops. My objective to display casual indifference is shattered by the image of her.

Delilah's beauty is captured in a single frame, a brief second in time that will haunt me for eternity. The gentle curve of her smile. The way her green eyes glitter with happiness. The softness of her skin taunting me.

I swear I'm going to lose my fucking mind over a group of pixels.

"Pretty, isn't she?" Benjamin remarks without dampening the pride and affection in his voice.

I scoff. "She's fucking gorgeous." It takes a huge amount of effort to tear my gaze away from the screen and hand the phone back to him. "But you knew that'd be my reaction when you asked me to look out for her. You also know our oath prevents me from fucking her."

He narrows his gaze. "Not just our oath, but our friendship."

"That too."

I grin at him, concealing the maelstrom of violence churning in my chest. The complexities of this situation will only intensify as I navigate the thin line between duty and desire. Between my oath and my obsession.

The tightness in his shoulders eases, as does the tension around his eyes. But they don't disappear completely. "The Order can't find out about her."

"No shit."

"I'm fucking serious, X. If they knew what she meant to me . . ." He scrubs his mouth with his hand. "I've seen what they're willing to do to keep members from refusing their orders. I won't let them hurt Delilah, but I don't know how to stop them if they were to discover her."

My blood ices over at the thought. "You can't."

"That's why it's important to keep them from noticing her. It's the reason I've never told you about her until now."

"I get it. But to be clear, that's not a long-term strategy."

Unlike mine. For years, I've weighed all the risks and considered every possible outcome. The reward is worth it.

She is worth it.

I will have Delilah.

Even if it means I have to kill my father first.

CHAPTER 10

DELILAH

"Here we fucking go."

I take a deep breath and look around in awe at the stately brick buildings and manicured lawns sprawling before me. Everything screams money and privilege. I don't belong here.

But . . . where Ben goes, I go.

I pull out my phone and check it for any unread messages, my heart sinking when I find nothing. I texted my foster brother the date and time I was arriving on campus. As a senior, I know he's busy applying for jobs and whatnot, but I can't ignore his dismissal of me.

Actually, this is more like the hundredth time. I knew things would change when he left for college, but I didn't think we'd grow apart like we have. Or that he'd stop contacting me altogether.

Ben and I came from the same place and experienced the same shitty childhood. He knows how much it means to me that I obtained a scholarship to *any* university, let alone the same place as him. All I've wanted since he walked out the door of our foster home is for us to be together again, like old times.

Okay, maybe not exactly like old times considering Frank *disappeared*. Murdered is more accurate, but I've had the hardest time wrapping my mind around that. And the dark stranger who broke into the house all those years ago.

Regardless of how much he freaked me out, that guy did me a favor. Not only did the girls and I not have to worry about being assaulted by Frank anymore, but we were moved to a nice foster home with Gloria. If I could choose a mother, she would be it.

I shoot her a text letting her know I've arrived on campus safely. She's quick to respond that she's glad and super proud of me. After that, she sends me a picture the littles drew to wish me luck. I smile, feeling loved despite Ben's lack of communication. Once I find him, everything will be fine.

Lugging my overstuffed suitcase up the stairs of the residence hall, I remind myself that I've dreamed of this day. My scholarship is going to change my life for the better. And not just mine, but everyone I'll end up helping with my education in the future.

The hallways echo with the chatter of students hanging out and loitering in the common areas. I make my way toward my assigned room and push open the door. A young woman with jet black hair snaps up her head to pin me with a stare. Her dark red lipstick accentuates her impish grin as she assesses me. I return the favor.

She's dressed completely in black, her dress clinging to her curvy frame, paired with ripped fishnet stockings and boots. An assortment of silver chains, beads, and pentagrams hang from her neck. Her forehead creases when she asks, "Excuse me, ma'am, but do you have a moment to talk about our Lord and Savior Edgar Allen Poe?"

I lift a brow. "Is this your way of telling me you enjoy poetry or that someone is buried under the floorboards? Either way, I'm down."

She chuckles with a tiny shake of her head. "You're unexpected, but that's a good thing. It means we'll get along great, and I won't have to find a way to get rid of you."

"Good to know." I smirk. "So, what happened to your last roommate?"

Her grin widens. "Wouldn't you like to know? I'm Bree, but everyone calls me Raven."

"Delilah."

"Welcome to the den of poetic chaos."

I can't help but laugh at her dramatic introduction. After closing the door behind me, I set my suitcase down next to the unoccupied bed and plop onto it. I scan the room, beginning with my side. The dorm room is large with plain white walls and one large window. The bed is queen size instead of the standard-issue twin, and the sheets look to be made of quality material. Certainly higher than the thread count I have back home.

There's a wooden desk and dresser set, their surfaces empty except for a pen and notepad with the university's logo on the top right. Damn, even the parchment is thick and luxurious. A girl could get used to having nice things.

Raven's half of the room is completely filled with color. Dark purple curtains trimmed with black lace outline the single window centered in the outside wall. Her bed is made up neatly with satin sheets and a matching black lace bedspread. Above the bed is a purple wall covered in posters depicting famous artistic interpretations of monsters and ghosts. Interspersed are prints of poems by Poe, Baudelaire, and Dickinson.

"What's your major? Besides murder," I say with a wink. "Obviously."

Raven picks up a well-worn leather-bound journal and waves it in the air. "I'm an English major. It was either that or I wasn't going to college at all. My parents just about died when I chose something that wouldn't 'further the family business,'" she says, making air quotes, "but they finally got over it. You?"

"I thought about going into information technology like my brother, but that's not for me. I settled on psychology. More specifically, I want to be a child psychiatrist. Plus, I'll need a good-paying job after I graduate."

Raven slaps a hand over her heart. "Ah, the woes of picking a practical major to please the parental units. I get it."

"It's not to please my foster mother, it's to make sure I can provide for myself. I never want to depend on someone else for my survival."

"I get that too. My family's business means money isn't an issue for me. No offense."

She looks at me with a guilty expression and I gesture for her to continue. "No worries," I say.

"But the trade-off is having to live under my parents' control and expectations. Not that I'm comparing situations. I'm just saying I get it." She sighs, idly flipping through her journal. "I don't know what it's like *not* to have parents breathing down my neck about lineages and legacies, while threatening to cut me off financially if I refuse to marry some man-child in a suit. Money doesn't always equal freedom."

This university is one of the finest in the country. I knew I'd rub elbows with the rich, and I'm prepared to have their money—and my lack of it—thrown in my face. At least this conversation shows me that Raven won't do that.

"I grew up not having enough money to buy food." I shrug. "The grass isn't always greener. It's just grass."

"Well, sometimes I want to piss on it. Water it a little, you know?" Her smile returns, as does the glint of mischief in her brown eyes. "Maybe people would be less likely to rain on my parade if I piss on theirs first?"

I burst out laughing. I understand her frustration with being in a situation you have no control over. More than she could ever know.

"Absolutely. But before you decide to urinate everywhere, can you point me to the nearest coffee shop? I woke up early and I'm exhausted. My excitement wouldn't let me sleep last night."

I was too busy thinking about my reunion with Ben. The very person who has yet to respond to my calls and texts. My good mood plummets at the thought, but I keep my smile firmly set. It's one thing for me to tell Raven about having been a foster kid, but it's another to share my doubts concerning Ben's silence.

Her eyes light up at the mention of coffee. "Oh, I know just the place. There's this super cool cafe off campus called Brewed Awakenings. Epic name, right? It has a goth vibe with the best espresso around. I basically live there."

"There's nothing on campus? I still have orientation to go to in a little while."

"Fine," she says with a roll of her eyes. "We'll go to the lame coffee shop by the library."

I tilt my head. "Aren't you a freshman too?"

"Yup! My older brother graduated from here, so I know everything about this place. Why don't I give you a quick introductory tour and after that, we'll go to orientation?"

"Sounds good."

She jumps to her feet, her black combat boots striking the floor with a thud. "Come on, Delilah. Let us fuel up, and then it's on to plotting our glorious piss-ridden path to infamy!"

Laughter bursts out of me, honest and refreshing. I can't remember the last time I felt this light and just . . . happy. Yes, I'm concerned about Ben's lack of communication, and I miss Gloria and the girls, but I'm on a journey to accomplish what few people with my background do: attend an Ivy League college on a full scholarship.

If that doesn't make me a badass, I don't know what would.

CHAPTER 11

DELILAH

"Dude," Raven says, nudging me slightly in the back. "Keep walking. It's just a coffee shop."

"Erm . . ." I mumble.

Crystal chandeliers hang low over the seating areas, their warm glow reflecting off the polished mahogany floorboards. One wall boasts floor-to-ceiling bookshelves with well-known literature and some nonfiction texts. Plush couches and leather armchairs provide cozy nooks for reading or quiet conversation.

The main counter is sleek dark gray marble with gold trim, displaying pyramids of brightly colored macarons and cream-filled pastries under glass domes. An intricate brass espresso machine takes center stage. Given the number of levers and buttons, I doubt I could learn to use it. Molecular compounds are more straightforward.

"This isn't just a coffee shop," I whisper to Raven as she bypasses me. "This is . . . a work of art."

What I really want to say is this is somewhere I don't belong. This coffee shop is the nicest place I've ever stepped foot in, besides walking across this campus. I thought I could handle people throwing their money in my face, but I wasn't prepared to feel inadequate because of a vintage-looking espresso machine, for fuck's sake.

Raven glances back at me with amusement sparkling in her eyes. "You just wait until I take you to Brewed Awakenings. This place sucks in comparison."

The employee behind the register purses her lips at Raven, and I shrug as if that'll excuse her rudeness. Note to self: Raven has a bigger mouth than I do.

She orders something that should put her into cardiac arrest. I end up getting a regular latte with caramel. It's fancy enough for me.

"Do you want to sip and walk or finish up here first and then go exploring?" she asks me.

"Let's sit for a little bit."

We settle into a couch located directly in front of the window, surrounded by the comforting aroma of coffee and the gentle murmur of conversation. I try not to moan when I take my first drink, but I'm totally a slut for caffeinated sugar.

Raven stirs a packet of sweetener into her cup. "So, are you ready for the inside info on navigating this pretentious institute of higher learning?"

"Bring it on."

"If I were you, I'd make nice with the baristas here on campus."

I scoff. "You haven't."

"That's because I go to the one *off* campus." She waves a hand in dismissal. "Trust me, you'll want the caffeine when pulling all-nighters writing papers on . . . whatever the fuck psychiatrists care about."

"What else?"

"Let me see your class schedule. That way I can tell you about the professors and which ones are assholes."

I pull up my schedule on my phone, ignoring the pang of disappointment that rises when I find there are no texts from Ben.

Raven takes my phone and stares at the screen with a hum. I swear my heart pounds in time with the tapping of her dark lacquered nails against the phone case.

"Okay, so definitely keep Dr. Yamamoto for English Composition. She's tough but fair. I also hear she's an awesome mentor if she's not already tied up for the semester. You have good teachers for College Algebra and Human Growth and Development." Raven hums. "Dr. Ames for chemistry should be avoided as much as possible. Sure, he seems charming with those custom-tailored suits and that Rolex watch, but everyone says he nitpicks papers to avoid giving A's."

I frown. "Damn. It doesn't sound like I can do anything except work my ass off and pray for a B. I was hoping college was less about power trips than high school."

Raven gives me an exasperated look. "This place is nothing but a gazillion power trips between students, professors, and the administration. Never underestimate the wealthy's love of power. Besides, academia breeds pretentious bullshit. Just make sure you don't step in it."

"Right."

"Raven!"

We both turn our heads in the direction of the speaker. A petite girl with a pixie cut and winged eyeliner stops in front of us. She's dressed up in a pleated skirt and cardigan, with the first couple buttons undone and exposing generous amounts of cleavage.

I can't tell if she's a sexy nerd or a porn star.

"Hey, Juniper," Raven greets with a friendly smile. "Did you have a good summer?"

"Oh my gosh, yes! I discovered three new obscure mathematical theories to immerse myself in. They kept me busy."

I blink at her. Is this girl a math genius? Niiiice.

Raven bumps my shoulder with hers, breaking my stare. "Don't mind my new roommate. Delilah is new, a fresh escapee from suburbia-land. Be gentle."

"I'm June. Nice to meet you." She tosses her blonde hair, and it bounces back in place. "Are you guys going to orientation?"

"Yeah." Raven rolls her eyes. "Must be nice to be a sophomore and not have to go. What are you up to? Want to come with us?" Raven asks.

"It'll be full of nerds." She pops her bubblegum and sighs. "All the hot guys won't be there. Have you heard of any parties happening tonight?"

I shake my head, although I'm positive she isn't asking me.

Raven does the same. "Sorry, girl. Looks like you're not getting laid tonight."

"Maybe."

My roommate turns to me. "June is riding on a full scholarship for her brain. A math genius by day and a femme fatale by night."

The blonde curtsies. "Keeps things interesting."

"I was just about to give Delilah a tour of the campus," Raven says. "Want to join us?"

"Sure."

We follow Raven from the coffee shop with the sound of June's heels clicking against the floor. Once outside, my roommate leads us past the library, a stately redbrick building. Weathered by centuries of harsh New England winters, the building shows signs of erosion. Ivy climbs along the sides as if wanting to obtain the knowledge within its walls.

"Do you see that garden in the back?" Raven asks. When I nod, she continues, "That's the perfect spot for studying, or letting someone into your secret garden."

June laughs. "Did you grow up reading Victorian romance or something, Raven? If you say manhood, I'm going to punch you in the face." The woman turns to me. "Delilah, people go back there to get their dicks sucked and to suck dicks. It's far from romantic, but it is fun though."

"Speaking from personal experience or speculation?" I ask.

She winks at me. "Yes."

I grin.

"Obviously, I know people go back there to hook up," Raven says. "I just meant it's good for privacy in general."

June waggles her eyebrows. "Oh, it's definitely good for privacy. Oh, my God. Look, it's him."

"Who's him?" I whisper.

Our conversation halts as a tall figure emerges from the garden, walking with an air of confidence. And possibly . . . satisfaction? His dark brown hair is tousled across his head in an artfully mussed style. Or someone ran their fingers through his hair a lot.

His eyes glint and a smirk plays about his generous mouth. In contrast to his light-colored eyes, his clothing is completely black. A fitted T-shirt that accentuates the muscles of his biceps and torso, as well as the expanse of his back. His forearms are covered in dark ink, matching the rest of his attire. The cargo pants are tucked into boots that make no sound when he walks on the grass. He wears a watch that looks expensive even at a distance, and a single gold ring.

From this distance, I can't tell if it's similar to Ben's. Given the fact that we're at a university, there's a high probability he's also part of the same fraternity.

June gasps, turning to me. "You don't know who Xavier Donovan is? He's only the most intriguing guy you'll ever meet. Mysterious, brooding, and a bit of a legend around here."

"Now who sounds like they read bodice rippers?" Raven says, jamming her elbow into June's side.

The blonde lets out a feminine grunt. "Fine. He's rich, hot as fuck, and supposedly has a gargantuan dick. Happy now?"

Raven looks over at Xavier and nods. "Actually, yeah."

"Everyone calls him 'X,'" June says. "I've heard it's because he's like the drug ecstasy. Once you've been with him, he makes you feel so good that you'll get addicted after one hit."

My mouth falls open. "Wow."

She nods with a dreamy sigh. "Yup. He's the one equation I can't solve."

"Don't be such a whore." Raven groans. "Yes, X is a challenge and everything, but like drugs, he's bad for your health. Get over him, June."

"I make no promises."

Our conversation halts for the second time when a young woman with long chestnut curls emerges from the garden entrance, discreetly adjusting her clothes. She calls out to Xavier. He stops and turns to look at her over his shoulder before walking away, leaving her to chase after him.

"Pathetic," Raven says. "I bet she'd be on her knees again if he asked, even though he just used her."

June purses her lips. "I don't know . . . There's a reason why girls want him, even though he's obviously a dick. Rumor has it that he's not selfish in bed. That he gets off on you getting off. Probably some male ego thing, but it works for me."

Raven nudges me and then June to start walking. "I have no doubt he's hard to get over, but I think it's better not to get involved in the first place. That man cares more about conquest than actually connecting."

"You're such a poet," I say.

"Thank you." She gives me a smile. "Now, let's continue the tour on our way to orientation. I know it won't get you laid, June, but Delilah wants to go so I'm going to support her."

The blonde shrugs. "I'll go. It's not like I have anything better to do right now."

I push all thoughts of Xavier out of my mind. Although I can't deny his raw sexuality paired with his confidence sparks something in me, I'm not interested in having my life fall apart. It was broken for years, and I have no desire to return to that dysfunction.

Still . . . the image of his ring won't leave my brain.

CHAPTER 12

XAVIER

A few moments ago . . .

The tranquility of the garden is a front. The secrets that people have whispered here cling to the leaves of the oaks and willows, and the wind has snatched the grunts and moans of people engaging in sexual gratification. This secluded area is nothing more than a place to hook up between classes.

I lean against the trunk of a nearby tree and cross my arms with impatience. Whatever logic led me to meeting Brenda clearly wasn't sound. However, the urgency in her voice, along with her past relationship with Eric Gage, was enough to convince me.

Just as I'm about to leave, she steps out from the shadows, the library shielding her from the sun. Brenda's dark hair is loose, framing her face and resting on her shoulders. As always, she's dressed well, embodying sophistication and elegance despite her humble background. I assume she's here on a scholarship. Not that I care enough to confirm.

"X," she says in greeting. Her eyes glint with something carnal when she runs her gaze over me. "Thank you for meeting me."

"What do you want?"

She stiffens slightly, her smile thinning but still bright. "I was hoping we could get to know each other a little bit better." When I quirk a brow, she pouts, her expression turning coy. "I know things, and I'll tell you what they are, but first you have to promise me something."

I blow out a breath of frustration as my impatience morphs into irritation. "If you think you can bribe me, you've snorted way too much cocaine."

She gasps with quiet outrage and her eyes widen. I scrutinize her thoroughly, taking in the dark circles underneath her eyes and the gauntness of her cheekbones that can't be completely hidden by makeup.

"I know that you used to be with Eric," I say. "I also know he's a fucking asshole, so that couldn't have ended well for you. Tell me what you're really here for, Brenda."

She reaches for the buttons on her shirt and slowly undoes the first one. "I don't want to talk about Eric. I'm here to talk about us."

Brenda takes a step closer and licks her lips, releasing the second button. The swells of her breasts come into view, and paired with her inviting smile, she makes an alluring picture. Or she would if I wasn't obsessed with a green-eyed, beautifully violent woman.

I hold up my hand. Brenda's reaction is immediate, a mixture of surprise and disappointment. She freezes, her fingers lingering on a button, her gaze locked on mine.

"I'm not fucking you," I say.

"We can take it slow, if that's what you want." Her lips curl. "Although I didn't think you were the type to wait."

Well, fuck, that makes two of us. Yet I have been waiting. Three fucking years to be exact.

I haven't been with another girl since the day I met Delilah. I value control, but I swear she's taken over my mind and body to the point I can't get off unless I'm thinking about her. Not that it's a problem. I think about that girl constantly.

Which means I fuck myself all the time because of her. If I make it through the day without groaning Delilah's name, it's a fucking miracle.

Seeing her on campus has been the worst and best thing in my life. Having her near soothes something chaotic inside me, but then there's the issue that I'm hard.

All. The. Fucking. Time.

It's difficult to concentrate on my classes or my combat training when my dick is urging me to find her. Soon . . . After I get through the Trials and become a full-fledged member, a crow of the Obsidian Order, Delilah will be mine. Not just in my thoughts and fantasies, but she'll share my last name.

Mrs. Delilah Donovan.

Fuck. Me.

"Um, X?" Brenda says, her voice dragging me out of my head. She drops her gaze to my groin and lifts it, her brows raised. "You say you're not interested, but *that* says otherwise."

"That isn't for you."

She scrunches her face in confusion. "Okay, sure."

"If you have information, tell me now."

Brenda narrows her gaze, and her nostrils flare. She buttons her shirt, her movements jittery. I scrutinize her, taking in subtle cues in her behavior and appearance that I initially overlooked because she's not important to me.

"You're going through withdrawal," I say. "That's what this is about."

She transforms right before my eyes as her mask falls away. Instead of surrounding herself with a seductive air, the atmosphere shifts to something desperate, a deep craving etched into her features. Her playful smile disappears, and her body language, once soft and welcoming, turns hard.

"I'm not like you rich kids," she says, her words venomous. "I can't snap my fingers and get whatever I want. I need money."

"No, you need to go to rehab."

She blows out a breath. "I don't have enough money for drugs, so how am I supposed to afford that?"

"I'll pay for it. Being with Gage fucked you, but you don't have to stay messed up."

"You won't fuck me, but you'll pay for rehab?" She squints at me, suspicion churning in her gaze. "Why would you help me?"

"You got caught up in a bad situation that spiraled out of control."

"If anyone finds out, I'll lose my scholarship."

I shrug. "I'm not going to tell anyone."

"I don't know if I can," she whispers.

Her confession reveals the depth of her struggle. I pity her. Gage runs a drug empire, so he's familiar with narcotics. He just doesn't care that they ruin people. He certainly doesn't give a shit about this girl and how it's wrecking her life.

"Make a choice," I say. "I'll pay for it whether you give me information on Gage or not."

There's a moment of silence between us, filled with unspoken words and hidden motives. Her gaze darts back and forth, her tumultuous thoughts flitting across her face, betraying the tension simmering under her skin.

"Eric took a phone call when he thought I was asleep," she says slowly. "I don't know if it'll be useful to you or not, but he did mention your last name."

I listen attentively as Brenda divulges the details of Gage's recent setbacks, her words painting a picture of vulnerability within his empire. The insight into his organization will allow me to tip the scales in my favor, especially now that I know he's seeking to negotiate arms deals with my competitors to protect his supply chain. The Order likes everything to stay "in the family," and the council will be pissed when they find out.

I relish the thought.

"Anything else?" I ask her.

Brenda shakes her head. "That's all I heard."

"Choose the facility you want to go to, and I'll cover the costs," I say.

"Okay." She eyes me warily, her expression guarded. "Are you sure you don't want to hook up? I'd do it for free." When I shake my head, she runs her gaze over me and gasps. "You're hung up on someone. That's it, isn't it?"

I don't respond.

She smiles at me, and for the first time, it's sincere, without any ulterior motives or deception. "She's a lucky girl."

Delilah is more than lucky, she's my obsession. Every recruit entered a vow of celibacy for their senior year, but my oath was made way before then, to a girl who doesn't even know my name.

Well, not yet.

When Delilah learns it, she'll be screaming it.

CHAPTER 13

DELILAH

It's time to fuck the *carpe* out of this *diem*.

At least I think that's how the saying goes.

I grab my cell phone and put it on silent, but not before checking it for new notifications. My excitement for my first day of college dwindles at Ben's lack of communication. I texted him yesterday several times about my new friends, the beauty of the campus, and how much I was looking forward to seeing him.

And . . . nothing.

We haven't talked on the phone since I told him the details of my pending arrival on orientation day. At this point, either my foster brother is erasing me from his life, or something's wrong.

The former is too painful to even consider. The latter leaves me with a sense of foreboding.

I need to find him. Someone at this university has to know Ben, and hopefully, they'll tell me where he's been hanging out. It's his senior year. There's no way he'd not attend his classes and graduate.

Unless he's no longer the boy I grew up with.

A tide of memories floods my brain, making my heart squeeze in on itself. I slap a hand to my chest and pull in a lungful of air to help me breathe. My mind fills with inside jokes and whispered secret dreams, the things that kept me from giving up in hopes of something better.

Ben, the one person who made me feel loved and valued, isn't here on the first day of a major achievement in my life.

Pushing the debilitating thoughts of him aside, I open my refurbished laptop on my desk in the lecture hall, praying the piece of shit doesn't die on me like it did the last time I tried to use it. After opening a blank document, I sit there and wait for Professor Ames to show. The blinking cursor on my screen reflects my anticipation and my racing pulse.

I'm going to get an A in this class or die trying. I've come too far to let someone derail my goals because of a god complex.

Raven's warning drifts through my mind as the imposing figure of Professor Ames walks through the door. He snatches the attention of everyone present, instantly killing all sounds of conversation. If a mouse farted, we'd all hear it.

His three-piece suit speaks of money, and it's made from materials that I can't name, let alone afford. Faint pinstripes are brightened by the overhead lights and his leather dress shoes gleam from the polish. But his gaze is where his true superiority lies.

In its depth is an understanding of how the world works. Might makes right. And in this day and age, money is everything. Power cannot be obtained and held without it.

I position my fingers on the keyboard and wait. My pulse ratchets up as he opens his mouth to speak.

"This is the Fundamentals of Chemistry. I am Professor Archibald Ames the Third. You will address me as Professor Ames, and nothing else."

He clasps his hands behind his back and starts to walk, my eyes glued to his every move.

"Let's establish some expectations before diving into the intricacies of chemical bonding. If your cell phone disrupts my lecture, escort yourself from the premises and straight to your academic advisor, who will drop you from my class. I don't tolerate irresponsibility. You are all legal adults, so act like it, or get out."

I grab my cell phone again, and check that it's on silent. Again. This man does not fuck around.

"Secondly," he continues, "I don't care what your reason is for taking my class. However, you will respect the subject matter, as well as my dedication to it. If you think you can turn in a paper that's been drafted within twenty-four hours, your grade will reflect your effort. You've been warned, so let's proceed."

Holy shit. Maybe getting a B isn't the worst thing after all.

I gather my things at the end of the lecture, my brain throbbing after trying to comprehend everything Professor Ames went over. The other students don't try to hide their relieved expressions as they exit the room and continue on with their day. I predict a long line at the coffee shop in the next five minutes.

Not wanting to fight the crowd, I wait until only a few people are left before I leave. Professor Ames gathers papers and places them into his leather briefcase. I drop my head to avoid his gaze as I shuffle past.

He shuts his briefcase, the movement drawing my attention to his hands. A hint of gold winks at me under the bright lights. I halt mid-step, and my eyes dart to the ring on his middle finger.

It's exactly the same as Ben's, except with the letter "A" right above the anchor.

My heart thunders in my chest. Not only at the prospect of what this could mean, but also because my professor is staring at me like I'm a puppy who just shit on the floor.

He raises a sardonic brow. "Yes, Miss . . . ?"

"Scott, sir. I mean, Professor Ames."

"What can I do for you?"

I take a deep breath and take the plunge, hoping it doesn't tank the grade I haven't even gotten yet. "I have a question about your ring. It's really nice. Is it from a fraternity or maybe a family heirloom?"

When he doesn't respond—or blink—my pulse kicks up a notch. "It's just that I've seen one like it, and I thought it was interesting. You know?"

The man locks his briefcase with a definitive click, his eyes narrowing. The look he gives me makes my insides shrivel and die. If I make it out of here intact, I'm going to yell at Raven for her understatement concerning his arctic personality.

"No, I don't know, Miss Scott. To answer your question, the ring is both a family heirloom and representative of the Obsidian Order, a fraternity that's been a part of this university since the first brick was laid centuries ago. Does that satisfy your curiosity, or would you like some more interesting facts that have nothing to do with chemistry?"

I shake my head so hard my hair slaps my cheeks. "No, thank you. But thank you, Professor Ames. Have a good day!"

I cringe at the high-pitched squeak that masquerades as my voice and spin around to practically run out the door. With his piercing gaze stabbing my back.

CHAPTER 14

DELILAH

It takes me the entire walk back to the dorms to shake off the icy temperament of my professor. He acts like he's had an icicle shoved up his ass.

When I open the door, I find Raven lounging on her bed, punk music blasting as she scribbles furiously in a notebook. She looks up with surprise when I step inside the room, but her expression quickly morphs into a frown.

"Damn it, Delilah." She turns off her music and crosses her arms over her ample chest. "It's the first day of class. Don't tell me you've already fucked up in some way."

"I haven't, unless you count talking to Professor Ames about his signet ring after class."

She slowly shakes her head, staring at me like I'm a terminal cancer patient. "What did I say about him? You know nothing, Jon Snow."

I plop onto my bed with a sigh and toss my arm over my face. "This is all Ben's fault."

"Explain."

"So, I grew up in the foster system. I'm not trying to get out my violin and play my sad song, but it was rough until the last three years. My foster mother, Gloria, is an angel. Before her, it was just me and Ben, my foster brother. There are also two little girls who came to live with us that are like my little sisters."

I pause when my eyes prick with tears. After clearing the emotion in my throat, I continue, "They were my family, and the only good things in my life. Ben got a scholarship to South Harbor, and he's been here for the last three years. The long distance was hard on us, but I thought that would change once I started school here. Except he hasn't responded to any of my texts or calls. It's been days now."

Raven nods solemnly. Then she gets to her feet and walks over to my bed, sitting next to me. "You'll hear from him soon. It sounds like you were in the trenches together, and that kind of bond doesn't disappear overnight."

"Maybe it did over the last three years."

She scoots closer on the comforter. "A ride-or-die doesn't just continue riding without you. So that leaves dying, which I would've heard about by now. Gossip travels through this place faster than a viral video on social media. So that means it's either a possessive girlfriend, or he's in an over-involved alumni group."

I smile at her. "You're brilliant. You know that?"

"Duh. Now tell me why."

"Ben has been wearing a gold signet ring for a while now. It's identical to the one Professor Ames wears, except there's a different letter engraved on it."

She taps her chin in thought. "And that's why you talked to him and risked failing his class. The things we do for love."

"Oh, no. It's not like that between us. I only see Ben as my brother."

"That's cool, but love comes in many different forms. Whatever label you want to give it doesn't matter. What's important is that it's strong enough to get you to take action, and with that comes risk."

When I scrunch my forehead and give her a side-eye, she waves a hand in dismissal. "Anyway, what did Professor Ames say?"

"That it's a family heirloom and part of the fraternity, the Obsidian Order."

She tilts her head. "And you're sure Ben's not part of the founding families?"

"The what?" I frown. "Ben and I were orphans, so that just leaves the social club."

"Hmm. What was the letter on his ring?"

"M."

Raven jumps to her feet and crosses the floor to grab her laptop. Unlike mine, it's brand new and top-of-the-line. She types rapidly, the clicking sound the only one in the room.

"Boom shakalaka!" she screeches. "Who's your mommy?"

"Erm . . ."

I slide off my bed to walk over and peer down at her screen. "'The founding families in South Harbor, Massachusetts, are as follows,'" I read quietly. "'Gage, Kent, Shipley, Felton, Emerson, Paine, Barnum, Ames, Donovan, and McKenzie.'"

My knees give out, and I sink onto the mattress beside my friend. "You don't think that's his real family?"

Raven shrugs. "It's possible, and an avenue of inquiry we shouldn't ignore."

"Avenue of inquiry?"

She grins at me. "You can call me Sherlock fucking Holmes, baby."

"If Ben found his biological parents, he would've told me." I press my fingers to my temples, applying pressure to ease the ache beginning to pulse there. "It's too important for him not to."

Like a group of scorpions gathered in the pit of my stomach, betrayal infuses its venom into my being. I hang my head in defeat. How could he keep this from me?

"We don't know anything for sure," Raven says. She places a hand on my shoulder and gives it a gentle squeeze. "Let's assume it was given to him for the sake of the fraternity, okay?"

I nod, unable to form words just yet.

"The Obsidian Order," she mumbles. "Let's see what this one is all about. I swear, everyone is in a fraternity or sorority now. For the students here, it's a social status thing. Very elementary, my dear Watson."

After a few keystrokes, Raven takes a deep breath. "'The Obsidian Order, nestled in the shadowed fringes of a historical campus, this fraternity lies behind the imposing wrought-iron gates that lead to a castle. After years of restoration, the place that was once a battleground during the famous British invasion during the American Revolution is now home to a number of South Harbor University students. The Order is the source of many legends. Its members claim lineage from the ten founding families of the South Harbor colony, who still hold power and influence today. The Gothic stone mansion is rumored to be haunted by British redcoat ghosts, as well as those of American revolutionaries, but only those initiated know the truth.'"

Raven looks at me, her gaze scrutinizing. "Okay, so I might've been wrong about the family lineage and all that, but I'm confident that Ben can explain everything."

"Yeah."

"You guys didn't have a fight or anything, right?" she asks. When I shake my head, she purses her ruby-painted lips. "Then there's only one thing left to do. We need to find him."

Even if Ben's feelings toward me have changed, there's no way he would abandon the littles. They have nothing to do with our relationship, and he's shut them out as much as he's done with me. Maybe he found his real family and felt too guilty to tell us because we haven't. And probably never will.

"I'm going to reach out to my contacts—"

"You mean friends?" I ask.

She rolls her eyes. "Yeah, that. Especially June. She dated one of them recently. The only guy she was faithful to. If anyone knows anything about the fraternity, it'll be her. Besides, no one loves men more. And a whole castle full of them? Might as well put her on a spinning table with her legs spread so she can get—"

"Oh, my God!" I shake my head. "It's too early in the morning for this."

"Honey, it's never too early or too late to talk about sex."

"This explains why June was so excited to see Xavier Donovan," I say, attempting to change the subject. "He's from one of the founding families. Does she just want to sleep with him, or is it like a revenge fuck against her ex?"

Raven glances at me. "Bingo. Tell her the prize she's won, folks."

"Makes sense."

"Well, that and the fact that he's gorgeous and forbidden fruit. Like a fly to a banana. And by banana, I mean—"

I throw up my hands. "Yup. It's too early in the morning for this."

"It's never too early to talk about dick."

"I knew you were going to say that."

CHAPTER 15

DELILAH

"What did I tell you?" Raven holds her hands to her chest and sighs. "Brewed Awakenings is the absolute best."

I nod. "I believe you now. If the coffee is anything like the decorations, I'll be blown away."

Vintage lamps hang from the ceiling like floating lanterns, casting a glow over the black velvet chairs and crimson settees strategically placed in the room. A huge marble fireplace boasts a roaring fire, its crackling threaded into the soft alternative music playing in the background.

Raven grins at my astonishment. "Told you. This place is a mix between punk rock and aristocratic aesthetic, drowning in goth."

I breathe in the familiar notes of coffee, chocolate, and sugar as I follow my friend to the counter. An employee with aquamarine hair smiles at us.

"Raven! Good to see you," she says. "Do you want your usual Death in a Cup?"

"You know it, Misty." Raven winks at the girl. "And for my friend, a Rainbow Rose Latte."

I browse the elaborate menu with wide eyes, impressed by the options. Edgar Allen Mocha and Nightingale Nitro Cold Brew are among my favorite names. The time and creativity that went into every detail of this place isn't lost on me.

When I open my purse and reach for my wallet, Raven places her hand over mine. "I've got you, boo."

"Are you sure?" I ask.

"Absolutely."

My cheeks burn at her generosity. It might be just a coffee to her, but to me it's a frivolous spend that I can't indulge in too often. "Thanks."

We make our way over to an empty corner, drinks in hand. I take a sip of mine and groan loudly. It's like cotton candy coffee. Or some other sugar-infested concoction that tastes like happiness. Either that or I'm about to get into a diabetic coma.

June arrives a few minutes later, manicured nails drumming against her cup. "You baited me, and I'm here." She gives Raven a pointed look. "You can't just text me 'Dick detectives' without any explanation. So spill."

Raven laughs. "Don't be mad because it worked. Anyway, long story short: Delilah hasn't heard from her friend Ben, who joined the Obsidian Order. We're not sure if the social club is the reason he's been MIA or if it's a girl who's got his balls in a vise. I figured we'd start with the fraternity because that's where he lives."

The math genius tucks a curl behind her ear. "I don't know how much help I'm going to be. Those guys stay locked up tighter than a chastity belt." A sly smile works its way onto her pink lips. "Not that they don't get around, but you know what I mean."

"You dated one of them for a while," Raven says. "Faithfully, I might add. You have to know something useful that'll help Delilah get in touch with Ben."

June drops her gaze to her coffee cup, her bottom lip trembling slightly. "Yeah, Declan and I were together for a long time. Then at the beginning of summer he dumped me. No warning, no indicators, nothing. One day I'm happy and in love and the next he tells me he's done."

"I'm so sorry." I reach across the table to cover her hand with mine. After giving her a squeeze to show my support, I withdraw my hand. "I can't imagine how hurtful and confusing that was."

She snaps her head up and her eyes flash. "Yeah, well, fuck him."

"Just for the sake of research," Raven says slowly, as though carefully choosing her words, "Declan did wear a gold signet ring with the first letter of his last name on it, right?"

"Yeah. He said every male in his family gets one made the day they're born, but they can only wear it when they join the fraternity. Something about tradition that goes back to the fucking pilgrims or whatever."

"Am I right to assume you've never been inside the castle?" When June nods, Raven taps her chin in thought. "I wonder what's in there? Besides a bunch of entitled douchebags."

"Every other fraternity holds parties in their buildings, but not them." June takes a drink of her coffee and sets it down. A little more forcefully than usual. "They don't allow anyone in their inner sanctum. Dicks."

My shoulders slump with disappointment. I thought the mysterious fraternity would lead me to Ben, but after this conversation, it could actually be preventing me from finding him. The idea of waiting for my foster brother to contact me for an indeterminate period of time is unbearable.

"So now what?" I ask. "I feel like I've wasted your time with this. Other than storming the gates and demanding an answer from Ben, it seems like there's nothing I can do except wait for him to reach out."

Raven's eyes light up with a mischievous glint that has me squirming in my seat. "I say we do exactly that, my dear Watson," she says, adopting a British accent.

I raise a brow at her dramatics. "Seriously?"

"But of course!" She grins, steepling her fingers. "A little bit of sleuthing never hurt anyone."

"First of all, Sherlock almost died during his *adventures*. Several times. Second, lurking around at night sounds a lot like stalking."

Raven waves a dismissive hand. "Pish posh! All I'm suggesting is we take an evening stroll and enjoy the night air. If we happen to spot something through the window or find anything suspicious, that's a bonus. But not illegal." Her voice drops conspiratorially low. "But if you want to break in, I'm game."

"Trespassing *is* illegal," I say.

"Semantics. The fraternity is on university property, and we attend said university."

"Your logic is sound," June says dryly.

I bite my lip. My need for answers battles with the risks and potential ramifications if I take this operation further than the school's administration allows. I may not have read the student code of conduct, but I'm pretty sure it doesn't allow good old fashion B and Es.

As if to soothe my reservations, Raven lightly touches my wrist. "We can turn around and go back to the dorm room whenever you want," she says without an accent, her tone serious. "No man is worth losing your mind over."

I exhale, letting my good sense flow from me. "Let's do it, but just a little recon from the outside. And if I say it's time to leave, we go."

Raven gives me a grin that could rival the Cheshire Cat's. "Deal. The game is afoot, Watson!"

"What about me?"

My roommate and I turn to look at June, who stares at us with raised brows. Raven is the first to recover.

"Do you fancy a little midnight stroll?"

June rolls her eyes. "Nothing like a little trespassing to get the school year going."

"Is that a yes?" I ask.

"It's a definite yes. If possible, I want to find out what Declan's up to nowadays."

"Hell hath no fury . . ." I mumble against my coffee cup.

"Right you are, my dear Watson." Raven gets to her feet. "Would you look at the time? I must leave for my next class. Be at the dorm tonight a little after eight. Cheerio, darlings."

I stand. "I have a class starting shortly. I'll walk with you." I turn to June. "You coming?"

She shakes her head. "We're going to do a lot of walking tonight, so I'll just wait until then. Oh, and don't forget to dress completely in black." When I frown at the idea of my limited wardrobe, she says, "Just borrow from Raven. She has more black clothes than a grieving widow."

My roommate scoffs. "What I grieve is your lack of appreciation for gothic attire, my fair lady."

June's tinkling laugh follows Raven and me from the coffee shop and into the brisk autumn afternoon. Pedestrians walk by on their way to classes or jobs, each of them lost in their own agenda.

Raven links her arm through mine. "Don't worry so much. This is going to be fun. I didn't take you for a goody-two-shoes."

"I'm not," I say, thinking of how I stabbed two men in one night back when I was fifteen. "I just have a lot to lose now, and it makes me more cautious."

My friend nods. "I wish I could say that I understand, but I don't really. If I fuck up, my parents will bail me out, make a generous donation to the school, and I'll be back in class the next day."

"That's so far removed from my circumstances that I can't even imagine having that much security."

"I promise I won't even let things escalate that high. Okay?"

"Sure, but what about June?" I giggle at the expression on her face when she spoke about her ex. "She sounds like she's one espresso away from blowing up the whole place."

Raven smirks. "All I know is this is going to be more fun than some stupid frat party."

I make a noncommittal noise. "We'll see. But first, Human Growth and Development starts in twenty minutes."

"I know you're a psych major, but when they say 'human growth,' could they be talking about the male anatomy by chance?"

I playfully shove Raven. "It's too early for that subject."

CHAPTER 16

DELILAH

I've lost my freaking mind.

I stare at the intricate wrought-iron gate stretched between two large brick posts with ivy crawling up their weathered sides. The posts are topped with ornate, black iron lamps that pierce the shadows with their light. Behind the gate is the castle.

Large trees stand tall like sentries, their branches shielding parts of the building under a leafy canopy. The structure itself is a behemoth of brick and mortar. There are a number of windows lit up inside, signs of life within something so ancient.

In the gentle breeze, the gate emits a soft groan like a warning. I blow out a breath and fight the urge to glance over my shoulder for the millionth time since we started this "adventure." When I shift my stance, the gravel underneath my shoes elicits a crunching noise that has Raven's gaze zeroing in on me.

"Isn't this exciting?" she whisper-shouts.

I nod. "About as exciting as the prospect of a pap smear."

"What about you, June?" Raven asks. "Are you having regrets too?"

The woman shakes her head. "Nope. I'm already trying to figure out how to scale the wall."

"Won't it be difficult in that skirt?"

"Skirts are good for straddling walls *and* men." She winks at me, but her humor is quickly replaced with a look of determination. "We can't see shit from here. The only option is to go forward."

Raven tilts back her head. "You mean upward. It's not too high though."

"I know this whole thing started because of me, but I feel like I should be the voice of reason," I say. "Shouldn't we be concerned with cameras and lights with motion sensors? Not to mention security and possibly dogs?"

"This is a fraternity, not fucking Alcatraz," Raven says with an eye roll. "Besides, I know a girl who blows a guy who knows a guy who was able to hack the cameras and make sure our entrance goes unnoticed. The game is afoot, Watson."

I think about Ben and how much he means to me. At one point my foster brother was willing to give up his scholarship to keep me safe. I can do no less. Something in my gut churns at his continued silence. This goes beyond paranoia and self-consciousness.

Ben is in danger.

"Listen," Raven says, pulling me from my musings. "*If* a security team spots us, we'll just say that we were dared to come here by some boys. They'll probably take pity on us. Right, June?"

"Probably." She shrugs. "A little flirtation goes a long way."

"That's the spirit. Let's do this shit!" Raven turns around and threads her fingers. "I'm the tallest, so you guys have to go first. Get your ass up there, June. Delilah, you're next."

With the grace of a ballet dancer, June steps on Raven's clasped hands and leaps up to catch the lowest branch of the nearest oak. The hem of her trench coat flutters behind her like a pair of wings. She pulls herself smoothly onto the wall and grins down at us.

My heart kicks into overdrive watching her standing up there. Too late for second guesses or common sense now. Raven turns to look at me.

"It's time to engage those happy chemicals or the panic ones. Either works."

"I don't think that's going to help . . ."

She laces her fingers to provide a foothold and then practically hurls my ass over the wall the second my shoe makes contact with her palms. I wildly scramble to grab onto the branch, with June assisting me by yanking on my arm. Once I'm standing on the wall, I look down at Raven with a shit-eating grin.

She returns it. "Onward and upward!"

Like a squirrel with glue on its paws, Raven launches herself at the branch, her height giving her an advantage. June and I steady her once she reaches the platform, and she giggles.

"That was awesome. I've never felt so alive." She does a quick sweep of the area and waves at us. "Follow me. Up ahead there's a tree we can scale down."

"'Scale down' and hacking security cameras . . ." I mutter. "It's like you're an undercover agent."

Raven glances at me over her shoulder. "Maybe I am."

"I think you guys should shut up," June whispers.

My roommate flips her off. Within seconds, she's shimmying along a branch and then drops down onto the grass with a muffled curse. Before I can ask her if she's okay, June takes off after her, landing like a ninja beside Raven.

Raven plants her hands on her hips. "Come on, Delilah. Don't be a pussy."

"I'm not," I grit out. "I'm just trying not to break my neck."

I take a deep breath and inch forward along the thick branch. My palms turn slick when I wobble precariously, but I manage to lower myself to a safe height. The only thing left to do is jump.

"Fuck it."

My tennis shoes hit the grass, and I grunt at the impact. Sweet relief floods my system, making me a little giddy.

"Who's the pussy now?" I ask Raven.

"Not my Watson. Now, let's go."

I glance up at the formidable structure of the castle, a monolith of strength and masculinity. As we get closer, the detailed stonework and peaked roofs come into view. Ivy clings possessively to the sides of the building in tangled vines. It's eerie and beautiful.

My footsteps falter at my brief distraction, and Raven glances at me over her shoulder. "I'll buy you the audio tour later, nerd. Focus."

With June behind me, we follow my deranged roommate to a darkened window on the far east side of the property. I plaster myself against the brick wall and frantically scan the area. There are still no signs of alarm or any indication we've been spotted.

Raven grips the edge of the window and tries to lift it with a grunt, pushing her shoulder against the flat surface. She blows out a breath of frustration. It fogs up the glass she's been unsuccessfully trying to raise for several seconds.

"Ugh, this thing won't budge," Raven says. Several profane but creative words flow from her after that.

I shift from one foot to the other. I'm not sure what my friend's plan was supposed to be. Did she really think a window would just magically open for us? I guess I'll have to question her methods beforehand next time.

Oh, my fuck. Do I really think I'll do this again?

"The window is either painted or nailed shut," Raven says. "We need something to pry it open. Any ideas, Watson?"

I open my mouth to inform her that she should've thought of that *before* we attempted to commit a crime, but June steps between us. She reaches into her coat and holds out a slim metal tool. My eyes widen when the moonlight catches it.

"Is that a mini crowbar?" I ask.

June nods. "How else did you think we were going to get inside? Witchcraft?"

I give Raven a pointed look. "Someone did." After turning back to look at June, I scrunch my face. "Where was that thing hiding? I never saw the outline in the material of your clothing."

"Wouldn't you like to know?"

Raven lets out a cackle and swipes the object from June's hand. Twirling the metal rod, my roommate wedges it under the window seam with a confidence I find disturbing. For a rich girl, she's familiar with shady shit.

Or maybe that's why.

After a few seconds of strained prying, the pane gives way with a loud crack, the sound like a gunshot in the quiet. Raven straightens with a maniacal grin while I stand there with my heart beating so hard my chest starts to ache.

"Huzzah!" she whisper-shouts. "We're in."

"There's no way someone didn't hear that," I say.

June nods, her gaze wide as it zips from side to side. "We better hurry. Raven, move your ass."

My roommate hands the crowbar back to June and retrieves her phone from her pocket. After turning on the flashlight feature, she inspects the dark opening.

"Damn. It's a long drop, and there's nothing to climb down on." She hoists herself onto the window ledge, wiggles a little, and leans forward. "Like, how committed are we, guys?"

"Committed enough to risk a misdemeanor." The deep masculine voice has all of us gasping. "Or maybe you're just taking the scenic route?"

CHAPTER 17

DELILAH

I'm going into fucking cardiac arrest.

My crazy imagination convinces me that my heart is about to jump out of my body. I slap a hand to my chest while sucking in gulps of air. The organ beats rapidly against my palm like a cry for freedom.

Raven freezes on the window ledge, her face pale and eyes wide, as the flashlight from her phone illuminates her features. "Where the fuck did you come from?"

June retrieves the crowbar and whirls around with the tool raised in defense. "Oh, it's you."

The familiarity in her voice gives me the courage to slowly turn around.

The owner of the deep voice stands in the shadows, wearing jeans and a black hoodie that conceals his face. My brain sparks with the memory from years ago when I faced a different hooded individual.

He still haunts me to this day.

I stand there, vacillating between panic at having been caught and a curiosity that always gets the best of me. June sounds unafraid. I focus on the identity of the stranger as opposed to what he's going to do.

"Come on, X," June says, waving the crowbar. "I'd recognize you anywhere."

He steps forward. "Interesting."

Raven, still perched on the window ledge like—well, a raven—shines her phone in his direction. "To answer your question, we're taking the scenic route. Obviously."

The light finally reveals his face. His mouth is twisted in a smirk, and his eyes are liquid silver, beautiful despite twinkling with something hostile.

His attention shifts to June. "Still unable to keep your nose out other people's fucking business?"

She shrugs. "Old habits die hard."

"What were you looking for?" he asks.

My roommate jumps down and stands next to me. "Now who's not minding their own fucking business?"

"Anything concerning the Order is my business," he says. "What are you doing here?"

"Why should we tell you? If you're going to be a narc, just go ahead and do it," Raven says. She folds her arms and lifts her chin. "My dad will make those charges disappear faster than you can bust a nut."

He shifts his gaze to me. "What about you? What the fuck are you doing here?"

I point to myself. Like a dumbass.

When Xavier nods, I snap out of whatever trance he's put me in. I said I wanted answers, and now that I'm face-to-face with someone who could actually give them to me, I can't walk away.

Like Raven said, don't be a pussy.

"I'm looking for Benjamin Johnson, um, McKenzie. I know he's part of this group, and I need to talk to him." I pause for emphasis although my worry is genuine. "It's an emergency. Have you seen him?"

Xavier's caustic expression shifts. It's slight, possibly a trick of the moonlight, but I swear I catch it. "Yeah, I have."

"Where is he? Is he okay?"

He shakes his head. "I'm not telling you anything. Unlike some people," he says, looking at June, "you need to learn to mind your fucking business. If I catch you here again, even your daddy's bank account won't be able to save your ass."

He gives Raven a mocking look. She flips him off.

His refusal ignites something fierce and primal in my soul. Benjamin could be hurt or in danger . . . and this guy is treating it like it's a joke. Well, fuck him.

Fury propels me forward to jab my finger hard against his chest. He blinks, surprise skating over his features.

"Listen here, asshole!" I say. "You better tell me exactly where Ben is, or I'm going to . . ."

I don't get to elaborate my threat as Xavier's brows draw downward. "You're going to what, exactly? Cry? Slap me? Or maybe you'll try and stab me, little raptor?"

The impact of those two words is like a punch to the gut. My breath wheezes from me while my insides clench until I'm shaking from lack of oxygen. My lips tremble with questions I'm too scared to ask.

Did I imagine what he said?

"She's not a fucking dinosaur," Raven says.

I guess I didn't make that up. This guy is the same one from all those years ago . . .

My roommate steps in front of me while Xavier continues to stare down at me. I peek at him from behind her shoulder, my body shaking uncontrollably. His eyes pierce me, carving into my mind like the knife I used to stab him. I'm unable to look away no matter how badly I want to.

"We're leaving," Raven says.

Her voice slices through the charged atmosphere, snapping me out of my stupor. I avert my gaze and focus on breathing to keep from passing out. His words echo in my mind, making my head pound.

This can't be happening.

Xavier flicks his wrist in a dismissive motion, but the air ripples with tension. I look at him one more time.

Memories of a hooded figure surface in my mind's eye, intertwining with the man in front of me, leaving me caught between the past and the present.

June places a hand on my arm. The unexpected touch sends a jolt through me, and I suck in a lungful of air, barely halting my scream at the last second.

Her brow furrows as her eyes search mine. Whatever she sees on my face has her putting an arm around me.

I probably look like a candidate for a psych ward. I certainly feel like I've lost my mind. All of this can't be a coincidence.

Right?

CHAPTER 18

DELILAH

The entire trek back to the dorm room is done in silence. Thank fuck. It gives me enough time to come up with a story to tell my friends. But it's not long enough for me to get my shit together.

The door clicks shut behind us and Raven whirls to face me. I sink onto my bed and mentally prepare myself for the interrogation that's about to commence. I'm not disappointed.

"What the fuck just happened?" She looks from me to June and back again. "Both of you have tea you need to spill. One of you better start talking."

The blonde plops down beside me with a sigh. "I'll go first. I know I said that I was pissed at Declan for dumping me for no reason, but I'm not . . ." She pauses and nibbles on her fingernail before continuing. "I'm not over him, okay?"

"So, what, you're a stalker?" Raven asks. "I mean, I approve, but is that why Xavier accused you of not minding your business?"

"Kind of. I didn't understand why Declan ended things all of a sudden. We were happy. Like stupid happy, and then it was over." She snaps her fingers. "Just like that. When I tried talking to him to get him to explain things, he outright refused. Naturally, I did what any woman would do."

Raven nods in understanding. "You tried to kill him."

"No," June says with a frown. "I followed him to see if he was with another woman."

"Or that."

"Anyway, Declan wasn't with another woman, but the place he went to was . . . weird."

Her hesitation has me reaching over to grip her hand. I give it a tiny squeeze to show my support. "It's okay. You don't have to share anything you don't want to."

Raven blows a raspberry. "The fuck she doesn't. Now I really need to know what's going on."

"It's fine," June says to me. "I've been holding this in for months. It was a medical research facility. It's known for its cutting-edge experiments and research. At least, that's what the internet said."

I retract my arm and fold my hands in my lap. "I'm still waiting for the weird part."

"Yeah, get to the good shit." Raven rubs her hands together. "Weird how?"

"There was a room, dimly lit, with some shady-ass looking people," June says. "I grew up poor, so I know fucked-up when I see it. Just because the men were wearing expensive suits doesn't mean they were legitimate. I only saw one person with a lab coat. In a research setting, that's not normal, but that's not what scared me."

"Zombies," Raven says. "I knew it."

"No. I saw several organs being put into containers, like for a transplant."

My eyes widen. "But there weren't any recipients there?"

"Not that I could see."

"Dude, organ trafficking is wild." Raven starts pacing, clasping and unclasping her hands. "Isn't the Kent family behind the funding of a shit ton of hospitals and research facilities? I swear, every time I turn around, I find their name on a Band-Aid or a clinic pamphlet."

June nods. "At first, I thought Declan dumped me because of another woman. Now, I'm thinking it was because I'm not good enough for his family. You'd think being a mathematical genius would score me some points, but I guess with him being from a founding family, they don't want to pollute the bloodlines."

"What does that have to do with Xavier?" I ask.

"They're best friends," June says. "I just assumed Declan told him. I only followed my ex the one time. After that, I left him alone."

She holds out her hands in supplication. "Let me be clear. I don't want to spread rumors, and this entire thing is complete speculation on my part. If Declan is actually involved in that shit, I don't want to know."

"Well, I do," Raven says. When I glare at her, she shrugs. "Fine. Your turn, Delilah."

I take a deep breath to compose myself. It doesn't work, but I continue anyway. If I don't, I'm positive Raven will bury me under the floorboards.

"I'm not sure how to say this without freaking you guys out," I say.

Raven squeals. "I love this kind of stuff." She sits on the bed next to me with a huge grin. "Talk dirty to me, roomie."

"Don't interrupt me, or I won't get it out," I say. When she mimes zipping her lips, I take the plunge. "I stabbed a guy three years ago."

Raven makes a strangled sound that's half shock, half glee. To her credit, she doesn't say a word.

"Long story short, I thought my foster parent was going to kill my foster brother, Ben. They were fighting in the kitchen, and I did the first thing I could think of to stop Frank from hitting him. I stabbed him. It worked."

I release a nervous laugh. "Then I waited at the top of the stairs all night in case he wanted to get revenge on me. Well, someone else walked up the stairs, and I stabbed him too."

"Holy . . ." June says.

"Fuck balls," Raven finishes.

"I know, right? Anyway, the intruder left, and I was moved to another foster home. That's pretty much it. But seeing Xavier in that black hoodie reminded me of that night. I think I was having a PTSD kind of moment."

The events from that night altered my life in a significant way. More than I can ever reveal to my friends. They exchange glances filled with shock and concern before they look at me again.

Raven pats my shoulder. "You are one badass motherfucker, and I'm proud to be your friend."

"I'm a little scared of you, but same," June says with a wink.

"Do you know why he called you 'little raptor'?" Raven scrunches up her face. "That was a random ass thing to say."

I shake my head. "No idea."

But I'm going to find out.

CHAPTER 19

DELILAH

The soles of my shoes make no sound on the asphalt as I chase after Xavier Donovan. However, my breathing is loud as hell. I sound like a pug being strangled.

Cardio has never been my thing.

Apparently, stalking is.

Xavier has been on my mind all of last night and every minute of today. I haven't been able to concentrate on anything except the questions that have haunted me for years. My need for answers from that night, and to know what's going on with Ben, have taken over, possessing me until I no longer recognize myself.

I'm following a man who has confessed to murder.

For *me*.

Maybe that's why I'm not as frightened as I should be. I mean, my legs are shaking, but I'm not scared enough to walk away. That'd be the smart thing to do.

I'm a fucking idiot.

Xavier weaves between the vehicles with a lethal grace, his steps confident and sure. I trail behind, struggling to keep up although I'm jogging. He leads me further into the maze of the parking lot. Row after row of expensive cars are lined up like soldiers awaiting a general. Only the occasional pair of headlights cut through the darkness surrounding me.

"Wait!" I call out, the sound of my voice startling me.

He pauses halfway down an aisle and slowly turns to face me. The moon hangs low in the sky, but it chooses that exact moment to break through the clouds, creating shadows all around him, except for a sliver of light that rests against his mouth. Like three years ago, Xavier smirks at me, lips twisted with amusement.

I come to an abrupt halt as memories of him flood my mind.

"Because no one *touches what's mine."*

"What the hell do you want?" he asks.

His question yanks me from my thoughts. I remain in the middle of the parking lot, unable and unwilling to get any closer. I'm not sure any amount of distance between us would make me feel safe.

Every question I've ever thought of rushes from my brain to land on my tongue. It feels heavy in my mouth, but I force myself to say something, anything that'll get this conversation going.

"Why me?"

He tilts his head. "Why not?"

I blink. "That's not an answer."

"It is, but not the one you want to hear."

He's right. What did I expect? I shake my head at my ignorance. And my ability to forget everything else when he's nearby. Even Ben.

Xavier leans against the nearest car and withdraws a cigarette. He lights it up and takes a slow drag, his silver gaze boring into me. Smoke spirals lazily from his nostrils like a dragon. My skin nearly bursts into flame from the heat of his gaze.

"Where's Ben?" I ask.

Xavier takes another long pull on his cigarette, his lips wrapping around the object in a way I find distracting. No man should have such a sensuous mouth. Or be this attractive.

It's just fucking rude.

"He's safe."

"That's not what I asked."

"But that's all you need to know." He puts out his cigarette by jabbing it against the hood of a Porsche before tossing it to the ground. "The next time you think to come looking for me, don't."

"Can you give Ben a message for me?"

Xavier continues to look at me with his arms folded across his chest. That's not exactly a yes, but it's not a refusal either.

"Tell him that I'm—"

The screech of tires and the smell of burning rubber assaults my senses. I spin toward the sound, my hair flying off my shoulders. The glare of headlights stabs at my eyes, forcing me to squint and raise a hand to block the light. The purr of the engine becomes a roar, getting closer with every breath.

My protective instincts scream at me to move. I lift my foot, but everything's in slow motion. Before I can take a full step, a powerful blow sends me flying. The impact squeezes the air from my lungs.

The world goes blurry, and I blink several times to put things into focus. I'm lying on something hard, but it's not concrete.

It's Xavier.

"Delilah?"

He says my name like a caress. It sweeps over me, his breath skimming my lips. I stare down at him, more in shock at the tenderness in his voice than the fact that the car could've killed me.

Gray eyes churning with concern meet mine. And something else I can't identify. Whatever it is, it has adrenaline flooding my system.

Xavier reaches up to frame my face with both hands. The slight shifting of his position reminds me that our bodies are flush, causing my heart to beat frantically. More so because he's touching me.

"Are you hurt?"

I continue staring at him, unable to form words. His expression has softened, but the lines around his eyes and mouth speak of deep worry. For me. Not in a good Samaritan type of way either. It's intimate.

"Answer me, or I'm going to lose my fucking mind," he snaps.

"Huh?"

He shakes his head, a wry smiling tugging at his mouth. "I guess that counts."

The haze from the shock begins to lift, the gravity of my near miss sinking in. I shake my head to dislodge his hold on my face so I can think clearly. "What happened?"

"Besides you trying to get run over? Not much."

I plant my hands on the asphalt and lift myself, peering around the parking lot. It's the same as it was before, quiet and void of pedestrians.

"It's really dark out here," I say, still scanning the area. "It was an accident."

He makes a noncommittal noise deep in his throat. Right before sliding his hands up to encircle my waist. I drop my gaze to him, my brows snapping together.

"Xavier?"

He drags his fingers along my sides, across my back and upward until he's lightly gripping my neck with both hands. I remain still throughout his exploration, but my heart ricochets in my chest like a wayward bullet.

"What are you doing?" My voice comes out breathy. Husky.

"I'm checking you for injuries."

"Oh."

That sounds logical. Considerate, even. *If* it was someone else . . .

I stare down at the man underneath me as he continues to trail his fingers along my body, leaving my skin tingling under my clothes. His scrutiny is like a touch all on its own. It runs over my face, stopping on my mouth before he drags his gaze back to mine. Only now, there's a glint in his silver eyes, making them shine like starlight.

"I'm fine," I say. The tiny whisper is all I can manage. Being this close to him has my mind deadening and my body coming alive.

"I'll be the one to decide that."

My lips purse. "You don't own me."

"Not yet."

"You shouldn't talk to me like that."

"Well, get used to it."

His fingers return to the column of my throat, stroking it slowly but deliberately. An unspoken message passes from him to me in that tiny caress. This man could kill me. But the reverence in his touch is what keeps me from running.

To be cradled in the hands of a demon is unsettling. And thrilling.

"I told you, I'm fine," I say, hardening my tone.

"I believe you'll live, little raptor."

His words send a shiver through me. I know the second he feels my body's involuntary movement. The barest smirk plays on his lips. The sensual expression makes me want to moan. And then punch him in the face.

"I have so many questions," I say. "Not just about Ben, but about that night." My confession fills the space between us. I take a deep breath as if I can pull it back into my body where it's safe from him. Xavier keeps stealing it from me.

The skin around his jaw tightens, but the sly expression remains. "Not tonight."

"When?"

His fingers, still lingering on my neck, tighten their grip. "When it's safe."

The intensity of his answer resonates somewhere deep. It's a cryptic promise, laden with the weight of secrets that I'm not yet privy to. Not yet.

"I just want to understand," I say. "Don't you get that?"

"I'm *very* familiar with wanting something I can't have."

My breath catches at the raw yearning in his voice, the hunger that ignites something inside me. The irrational allure that surrounds him snakes around me, coiling and unmovable. Leaving me helpless.

Xavier lifts his hand to brush a tendril of hair away from my cheek, tucking the errant strand behind my ear. Our eyes stay locked as he lightly grips my jaw and strokes my bottom lip.

"A predator should never desire its prey."

"I'm not prey." My voice betrays me with the smallest warble. Is the tremor from fear? Or fascination? "And you're not just any predator."

Xavier smiles. It's wistful, pricking my heart, making it bleed the tiniest bit for him. What has he gone through to think this way?

And what's wrong with me for being drawn to him?

"Are you going to get off of me now?" he asks.

My cheeks blaze with embarrassment. I look down at our bodies, flush against each other and our legs entwined. I've been lying on this man like a pillow-top mattress. Except he was hard.

Everywhere.

I scramble to my feet and wrap my arms around my middle to fortify myself. And create a barrier between us. The awkwardness that prickles my skin quickly removes all thoughts of attraction.

"Sorry," I mumble, unable to meet his gaze.

Xavier gets to his feet in one fluid motion that has my eyes widening. He has control over his body in a way that most people don't. It's the reason he was able to save me from getting run over, while also landing with me on top to cushion my fall.

"No need to apologize." He pulls the black hood over his head, his gray eyes gleaming at me from underneath. "It's not every day a beautiful woman sexually assaults me."

I look at him, not bothering to hide my appreciation of his physical appearance. "I doubt that."

He shrugs. "It's never the one I want. Until tonight."

I open my mouth to say something sarcastic, or possibly stupid, but he juts out his chin in a silent command. "Go straight to your dorm. I'll know if you don't listen to me."

His authoritative response has me flipping him off. He laughs at my act of rebellion. The sound is like melted caramel, sinking into my stomach and making me jittery.

"What about Ben?" I ask. "I need to speak to—"

Xavier shakes his head. "Good night, little raptor."

He turns his back to me and walks into the darkness, blending in with the shadows. The only reason I know he's there is the sound of his footsteps. They gradually fade, taking my answers with them.

CHAPTER 20

XAVIER

Once Delilah can no longer see me, I spin around, my gaze immediately finding her. I stand there, torn between following her back to the dorms and searching for her attacker. Knowing the identity of the driver, I'm certain it wasn't a fucking accident. The thing I don't know is why he did it.

I'll find out.

I've taken the necessary precautions to keep Delilah off the Order's radar, but that woman is stubborn and keeps showing up in places she shouldn't. I'll have to be firmer with her going forward. Although I enjoy interacting with her in any capacity, I won't risk her life just for the sake of my obsession.

Delilah walks swiftly toward the dorms, and I stay behind her like a shadow. It's unlikely that she'll be accosted on the way there, but I'm not willing to take the chance. As soon as she's safe behind a locked door, I'll confront that asshole who thought he could take her from me.

I keep my head on a swivel as she walks, the girl completely oblivious to my presence. Well, maybe not completely. A couple of times she pauses and looks over her shoulder. She scans the area, but I remain hidden.

What kind of assassin would I be if she were able to spot me?

The entire way back, Delilah is alert and tense, but the second she steps through the doorway of the building, she relaxes. So do I.

After retrieving my phone, I unlock the screen and bring up the live feed from her room. She appears a minute later.

My girl kicks off her shoes, sits on the bed, and grabs her laptop. Her eyes are glued to the screen as she types on the keyboard. I adjust the settings on my phone and zoom in as much as it'll allow. The image focuses, revealing a social media app and a profile picture that's familiar.

It's mine.

Satisfaction has my dick getting hard. She's interested in me. Not as much as I am in her, but this is a good start.

As I watch her scroll through my profile, I fist my hands, the need to touch her overwhelming me. The memory of the first time my fingers brushed her skin rises in my mind. Not the time I grabbed her wrist three years ago, but the gentle touch from earlier. Her skin was impossibly smooth, but it was her reaction to me that etched the moment deep into my consciousness. In my soul.

If I even have one.

There was a hesitation in her gaze, a wariness skating over her face when she looked down at me. However, the second I wrapped my hands around her slim neck, she softened. Submitted. Despite her unease, her eyes were bright with curiosity, and a tiny spark of attraction.

That's all I need to make an inferno. To make her burn for me.

She tried to mask her body's reaction to me, but her uneven breaths blew across my lips, making me hungry for more than just a touch. I wanted to fucking devour her. With Delilah's curves pressing into me, it took every ounce of discipline I possess not to flip her over and fuck her on the asphalt.

My obsession extends beyond sex, but that doesn't mean I don't think about the day I'll take her innocence, make her bleed on my cock. She'll mark me just as much as I plan on claiming her.

My gaze zeroes in on her mouth. Her lips move, but there's no audio. With a frown, I turn on the microphone on my phone and wait for the red light to appear. It's connected to a Bluetooth earpiece in her room. It took me a few days to find a pair that was compatible and discreet, but it was worth the effort. Having chosen Delilah's dorm room for her before she arrived helped immensely.

"Why are you being such a fuck nugget?" Delilah mutters to my picture, her voice filling my ear.

I laugh at her name for me. It's not the worst thing I've been called.

She sighs, the sound forlorn. "Ben, why won't you talk to me?"

The mention of the recruit sobers me, erasing all traces of amusement. Her concern for him is understandable. What isn't rational is the fury that builds in my gut. The possessiveness I feel for her is like a feral animal wanting to kill any other man that approaches her. It's a primitive urge.

One I won't be able to contain forever.

She sits up. "What the hell?"

Delilah squints down at the screen and clicks something. It's the direct message I just sent her through the app. I smile in the darkness at her look of confusion. She's fucking adorable when she scrunches her face like that.

Xavier: You're a stalker.

Delilah: I have no idea what you're talking about.

Xavier: So you didn't just view my profile?

Her eyes widen. She bites her lip, uncertainty covering her features. I groan and run the heel of my hand over my dick. The things I want to do to that mouth of hers . . .

Delilah: No, I didn't. The app must've sent you a notification by mistake.

Xavier: So you're not looking at my profile pic right now?

She sucks in a breath and lets it out slowly, her nostrils flaring. "How in the fuck . . . ?"

Her head swings back and forth as she searches for a logical explanation for my message. Finding nothing out of the ordinary, she returns her focus to the screen and types a response. It pops up on my phone a second later.

Delilah: No, and even if I was, I wouldn't admit it.

Xavier: Did you miss the part about you being a stalker?

Delilah: Did you miss the part where I think you're an asshole?

Xavier: That's true, but it hasn't stopped you from talking to me. This is the last time I'm going to tell you to stay away from me.

Delilah: And if I don't?

Xavier: Then I'll notify the administration about your stalking activities. Not only the way you followed and sexually assaulted me in the parking lot, but also the way you and your friends trespassed onto the fraternity's property.

Delilah: 🖕

Xavier: Not yet.

Delilah: Not ever.

I grin in the darkness. My girl has a fire in her that I can't wait to tame. She might burn me in the process, but I'm all too familiar with pain. At least it'd be worth it.

With Delilah safe and my warning to her delivered, I make my way to the fraternity house. As expected, the place is filled with guys, music, and booze.

I head straight for Eric's room, ignoring everyone else. After knocking on the door, I step back and wait.

He appears, his gaze narrowed, his pupils blown. "Donovan."

"Gage. I have a couple of questions that you're going to answer."

"Not fucking interested."

He moves to slam the door in my face, but I stop him by planting my boot in the doorway. "You tried to kill someone tonight,"

I say, my voice low. "I recognized your car. Was the girl part of a summons?"

Eric freezes. "Doesn't matter 'cause I'm sworn to secrecy. I'm not telling you shit."

"I don't need details. Just tell me if the hit came from the Order."

"Fuck off."

I tilt my head, struggling to keep a rein on my building temper. "You don't want to do this with me, Gage. Especially not when you're fucking high."

Eric, undeterred, amped by the drugs, studies me with a defiant expression. "Yeah, and why's that?"

The hard resolve in my voice doesn't lessen. "Because I'll torture the information out of you if I have to."

It's not a threat; it's fucking statement of fact.

He scoffs, a smirk pulling at the corner of his lips. "I'd like to see you fucking try."

Acknowledging his challenge with a slow, deliberate nod, I let the silence hang heavy between us for a moment. "I can make that happen."

Without another word, I close the distance between us. My fist connects with his diaphragm in a sudden, forceful impact, designed to incapacitate.

Eric's eyes widen in shock, the air whooshing out of his lungs in an involuntary gasp. He staggers back and clutches his abdomen as he struggles to draw breath. The surprise in his eyes is quickly replaced with rage.

With a sudden burst of energy, he lunges at me. His shoulder slams into my chest, a clear attempt to catch me off guard and push me back. I counter his advance, grabbing his shoulders and using his momentum to spin him away from me. Eric whirls around, fists clenched, ready to draw blood.

"If you keep this up, I'm going to kick your ass," I say. "We both know it. Your coordination is fucked by the drugs."

Eric throws a punch, a clumsy swing that's easily dodged. He's one of the best fighters out of all the recruits, but the drugs have slowed his reflexes, and his movements lack coordination. The only thing he has going for him is the stimulant to his central nervous system decreasing his perception of pain.

I deliver a solid kick to his midsection, sending him reeling backward. Eric recovers his balance and lunges at me again, his eyes wild with fury.

We dance like this for several minutes, trading blows. The sounds of our struggle echo in the room, the rhythmic thuds of flesh against flesh punctuated by the occasional grunt.

Finally, I land a solid blow to the side of Eric's head, dazing him. I seize the opportunity and throw him against the wall, pinning him in place with my forearm against his throat.

"Now, for the last fucking time, I'm going to ask: Was the girl a part of a summons?"

Eric's eyes are glazed, the effects of the drug-induced rage slowly fading. "No," he croaks.

"Then why did you try to kill her?"

"I—"

Before he can finish the sentence, I slam him against the wall, my patience waning. "Listen, motherfucker, you're going to tell me the truth, or I'll kill you. Right here, right now. Fuck the Order."

His eyes widen in alarm, his gaze clearing for the first time since the altercation started. "Okay, okay. Just calm the fuck down. I did it to see what you would do."

I frown. "You were going to kill her to see how I'd react?"

"Yes."

"Why?"

Eric stares at me, the confusion on his face matching my own. "To see if she's important to you."

"She's not," I lie. "No one is."

He laughs. It's unhinged, and not all of it can be blamed on the narcotics in his system. "Then why the fuck did you come here tonight, threatening to torture me for information? Why are you willing to risk the wrath of the Order, the same organization you're pledged to serve, if the girl means nothing to you?"

My jaw tightens. "Because we don't shit where we eat. That girl is a student here, so if she's a threat to the Order, I want to know."

"Bullshit. There's something else. You want her."

"I'm not breaking my vow to the Order for a fucking piece of ass."

I shove off of him. He loses his footing and laughs again, the sound mocking. "You can lie to yourself all you want, Donovan."

"I don't give a fuck what you think."

"No, but you do care what the council has to say."

I pause at the door. "Watch your back, Gage. What happens during the Trials can be . . . accidental."

CHAPTER 21

DELILAH

I bite my bottom lip, focused intently on the chemistry exam in front of me. I don't allow myself to think of Ben, or the fact that I haven't heard from him in two weeks. And I refuse to let my thoughts wander to a silver-eyed *and* silver-tongued devil.

In my peripheral vision, I catch the student next to me angling his body toward me. More specifically, my paper. He glances repeatedly between his exam and mine, his pencil scratching away furiously.

Frustration has me gritting my teeth at his obvious cheating. I shift in my seat to conceal my paper, but that doesn't work. If it did, this wouldn't be the second time this guy has copied me.

I clear my throat loudly and cover my answers with my arm. The student pauses, his brow furrowing, before he leans forward even further than before. I shoot him a pointed glare, which he promptly ignores.

With a sigh, I do my best to rush through the test, hoping he'll be too slow and get the last section wrong. I worked hard last night studying the binary ionic compounds instead of joining Raven and June at a club. Not that it's my scene, but anything is better than chemistry.

I make a mental note to speak to Professor Ames about this during his office hours. Integrity matters to me. Also, I can't afford to lose my scholarship because of some random twat cheating off me.

As soon as I finish the test, I gather my things and give the student one final dirty look. He has the grace to look sheepish, but I don't care. He's still a liability.

I place my test on Professor Ames's desk, avoiding his gaze. Ever since day one, I haven't been able to look this man in the face. There's a coldness in his eyes that chills me to the bone, like he's one manic episode away from becoming a psychopath.

"Wait a moment, Miss Scott."

His voice stops me cold. I turn back to meet his stare and immediately regret it. His eyes are bright with anticipation, similar to the way I look at a spider before smashing it. Repeatedly.

He leans forward and lowers his voice. It takes everything inside me to hold my ground and not take a step back.

"I couldn't help but notice some concerning behavior this morning," he says. "I'll be reporting your academic dishonesty to the Academic Integrity Board. Today."

"What?" I cringe at the volume of my voice. It wasn't a screech per se, but it wasn't far off. "I didn't do anything wrong. *He* cheated off of *me*. Today isn't the first time either."

Professor Ames tilts his head. "And yet you haven't mentioned it. This means you were assisting him." He holds up a hand when I start to protest. "I understand this is upsetting, but we take integrity very seriously here. I suggest you speak with your academic advisor as quickly as possible."

With my mind spinning, I leave the room and head straight to the administration building. My panic over this unjust situation has my stomach tied in knots, and by the time I'm sitting in Mrs. Shipley's office chair, I'm close to fainting.

"Delilah," she says, her forehead wrinkling with concern. "What's wrong?"

It takes me several deep breaths to clear the spots from my vision and to steady my racing pulse. I grip the armrests to ground myself and to keep from falling on the floor.

"I was just accused of cheating during Professor Ames's exam, which is complete and total horseshit, bullshit, and pigshit."

The woman delicately clears her throat and tucks a gray strand of hair back into the bun at the base of her neck before adjusting her glasses. In their reflection I can see myself, my expression borders on hysteria. The opposite of her professionalism.

She laces her fingers and sets them on the desk. "Start from the beginning."

I tell her everything about the other student and my attempts to discourage him from copying. "Now I'm in danger of losing my scholarship. I can't stay here without it."

"This is very serious, my dear."

I cover my face with my hands and groan. "I know."

"Accusations like this can have severe consequences."

"I know," I repeat. I drop my hands into my lap and hang my head. "Is there anything I can do? I mean, there has to be a way to prove my innocence."

She nods slowly, her gaze narrowing in thought. "Let me look into this."

After reaching for the phone on her desk, she dials an extension and engages someone in a brief conversation. I watch her like she's going to disappear if I so much as blink. My heart rate skyrockets again, and I have to concentrate on breathing evenly to avoid passing out.

Mrs. Shipley hangs up the phone. "Professor Ames is willing to reconsider the situation, but he still believes that you are at fault for failing to report the other student. To resolve this issue without escalating it to the Academic Integrity Board, he's proposing an alternative."

"What is it? I'll do anything."

The woman nods. "Instead of facing a formal investigation, he suggests you sign a contract."

"What?" I narrow my gaze. "Like a promise to narc on pieces of sh—" When her mouth thins with disapproval, I clear my throat. "What does the contract entail?"

"This would involve you taking on a role as a model student. You would participate in campus events, and attend ceremonies and various university activities left up to the discretion of the Obsidian

Order. It's a way for you to demonstrate your character to your professors, as well as your fellow students."

I open my mouth, close it, and then try again. "The Obsidian Order . . . as in the fraternity?"

"Yes, dear. It is our most prestigious foundation on campus. It dates back to before the university was even built."

"So, this whole ordeal is like a community service thing?"

Mrs. Shipley nods. "In a sense. It's a good way to show your commitment to the university's values and prove you're an asset to the community. Signing this contract would also be an acknowledgment that you understand the seriousness of the situation and are willing to take responsibility for your part in it."

I fold my arms and sigh. "I don't see any other option for me."

"It'd be in your best interest to do this."

The older woman shifts her attention to her computer, types for several minutes, and clicks the mouse. Every time she presses a button, my stomach knots a little more. I don't know what else I can do except go along with this stupid contract. As much as I'd like to tell everyone to kiss my ass, it won't do me any good.

I silently curse Professor Ames and the other student. Calling them all sorts of profane things almost makes me smile. Almost.

The hum of the printer interrupts my internal barrage of insults. Mrs. Shipley grabs several sheets of paper which has me frowning. How many pages is this contract? After the tenth page, I begin to lament the tree that sacrificed itself on my behalf.

"Here you go," she says, sliding the stack of papers to me. "Legal documents are very thorough. Read it carefully so you're fully aware of what you're committing to. If you have any questions, I'll be happy to answer them."

"This is longer than I expected," I mutter.

I quickly scan the words on the first page. The legalese on the document is mind-numbing. It's paragraph after paragraph filled with dense language that seems designed to confuse more than inform.

After a few seconds, my eyes glaze over as I try to decipher the tiny font outlining the clauses and obligations in the contract. My academic advisor watches me with a smile, but her attentiveness is a little overwhelming. She's not rushing me, but my intuition says she wants me to hurry up. I'm sure she has other tasks to complete that don't include managing my crisis.

"I think I get the gist of it," I say. "I sign, do my time, and keep my scholarship, right?"

She nods. "That's the general idea. Make sure to note that your point of contact will be Professor Ames. Unless he appoints a senior to direct you, he's the one who will reach out with the details of the upcoming events."

I'm sure that dickhead will have me picking up trash alongside the road just to humiliate me. As long as my duties are nothing unconventional, I'll handle them just fine. Growing up in the foster care system isn't for the weak.

I pick up the pen, eyes widening at my shaking fingers. This situation is grossly unfair and pisses me off, but it's fear that's wrapping around my hands and making them tremble. I flip to the last page and scrawl my signature across the dotted line before I lose my nerve.

After shoving the document back at Mrs. Shipley, I blow out a breath. Instead of feeling relieved that I'm doing everything to save my future, a sense of doom hovers over me like a rain cloud.

She snatches the papers from the desk. Almost like she doesn't want me to change my mind. "Although you'll be on probation with Professor Ames for the rest of the semester, your obligations will last for the entire school year. Take this seriously, and you might find it more rewarding than you expect. It's an honor to be affiliated with the Obsidian Order."

I get to my feet, shift my gaze from her face, which is alight with pride and sophistication, and concentrate on the nameplate on her desk. "Thanks," I mumble. "Shipley, as in one of the founding families?"

She beams up at me. "That is correct."

That explains why she's drinking the Kool-Aid the fraternity is serving. Too bad she's snorting it as well.

CHAPTER 22

DELILAH

Subject: Urgent: Obsidian Order Ceremony Details

Delilah,

I trust this message finds you ready and willing to perform your contractual obligations. The Obsidian Order ceremony is slated for this night, September 3rd, commencing sharply at 9:00 p.m. The venue is discreetly tucked away at 124 Oak Street, within the walls of our fraternity house.

Arrive punctually to avoid unnecessary complications. The dress code is formal. Discretion is paramount, as was indicated in the contract.

This event holds significant weight within our fraternity. Your presence is not only anticipated but crucial. Failure to comply may have unforeseen consequences.

For any queries or concerns, do not hesitate to reach out. Your cooperation is expected.

Regards,
Professor Ames

CHAPTER 23

DELILAH

I slip in my earrings, wishing I could admire the way they complement my silver dress. It's from a secondhand shop, but no one would ever know because of the label inside. Tonight calls for an elegance I don't usually get to participate in, and I couldn't care less. My heart has been racing ever since I got the email from Professor Ames this morning, and now that it's almost time, I want to puke.

The door swings open to reveal Raven. She runs her gaze over my shiny dress and arches a brow. "Hey, sexy. Hot date tonight?"

I shake my head. "I wish. This," I say, running my hands down my sides, "is for extra credit."

"As a prostitute?"

A laugh slips out of me. "No. This place doesn't allow bribery, so I'm pretty sure prostitution is off the table."

"That's a shame." She steps fully into the room and shuts the door behind her. After tossing her purse on the floor, Raven throws herself on her bed and folds her arms over her chest. "That outfit of yours screams, 'Do me, daddy' instead of 'university event.'"

"I don't care if it's boring, as long as it allows me to keep my grades up."

"Where is this thing anyway?"

I pick up my lipstick and apply it before speaking. I'm unsure how much I'm allowed to disclose about my contract, but keeping Miss Sherlock Holmes from suspecting anything is going to be a challenge. I'm pretty confident she wouldn't tell anyone if I told her my situation, but that's not my only issue. I'm not just scared of losing my scholarship, I'm beyond embarrassed this is happening.

"It's at the student center," I say.

"That's for nerds. I wouldn't be caught dead there."

I know. That's why I chose it as my answer.

"You were right about Professor Ames," I say, attempting to steer the conversation in a different direction. I secure a diamond-tipped hairpin in my updo. "He's a hard-ass when it comes to grading. If I want an A in his class, then I have to do this extra credit."

"As long as it doesn't include sucking his dick, then you should be okay."

I make a face. "That's not happening. What are your plans tonight?"

"Well, I was going out with June, but she canceled on me this morning. Bitch." Raven sighs and rolls on her side to face me. "She said she had some mandatory thing for her math club. Talk about boring. I bet she'll be at the student center too."

"Maybe," I say, avoiding eye contact with my roommate. "All right, I'm out of here."

"Have fun, if you can."

"I doubt it."

She snorts. "Me too."

"Don't wait up for me."

Raven blows me a kiss right before I shut the door behind me. Within moments, I'm outside, the cool evening air brushing my cheeks. I stay on the sidewalk to avoid breaking an ankle in my heels. The click that sounds with every step I take is like a metronome, ticking away toward my doom.

The only silver lining in this whole ordeal is the possibility that I could see Ben. Whether or not he wants to see me is something I won't allow myself to think about for long. It's been weeks since we last spoke, and now the prospect of encountering him stirs so many conflicting emotions.

If I walk up to him, will he ignore me? Would there be tension or a familiarity that's been constant most of my life? What's the reason he's been avoiding me?

My tumultuous thoughts keep me company as I make my way across campus. Eventually, the glow of the fraternity's castle comes into view, guarded by the ornate wrought-iron gate. I slow my steps on the gravel-filled driveway and then stop in front of the entrance.

Like magic, the gate slides open. They have great security . . . or someone's anticipating my arrival.

Hesitation slithers down my legs, keeping me from moving. I shake it off and pull my coat tighter around my shoulders before marching forward. The faster I get in there, the faster I can get this over with.

The heavy wooden door of the castle opens without a sound just as I reach the threshold. A figure emerges, backlit by the lights from the foyer. It's an older man with salt-and-pepper hair, dressed in a black suit with a crisp white shirt underneath, and polished onyx shoes.

The man inclines his head and extends his arm with flourished movement, his gloved hand pointing in my direction. "Welcome, Miss Scott."

I nod, too unsettled by everything to form coherent words. It's one thing for the gate to swing open when I show up, but to have this man open the door before I knock is another. Not to mention he said my name, which means he knows my identity. The security in this place is either epic or really fucking scary.

"I am Mortimer. Mrs. Emerson has asked me to escort you to the lounge. Right this way, please."

My mind instantly hones in on the founding family name of Emerson. Another bitch who's probably drinking the crazy Kool-Aid. I suppose I should be grateful I'm not dealing with Professor Ames. He's like a not-hot Professor Snape: smart, creepy, and a dick.

As Mortimer leads the way, the grandeur of the castle's interior momentarily diminishes my nervousness. The entrance hall is adorned with colorful tapestries depicting different coat of arms and battle scenes from the Revolutionary War. I glance up at the chandeliers, now with electric bulbs instead of candles, and their sparkle momentarily dazzles me.

We climb a wide staircase that's covered in a rich burgundy carpeting. The carved banister is smooth to touch, worn by generations of hands. At the top, he guides me down a long hallway and my heels sink into the cushioned material underneath my feet.

I scan the area and frown when I find we're completely alone. Although I have no idea how many fraternity members live in this building, I figured I would've seen at least one by now.

"Where is everyone?" I ask.

The butler never stops walking but turns to briefly look at me over his shoulder. "All will be revealed in time, Miss Scott. You'll see."

His cryptic response makes my nervousness return in full force. I'm not sure why I'm so jittery. This event is sanctioned by the university, at least to an extent, so it has to be safe.

Right?

Mortimer stops in front of a pair of double doors at the end of the corridor before pushing them open. I peek around him to find a room draped in blue and gold.

"Mrs. Emerson will be with you shortly," he says.

I nod and step into the room, finding it empty. The large fireplace takes center stage and gives the space a welcoming glow. Plush sofas have been placed in front of it, the flames from the fire dancing along in their deep blues and bright golds. The walls are draped with swaths of cream-colored silk and accentuated with golden filigree patterns.

My inspection of the decor comes to a halt when the doors open. I immediately take a step back, my gaze focused on the newcomer. Mortimer guides her inside, giving her the same speech he did to me, and shuts the door once more.

June glances around the room, taking in the antique furniture, but when her gaze lands on me, it widens. My friend hurries over to my side, her long legs scissoring gracefully. The black dress she wears is similar to mine in style, straps lining her shoulders and the hem stopping just above her knees.

"What are you doing here?" I ask.

"You first." She eyes me up and down. "Though it looks like we're here for the same party."

I bite the inside of my cheek. The uncertainty of the situation rushes through me, loosening my tongue. "I, uh, had a little *incident* involving a certain asshole professor. Signing up for this event was my way of getting out of trouble. Your turn."

June folds her arms with a sigh. "My academic advisor called me into the office yesterday and told me that my 'failure to participate in community activities could lead to my scholarship being revoked,'" she says, making air quotes. "I can't afford the tuition, so here I am, despite the fact that I was never told about this."

"I was accused of cheating. Well, not me, but helping the guy next to me do it."

"Seriously?"

I nod. "Yeah. I'm here to exemplify a model student."

"Join the club. Do you know what we're supposed to do exactly?"

"Not a fucking clue. The email I got from Professor Ames was short and didn't tell me anything important other than the date, time, and what to wear."

June purses her lips. "Honestly, this is the biggest load of bullshit. I don't get how us attending a fraternity's initiation ceremony makes any difference."

I open my mouth to respond, then promptly shut it when the door opens. Another young woman, clearly a student like us, walks into the room. Her hair is dark brown, but her eyes hold the same apprehension as ours.

It takes me a moment to recognize her. An image of her adjusting her clothing before she chases after a disheveled Xavier fills my mind. A rush of heat sweeps over my cheeks before I can stop it. Jealousy, an unwelcome intruder, wraps its fingers around my heart and squeezes.

I stare at the young woman while reminding myself that I'm not interested in Xavier. Never mind the fact that he's a grown man and free to sleep with whomever he wants. It's not like him saving my life means I'm indebted to him or that I've stopped being pissed at him for keeping secrets about Ben.

Even with that logic running through my mind, I find myself studying her features, trying to understand what he sees in her. In comparison, her clothing is better quality, and she carries an air of sophistication I can never replicate. Maybe she's his girlfriend and one of the reasons he keeps telling me to stay away from him.

"Hi," she says with a tiny wave, bringing me out of my grim thoughts. "I'm Brenda. You guys here for the ceremony?"

"Yes," June says. "I'm June and this is Delilah."

Brenda comes to stand beside us, wringing her hands. "This place is wild. They don't allow anyone on the property, let alone inside. It's crazy that they want us here to begin with. My roommate is super jealous."

"It doesn't add up," June says. "I'm saying that as a woman and as a math genius."

I nod. "Agreed."

That is what's been bothering me since I received the email from Professor Ames. Nothing about me being here makes any sense. My presence should have no bearing on the proceedings, yet there's three of us standing in this room.

The doors open, and I jerk my head in that direction. My gaze lands on a middle-aged woman as she strides into the space with a commanding air. She's wearing a fitted navy gown that combines opulence and a hint of sensuality. Her chestnut hair is swept up into a bun atop her head and artfully arranged curls frame her face.

She stops two feet from our group and claps her hands sharply. "All of you need to remove your clothes. *Now.*"

CHAPTER 24

DELILAH

"Listen," I say, "it's more likely that tiny cherubs will fly out of my ass before I take this dress off."

June nods. "Same, but not cherubs. I'm going with oranges. It's a healthier option."

Mrs. Emerson lifts a brow, clearly not amused. "I don't have time for your antics. The Order has charged me with the task of preparing you for the ceremony. I haven't been late in my duties for over a decade, and I'm not about to start now."

I look to June, not bothering to hide the shock that has to be written all over my face. Mrs. Emerson's authoritative tone leaves no room for negotiation, but that's not what has fear coiling in my gut. It's the fact that this ceremony has been taking place for over a decade. At least.

"Look, lady," June says, "I signed up to participate in a community event, not a nudist colony."

Nervous laughter bubbles up in my throat and I stifle it. My discomfort over this turn of events is like drinking champagne, and now I'm drunk on fear.

The older woman tilts her head, her expression unfazed. "Your concerns are duly noted. However, let me be perfectly clear. You signed a contract. A legally binding one that will have you stripped of your academic funding if you refuse to follow through with your obligations."

"You can't do this," Brenda says. Her voice takes on a higher pitch, filled with hysteria. "I never would've signed if I'd known you were going to ask me to participate while naked."

"You won't be nude, silly girl," Mrs. Emerson says. "You are going to wear the proper ceremonial clothing."

She walks over to a large armoire and pulls open the door. Inside are several white gowns. The woman selects one and holds it away from her body, her gaze darting to me.

It's a wedding dress.

"I think this is your size." When I don't move to retrieve it, she thrusts it in my direction. "All you have to do is put it on. Before the event starts, you will be given a chance to get out of your contractual obligation, but until then you have to be dressed in the appropriate attire."

A heavy silence drapes over the room like a velvet curtain, suffocating me. I drop my gaze, unable to look at June as I give in to the demands weighing on me and take a step forward. This might be just a scholarship to some people, but to me it's my entire life.

When June and Brenda also take the dresses handed to them by Mrs. Emerson, I highly suspect I'm not the only one who has much to lose.

I inhale a deep breath before removing my silver dress. The rustling of fabric echoes throughout the room as each of us complies with the unusual directive. Mrs. Emerson's gaze stays locked on us, completely unaffected by our distress and discomfort.

The cool, pale material slides over my skin like a gentle breeze. Intricate lace patterns cascade along my arms and down my entire back, leaving me feeling exposed. The skirt only billows out slightly, providing enough room for me to walk comfortably, but still clings to my hips in an enticing manner.

"The removal of your old clothes is symbolic," Mrs. Emerson says. "It represents you shedding your preconceived notions about control and embracing the Order's authority over you."

I grip handfuls of my skirt and yank on them. "Why a wedding dress? That's pretty fucking specific."

"You're a bride." When my eyes nearly pop out of my head, she waves a hand in dismissal. "Relax. The only contract you're fulfilling is the one you signed, not a contract of marriage."

"Let me guess," June says, folding her arms. "The wedding dress is symbolic?"

The older woman nods. "However, not in the way you think. Yes, it's associated with loyalty, in the way a bride must remain faithful to her husband. But it also represents the power the recruit has over you. If he claims you, he will be your master, and you will be his property."

I make a choking noise before throwing up my hands. "I'm out, like a vegan at a fucking barbecue."

"Same." June marches behind me. "No scholarship is worth this shit."

"Failure to fulfill your duties doesn't just have repercussions within these walls."

Mrs. Emerson's words have me coming to a halt mid-step. I plant my feet and slowly turn to face her, my heart thundering in my chest. "What do you mean?"

"The power wielded by the Order extends far beyond the realm of academia." The older woman's brow furrows, a pitying expression on her face. "Did you really think you could walk away? The founding families of the Obsidian Order are no ordinary individuals. They control industries that permeate every facet of society. Technology, firearms, medicine, finance—their influence is beyond comprehension for those outside its confidentiality."

The gravity of her revelation has my legs trembling. I reach out and grip June's hand to keep from falling to the ground.

Mrs. Emerson continues speaking, every sentence like a guillotine above my head, getting closer and closer. "Your actions and involvement within this place are not isolated. The power behind these men is not only extensive but pervasive. You can't escape it, no matter where you run. It's better for you to save your energy for the chase in the Bride Hunt."

"Chase?" I repeat the word in a whisper, barely discernible to my own ears. "What chase?"

Mrs. Emerson nods. “That is the part of the ceremony you were summoned for, bride.”

“But we’re not actually getting married, right?” Brenda asks. She wrings her hands until her skin blanches, similar to the pallor of her face. When the older woman nods, she exhales. “What about the chance to get out of this?”

“If you can make it to the forest’s edge, your contract will be null and void.” Mrs. Emerson shrugs. “It’s as simple as that.”

“And if we can’t?” I ask, my words sharp with fear.

“Then, my dear bride, your recruit will be a *very* happy man.”

CHAPTER 25

DELILAH

The forest is eerie at night.

Ancient trees cast elongated shadows in the moonlight, turning the grass-covered earth into a sea of black. In contrast, Brenda, June, and I stand there, covered in snowy white dresses that are blinding against the dark background.

There's no way we can hide.

My heartbeat echoes in my ears, growing louder with every passing moment until I'm deafened by my fear. The other girls' expressions mirror my own, a mixture of horror, reluctant acceptance, and anticipation. No one has said it out loud, but we're all determined to get out of our contract by reaching the edge of the forest.

If not, we're fucking fucked.

I glance at the trees, waiting for someone to emerge from the shadows. Although I've been waiting for their arrival since I first stepped outside, I'm still shocked when it happens. One by one, each man appears, completely covered in black clothing.

And a mask.

Every single one has a white background with black designs. Some have splotches over the eyes, while others have streaks or tribal-like markings. One has nothing except black dots on it, reminding me of an old-school hockey mask.

I'm sure the masks and the colors symbolize something. I just don't know what. And I have no intention of staying long enough to find out.

The group enters the clearing and forms a semicircle around us. Mrs. Emerson watches from a distance, clearly waiting for something. Or someone.

I squeeze the shit out of June's hand, and she grunts but doesn't pull away. In fact, she returns the gesture. Brenda stays close to me, pressing her side to mine, lending me her body heat.

The wind chooses that moment to stir, creating gooseflesh on my skin. I shiver from both the cold, the damp grass under my bare feet, and the gazes of the men staring at me. Their eyes, the only visible feature, glint with intensity.

And hunger.

Even though I'm mentally one scream away from a padded room, I hold my ground and lift my chin. Fuck these guys.

And Ben, if he's willing to participate in this type of thing.

I scan the men, searching for anyone similar in build and height to my foster brother. There are nine of them, and three could be him based on hair color.

"Ah, fuck," a recruit mutters.

My ears perk up. I recognize that voice. I know that "fuck."

I hone in on the speaker, narrowing my gaze as if I can see through his mask, the one that has a black patch over the left eye. It has to be Ben. Adrenaline combines with betrayal in some fucked-up cocktail streaming through my blood.

Right when I'm about to walk over to him, another figure appears. This one is different from the rest. He has a mask on, but it's pure black. There's also a black cloak covering him from head to foot, concealing his imposing frame.

Every member of the fraternity looks in his direction. And by fraternity, I mean a fucking cult.

There's an aura of power to this man that sends chills running down the back of my neck. The recruits keep their focus on him, their gazes never straying. He comes to stand in the gap between us and the younger men, and gestures for us to kneel.

I stiffen in disdain, but June yanks on my arm, pulling me down.

The grass beneath me is cool and slightly damp, the moisture clinging to my skirt. I dig my nails into the dirt to keep silent and to stop myself from flipping this guy off.

"*Mors solum initium,*" he says.

Every recruit repeats the phrase, their voices becoming one sound. It's melodic, a deep baritone that echoes throughout the clearing. I know it's Latin, but I have no clue what it means. Or if I even want to know.

The man clasps his hands behind his back. "You will be ranked according to skill and execution. Not only tonight, but in the upcoming Trials and every area the council deems worthy. The top three recruits will automatically be selected as crows and given first choice in assignments. These brides are my gift to you."

He points in our direction. I glare up at him, not bothering to hide my irritation until June sways into me. I'm quick to steady her. We exchange a glance, and her eyes beg me to stay quiet.

"Let there be no misconceptions," he continues. "A bride will never be a crow's wife. But she can be a recruit's prize. She represents your standing within the ranks, as well as the victories you've earned through prowess, cunning, and strength. How *she* acts is a reflection of you. This arrangement is temporary but highly indicative of how you will utilize power once you've been given a taste. And this, gentlemen . . ."

He leans down and snatches my upper arm, yanking me to my feet. "This type of power is only the beginning."

When I rear back, he tightens his hold, his fingers digging into lace and skin. I suck in a breath at the pain, and the scent of his cologne fills my nose. It's expensive, soothing to the senses, yet crisp with a hint of smoke.

"What if we get out of our contract?" I ask through clenched teeth. "Will you leave us alone?"

He laughs, the sound like poison in my veins, making me ill. "I might be a man without morals, but I do have a code of justice. *If* you can break the tree line, you will walk away from this, sworn to secrecy for the rest of your life. Or it'll be forfeit."

"I'd rather be sworn to secrecy than to a year of servitude."

"This one," he says, shaking me, "is going to be fun to break, recruits."

"*If* they fucking catch me," I snap, raising my voice for everyone to hear.

He yanks me to him, and I slam against his chest, the impact jarring me. My bare feet struggle to gain purchase on the grass. When I'm standing, I jerk up my head and stare into his eyes. The gray behind the mask pierces me, stabbing my vulnerability and making it bleed.

"One of them *will* catch you, bride. And when they do, I'll enjoy watching you be tamed."

My stomach heaves at the implication. I'm not certain what he means exactly, but it doesn't matter. I'm going to run like fucking Forrest Gump or die trying.

Before I can come up with a response, the man releases me. I stumble backward and immediately right myself, lifting my chin with a glare aimed in his direction. He ignores me and goes back to addressing the recruits.

"Remember the rules. No killing. Everything else is permissible."

Is he talking about us? Or them, in regard to one another? Neither answer gives me comfort.

I take my spot next to June. She stares at me, stark terror gripping her features, while Brenda trembles next to me. I wish I could say something reassuring to them, but nothing comes to mind. The only thing I can focus on is getting out of this contract by whatever means necessary.

"Brides," the leader says, "your time begins in five . . ."

My heart lurches in my chest as I bend my knees in preparation to bolt.

"Four . . ."

I look at June, encouraging her without words that we can do this. Although fear is like a corset around my rib cage, making it hard for me to breathe.

"Three . . ."

With my fists by my sides, I stare straight ahead, ignoring the men around me. Their gazes are ravenous, like a pack of wolves about to be set on a lamb. I might be wearing white, but my soul is dark enough to give them hell.

"Two . . ."

Fuck this guy.

"One."

I take off.

In that moment, I forget about everything and everyone except myself and my need for freedom. If I get out of this nightmare, I'll be in a better position to help June and Brenda. Maybe.

The wind whistles past my ears. It blows loose strands of hair across my face, the silky pieces sticking to my lips. I don't take the time to fix it.

Every second counts. I can't spare a single one.

My feet pound against the earth in time with my rapid heartbeats. Every sound is now heightened. The rustling leaves. My breaths. A snapping twig. But the loudest noises are my thoughts.

Faster. FASTER. *FASTER.*

Overhead, the moon casts a spotlight through the treetops. It's beautiful, peaceful, and completely at odds with the terror streaming through my body.

I continue onward, keeping my path straight to achieve the shortest distance to my goal. The forest plays tricks on my senses, casting menacing shadows on uneven terrain.

I trip and stumble. Then push through, never stopping as fear bites at my heels like a rabid animal. The forest is a blur as I weave through the natural labyrinth. However, my motivation is clear.

Don't get caught, or I'll face something worse than death. A complete loss of freedom.

A flash of movement catches my eye.

My heart stops. Panic takes over, and I pivot, making a hard left turn. And then another.

The recruit chasing me mimics my steps, his speed eclipsing mine. He closes the distance between us and grabs my forearm.

The pull on my arm causes me to come to an abrupt halt. Pain erupts in my shoulder like the shooting of fireworks.

"Fuck!" I gasp.

The masked figure yanks me in his direction. I lean into the momentum, spinning toward him with my other arm raised. My elbow connects with his stomach, and he grunts.

Before he can trap my arm between our bodies, I reach up and grab my hairpin. The man's eyes widen in surprise when I drive the pointed end into the soft skin of his neck, just under the dotted mask.

The leader said no killing, but everything else is fair game, including stabbing.

"Bitch!"

His expletive is followed by a sharp inhale as his hold loosens. I capitalize on his momentary weakness and break free, ripping the hairpin from his flesh. Then I spin on my heel, only to find another masked recruit materializing right in front of me, blocking my path.

Trapped between two men, I frantically scan my surroundings for the best escape route. The first recruit quickly recovers from my attack and lunges for me. I shriek in outrage and leap back.

Just as he's about to grab me, a blur of movement disrupts him. The newcomer knocks his arm away and plants himself by my side, so close I can feel the heat of his body.

"She's a fighter," the newcomer says.

Recognition zips through me like an electric shock.

He cocks his head and the black gashes on his mask glint under the moonlight. "You sure you can handle her?"

The other recruit with the dotted mask flips him off. "I'll do more than handle her. I'm going to fuck the fight right out of her."

I retreat a step. The action has both men shifting their attention to me. Despite the tremors wracking my limbs, I stand there, keeping my head held high. "Why don't you guys fuck each other? I'm sure your holes are tighter than mine."

The newcomer laughs. "This bride is definitely mine."

"Fuck off, X. If you're lucky, I'll let you have her." He looks at me with a narrowed gaze, his eyes blazing. "After I've stretched every one of her holes."

"No names," Xavier says, a hint of warning in his voice. "That'll cost you." He turns his head to stare deep into my eyes. "Run, little raptor. I'm coming for you."

CHAPTER 26

DELILAH

Un-fucking-believable.

Xavier and the other masked man engage in a struggle, each one trying to gain the upper hand, creating a window of opportunity for me. I sprint away from them, legs burning and lungs shuddering. The echoes of their fight follow me as I push past my discomfort and fear.

My muscles protest with each step, and thorns from the underbrush cut my skin. A low-hanging branch scratches my cheek. All of these injuries are but a sample of the pain I'll experience if I give up.

With each stride, I replay the recent interaction, my thoughts centered on Xavier. I recognized his voice. It's haunted me since the other night in the parking lot when his body was pressed against mine and his whispered words grazed my ears.

I knew he was part of the fraternity, but to come face-to-face with him under these circumstances is something else entirely. Then for him to say I belonged to him while using that stupid nickname? There's no doubt in my mind who he is.

He won't catch me.

I force myself to run faster. The canopy of leaves overhead signals my lack of freedom. The edge of the forest can't be too much farther. I hope.

A quick glance over my shoulder reveals nothing but impenetrable darkness.

The idea of being caught makes me push my body to its limits. My chest heaves, the burning of my lungs searing me from the inside out. They spasm, robbing me of breath until I stagger, falling to my knees.

The hairpin lands in the grass beside me. I hang my head, gulping in air like a fish on land. My vision blurs with tears, and I blink them away. I can't afford to cry, despite having every reason to.

When I lift my gaze, I gasp. The scream on my tongue never reaches the air. Xavier's voice wraps around my throat like a fist, choking me.

"You're beautiful on your knees, little raptor. Crawl to me and I might let you come."

"Fuck you."

His eyes brighten behind the mask. "That's the idea."

Adrenaline shoots straight to my heart. I grab the hairpin before jumping to my feet. Then I take a step back. He doesn't follow. Instead, he stands there and watches me, his silver gaze gleaming with yearning. Is it pure lust, or is it something deeper? Something darker?

"Don't touch me," I say.

"When I catch you, I plan on doing more than that."

"Not a fucking chance. You'll have to force me."

He stalks forward. "I'm happy to oblige."

"X, wait!"

The voice, as familiar as my own, causes me to halt. I spin around to find Ben, his features hidden behind a mask with a black patch over the left eye. Xavier studies Ben while coming to stand in front of me, creating a barrier.

Is he trying to protect me from my foster brother?

"Ben," I whisper, searching his gaze for tenderness, familiarity, something that'll tell me the man I know and love is still there.

Xavier's entire body goes rigid, his shoulders stiffening with ire right before my eyes. I peer around him to find Ben clenching his fists. Tension fills the air like a perfume spiced with contempt and violence.

"Delilah, you need to come with me," Ben says. His tone is cold, but the urgency underneath prickles my skin. "I'll keep you safe."

"I don't fucking think so." Xavier's voice cuts through the air. He reaches back and grabs my wrist, the warmth from his fingers seeping into my body as he pulls me to his side. "She's mine."

Ben's eyes widen behind his mask. "Are you fucking serious, X? I asked you to watch over her, and now you think she's yours?"

Xavier slides his hand from my wrist, up my arm, until he's gripping the back of my neck in a show of possessiveness. His silence is a challenge, a refusal to yield. The dominance in his touch has my pulse racing quicker than when I was running at full speed.

Ben curses and reaches up to grip his mask, ripping it from his face. "Now that the Order knows about you, you're in danger, Lilah. Come with me and I'll keep you safe."

"She'll be safest with me," Xavier says. He strokes the curve of my throat with his thumb. An awareness unfurls in my belly. I'm of half a mind to stab him just for that. "You know it's true, Benjamin."

"For the record, I don't belong to either of you," I say. I take a deep breath and gentle my voice. "Please let me go. Then I'll be out of my contract and done with this bullshit."

Both of them ignore me, their heated gazes locked on each other.

My foster brother extends his hand. "Come here, Delilah."

Xavier squeezes my neck in warning. Instead of being pissed off, my body betrays me. I tell myself that my nipples hardened because of the cool night air. It can't have anything to do with the man gripping me like I'm his actual bride.

When Ben takes a step toward us, Xavier lets out a growl and releases me, pushing me behind him. "I swear to fuck, if you come any closer, I'll fight you for her. And we both know I'll win."

"Lilah," Ben says, his expression pained, "please come here."

"No." My lips tremble, regret pricking my eyes with tears. "I can't, Ben. I won't let the Order control me. If you love me, let me go."

Xavier angles his head to look back at me. "He *does* love you, little raptor. That's the problem."

"What?" My question is nothing more than a breeze, a whisper that hits Ben with the force of a hurricane. He averts his gaze, his mouth pinching. "Ben?"

"We can talk later," he says. When he finally brings his eyes to mine, there's a vulnerability in them that makes me want to weep. "Delilah, please."

I take a step back. "I can't do this."

A whirlwind of emotion sweeps over me. The atmosphere is thick with unspoken words, hidden secrets, and danger. It coats my skin like fine mist, making me cold.

"I have to get out of here."

Ben shouts my name as I turn and run, my hairpin clenched in my fist. Xavier responds with a taunt before the sounds of an altercation reach me. I grip my skirt and hike it up to free up my legs so I can run faster.

Once I can no longer hear the fighting behind me, the tears come.

They fall in a steady stream, blurring the trees around me. Roots and leaves crunch beneath my feet, the noise is how I imagine my heart sounds as it breaks. I'm not even sure what I'm crying about, but the wind whips through my hair and carries my sobs away, slowly drying my cheeks.

The trees around me begin to thin in number and the canopy of leaves above me lessens, allowing moonlight to clearly light my path. Ahead is a clearing that could be the forest's edge. The very thought of ending this nightmare has my steps quickening.

My breathing turns into wheezing that has me grimacing. My pulse hammers in my ears, each thump like a fist to my rib cage. I clutch my chest and pray I'm not having a heart attack.

Hope fills me the moment I realize I've almost reached the forest's edge. A meadow stretches before me, offering safety from the darkness. The stars twinkle overhead, sparkling promises of freedom, making me smile.

Just as I'm about to burst through the final cluster of foliage, my sense of exhilaration fades.

Xavier stands there, arms folded, silver eyes narrowed on me.

"Did you really think I wouldn't catch you?"

His deep, smooth voice has shivers dancing along my flesh. And warnings clanging in my head. I come to a hard stop, my eyes wide and breaths ragged.

How can he be standing here when I left him behind with my foster brother?

I quickly scan the area, looking for him. "What did you do to Ben?"

My voice is shaky, fear coating it all over. Do I trust Xavier to tell me the truth? Do I even want to hear it?

"He's fine." Xavier waves a hand in dismissal. "Benjamin will be embarrassed when he wakes up because he got his ass handed to him, but that was inevitable. I'm not letting anyone get between us. Not even you."

I squeeze my hairpin, finding little comfort in the bit of metal. Xavier has taken down two recruits in order to get to me. My chances of escaping him are laughable.

That doesn't mean I'm going to give up.

"Come here, little raptor."

CHAPTER 27

DELILAH

I don't move. I'm not sure I can.

"It wasn't a request," he says, his tone firmer than before.

"I'm still not coming."

"You will be."

He rips off his mask. With fear clawing at my insides, I dart to the side, attempting to slip past him.

Xavier moves with a speed that defies the laws of nature, intercepting my path effortlessly. Before I can process his nearness, he yanks my body against his, sending the hairpin flying out of my hand.

I slam into him, my back to his front, the scent of him flooding my nose. It's like a secret in the dark, mysterious and alluring with a hint of citrus and leather.

The warmth from his body seeps through the thin fabric of my dress, his strength evident with every corded muscle that presses into my soft curves. He brushes his lips over the shell of my ear, and I stiffen in his embrace to prevent my body from melting into his. The traitorous bitch.

"You can't escape me, no matter where you run," he murmurs. "The Order can't have you. And neither can your foster brother. You're mine."

His voice is a seductive purr. With each word, his breath fans over the sensitive skin of my neck, causing tingles to shoot through my body. He drags his hand up my spine until his fingers tangle in my hair, pulling my head back to rest against his shoulder. When he stares down at me, his eyes burn into mine, stealing the air from my lungs.

"Why?" I whisper.

"Because," he says, his lips a mere inch from mine, "I've never wanted anyone more."

With the moon hanging overhead and the stars as witnesses, Xavier sweeps his lips over mine. I tense, waiting for the brutality, for his kiss to be nothing more than a weapon. Instead, it's an act of gentle persuasion, a subtle pleading that catches me off guard.

And it's with complete reverence.

His every point of contact, from his lips to his touch, is a contrast to the harshness he's always shown. This contradiction surprises me, leaving me frozen. How can he threaten me in one breath and in the next treat me as if I'm precious?

He only kisses me once. Then he's lifting his head before I even consider pushing him away. He wraps his long fingers around my throat and brushes his thumb over my jaw, making my heart stutter in my chest.

"What was that for?" I ask, my words thin and airy.

"A test."

I blink up at him in confusion. "For what?"

"Your response. Or lack thereof."

"Listen, I do—"

He uses his hand on my throat to silence me. This time when he brings his mouth to mine, it's different.

The kiss is possessive.

He sweeps his tongue over my bottom lip before darting it inside my mouth, laying claim to every inch.

I don't even realize I'm kissing him back until he growls low in his throat and rubs his erection against me. He fists the material of my dress before his hand drifts downward . . .

I gasp at the feel of his fingers on my bare skin as they snake under my skirt. With the same gentleness as before, he trails the seam of my thighs before cupping me fully, his thumb pressing against my clit. Arousal sparks a flame inside that could burn me alive.

The intensity of my reaction causes me to rear back, breaking the kiss. He continues to hold my throat, forcing me to look up at him.

"Stop." My voice is nothing more than a wheeze. He's stolen my ability to breathe. To think. Unless it's about him.

Through my panties, Xavier teases my clit with his thumb, making me clench my thighs. "I will . . . when you mean it."

He pinches my clit. It's the perfect combination of pleasure and pain. I groan. The sound is one of submission, and a plea for more.

"Good girl." He dips his hand inside my panties, rubbing my tender flesh. "Keep being honest with me, and I'll give you anything you want. You're mine. Your body knows it, and your mind will too. That's my vow to you, bride."

I shake my head and pull away from his grip on my neck. It doesn't budge. If anything, he tightens it.

I glare at him. "You're fucking crazy."

"And you're dripping for me." He presses harder, making me writhe. "Tell me who owns this pussy, and I'll let you come."

I shake my head in rebellion, even as my body hums for him.

He dips his head and grazes his teeth over the shell of my ear, nipping at the sensitive skin. "Deny it all you want, but this," he says, pressing his thumb hard against my clit as I suck in a breath, "belongs to me. Now, you're going to prove it to both of us. Be a good girl and come for me."

He tightens his fingers on my neck before working me harder and faster. My body trembles, a physical response to how much his touch affects me. When he grips my throat to the point I can't draw breath, panic combines with pleasure, heightening all my senses.

I reach up and yank on his hand to release me even as my orgasm builds. Xavier doesn't move. He grips me harder, making dots appear before my eyes.

"Shh. Trust me." He presses a kiss to my temple, a gesture so tender and at odds with him choking me. "I'm thirsty, Delilah. I want you to fucking drench my hand."

My vision blurs from the lack of oxygen, but my need to come has never been clearer. That doesn't stop my instincts from taking over. I know I'm drawing blood from him as I claw at his hand, trying to wrench it from my throat.

Something about the violence spurs him on. As it does to me.

Xavier bites down on my ear, and the pain is the catalyst that sends me over the edge. Only then does he release his hold on my neck, allowing me to suck in a breath. So I can scream.

And come.

Hard.

"Such a good fucking girl," he rasps against my ear, grinding his cock into my ass.

I buck my hips as wave after wave of ecstasy rolls through me. The pleasure is so intense, my legs shake uncontrollably, and I collapse. The only thing keeping me upright is Xavier's hand on my pussy. He continues to stroke me, his touch prolonging the high, wringing out every bit of my release until I slump against him, still trembling.

The entire time, he murmurs words of praise. It's the tenderness in his voice that has me looking up at him. The expression on his face is a mixture of arrogance and awe. I can handle his ego. It's the amazement that throws me.

No one's ever looked at me like they wanted to worship and fuck me at the same time.

"What are you staring at?" I snap.

"My bride."

"I'm not your fucking bride. I don't belong to anyone, least of all you."

Xavier reaches out and brushes his knuckles across my cheek, the gesture almost affectionate. He removes his other hand from my panties and holds it in front of my face. It glistens with my cum.

He leans forward to lick the entire length of his palm. Slowly and thoroughly. When I imagine his tongue on my clit, I flinch in shame at the renewed desire pooling in my belly.

"So fucking good," he says with a groan. "I'll never forget the way you taste. Now that I know, I'll crave it."

I squeeze my thighs together, still feeling the effects of my orgasm. And his words. They shock me, scandalize me. And make me burn. I want to hate him and myself, but I'm too lethargic, too satisfied to care.

"Open," he commands.

I part my lips. My obedience is immediate. I blame my bewildered state on him and how he took control over my body. He's right: I didn't want him to stop.

Before I can close my mouth, his fingers slip inside, and I taste myself on his skin. He growls in my ear, the sound full of praise and frustration. After removing his fingers, he grabs my jaw and crushes his lips to mine, making me taste myself on his tongue.

The salty taste is a reminder of what just happened, of the pleasure I experienced. And the weakness I showed.

I shove him away. Surprisingly, he lets me go. When I wipe my mouth with the back of my hand, he grins.

"Delilah—"

"Get fucked."

He chuckles, the sound a rumble in his chest. "I'll take that as an invitation for another round."

I flick my gaze to the clearing. Freedom is so close I can feel it, but I have no idea how to get there with Xavier in my way. After what I let him do, after the way he made me feel, he's more dangerous than the Order.

"Don't even think about it," he says. "If you run, I'll catch you. And this time when I do, you won't be the only one who *comes*."

I shiver at his threat, at the intensity in his words. As well as the truth behind them. "You're an asshole."

"Yeah, a horny one, thanks to you." He adjusts his cock, and I stare, unable to help myself. When he catches me watching, he smirks. "Don't worry, little raptor, soon enough you'll know what it feels like to have it fill that tight pussy of yours."

My mouth goes dry. I want to tell him to go to hell, but my voice deserts me. I don't want to think about why that is.

I avert my gaze. The clearing is so close. If I could just slip past him, this would all be over. But there's no way he'd let me. This man is too determined. And powerful. That only leaves me with one choice.

"Let me go," I say, softening my voice. "Please."

He shakes his head. "Never."

"Why are you doing this? What does any of this have to do with the fraternity?"

"This isn't about them. It's about you."

I blink up at him, confused. "Me? How?"

"I'll explain everything later. But right now, you need to understand that I'm the only one who can protect you."

I shake my head, unable to wrap my mind around his words. "I don't want your help."

"I know. You want your freedom. However, you need my protection, even if you don't want it. The Order has made you a person of interest, or else you wouldn't be a part of this ceremony for the recruits. The only way you'll get your freedom is through me."

"That doesn't make any sense."

He shrugs. "It will."

"So, you're saying I'm stuck with you?"

He nods, a smile curling his lips. "Until death do us part, bride."

I lift my chin. "My contract is only for a year."

"For now."

CHAPTER 28

DELILAH

Xavier grips my arm and hauls me against him. I slam into his body, the contact jarring me. Before I can recover, he reaches down to retrieve his mask and shoves it in his back pocket.

Then he takes off.

My feet trip over each other as he drags me with him. I look back at the tree line, my eyes prickling with unshed tears. Part of me still wants to try to get away from Xavier, from this messed-up situation. But his threat to fuck me still rings in my ears.

I immediately shove that image away. As well as what transpired between us. The only thing that matters now is figuring out how to get Xavier to release me from my contract. If I'm to be his bride, then he's the only one who can help me now.

"Are you taking me to the frat house?" I ask.

He corrects me with a chilling finality. "The altar. It's where the recruits take their brides to complete the ceremony."

"Like a wedding?" I try to dig my heels in the dirt, but it's useless. Xavier never breaks his stride. His determination is relentless, his grip unyielding. "I was told this wasn't a real marriage."

"It's not."

"Then what is this ceremony for, exactly?" I ask.

He doesn't respond immediately, and every ounce of nervousness in my stomach twists into a ball. From what I can tell, he's been honest with me so far. Blunt and crude are more accurate. Then why is he hesitating?

He glances over at me, silver eyes glittering in the night. "The ritual symbolizes our commitment to the Order, in the same way the bride will be faithful to her recruit. It's a binding ceremony, a pledge of loyalty witnessed by all. Once you're mine, no one can touch you without my permission."

"Without your . . . ?" I scrunch my face in confusion and irritation. "Are you saying other men will touch me if you *let* them? What about *my* fucking permission?"

He slows his steps to turn and face me. I stare up at him, my chin lifted. His eyes darken and the expression on his face hardens, weakening my mental armor.

"No one will fucking touch you, with or without your permission," he says, his tone cold yet heated at the same time. "Not if they want to live."

My pulse quickens at the fury in his voice and the threat of violence behind it. The blatant possessiveness has my body responding before I can stop it. My breath hitches, and my breasts rise as my nipples harden.

It pisses me off.

"Lucky for you, little raptor, I'm not the sharing kind."

"I think you've made that clear."

He tilts his head. "Have I? Good."

Xavier releases my wrist before grabbing my hand and lacing our fingers. I drop my gaze to our joined hands, my lips thinning. This is the way a boyfriend might show affection to his girl, a small physical intimacy that announces to the world that they're a couple.

I might be called a bride, but we are *not* together.

Oblivious to my thoughts, Xavier pulls me forward and deeper into the forest. Ahead is nothing but darkness occasionally pierced by the moonlight. We walk in silence, but my thoughts are loud.

What is he going to do to me?

I steal a glance at him before averting my gaze. His face is a mask of concentration that gives me no insight into what he's thinking. I tell myself I don't want to know, but it's a lie.

He fascinates me. In some twisted way, this man with his tenacity and arrogance has piqued my curiosity. I want to know why he's so intent on having me. Is this just about sex? Power? Or both?

Nerves ripple along my arms and up my throat, making my lips part. "Are you going to rape me?" I blurt out.

Xavier stops and whips around to face me. "Is that what you think?"

"Honestly, I don't know what to think."

He studies me for a moment, his gaze digging into my soul. "No, Delilah. I'll never rape you. When it comes to sex, you will *choose* me."

I jerk back, tugging on our joined hands. He tightens his grip and pulls me closer. I glare up at him.

"No, I won't."

"Yes, you will."

"How can you be so sure?"

He leans down and places his lips next to my ear, and his warm breath skims the side of my neck. I resist the shiver his nearness creates.

"How do I know?" he murmurs. "Because the cum on my hand tells me so."

My face heats and the sensation spreads to the rest of my body. I can still taste his kiss, feel his touch on my skin. On my clit.

I squeeze my thighs together, hoping my skirt hides the telltale movement. "Are you using me for some weird kink?"

"No." He gazes down at me and slowly shakes his head. "This isn't just a kink."

"Then what is it?"

"A need."

His tone is soft, but his admission is like a slap in the face. I stand there with my lips parted in surprise while my mind tries to make sense of what he just told me. Is this just a sexual need?

Or does he need *me*?

"We're almost there," Xavier says.

I squint, not recognizing the trees in front of me. That isn't surprising, considering I ran through the forest like a bat out of hell.

All for nothing.

Tears of frustration gather in my eyes at my failure.

He stops and releases my hand to put his mask back on. I watch him, silently debating whether or not to make a run for it. It's a stupid thought, but I can't help it.

I'm so fucking scared. Of everything. Him. The Order. The ceremony.

If I try to escape, Xavier will catch me. And then he'll fuck me with everyone listening. Or even watching. I don't want my first time to be like that.

"Listen carefully," he says. He stares down at me, the slashes on his mask making my stomach churn with foreboding. "The recruits want to see you suffer. They get off on that shit, especially the council member. Everyone saw the fight in you, and now they want to watch you break. Don't give them the satisfaction."

I narrow my gaze, tears long gone. "I heard your leader say that my behavior is a reflection on you. Is that why you're telling me? So I don't make you look bad?"

"No. I don't give a fuck what they think."

"Then why?"

He steps closer. "This is a test, and the Order expects you to fail. They *want* your fear," he says.

"And what do you want?"

"Everything else."

My breath hitches. Just as I'm about to ask him the question burning on my tongue, he takes my hand in his. The feel of his touch breaks my concentration.

What is it about him that has my mind going blank and my body becoming alert?

A woman's scream shatters the night, echoing in the trees like the wail of an ambulance siren. The agonizing sound is immediately followed with masculine cheers and clapping. My heart slams against my rib cage. Was that Brenda or June crying out?

Xavier doesn't so much as flinch. He squeezes my hand. I can't tell if it's a warning or to comfort me.

He pulls me behind him while anxiety claws at my insides. The trees around us create a wall of black spikes, their trunks covered in shadow. Too soon, the clearing comes into view, along with the recruits.

And the altar.

It's a rectangular slab of stone. Possibly marble or granite, a dark gray speckled with silver and black flakes. Moss covers the base and the sides, hiding the weathered edges and some of the intricate carvings of long-forgotten symbols. Adjacent to it stands a single brazier, wrought from iron, its curved design hinting at ancient elegance. Smoldering embers cast an eerie glow upon the altar's surface.

And June.

The sight of my friend lying on top of it almost makes me vomit. She sobs uncontrollably, her entire body shaking as though she's having a seizure. The flames from the brazier dance on her tear-stained cheeks and torn dress, etching a haunting, sorrowful portrait of her distress and suffering.

The recruit with the checkered mask standing directly behind the altar extends a hand to June. His masked face conceals whatever thoughts lie behind the cold demeanor that lines his shoulders. When she doesn't take his hand, he reaches for her, assisting her down with his arm wrapped around her waist.

June stands on shaky legs and her hair sways back and forth like a curtain in a breeze. She clings to him, her sobs gradually subsiding as he whispers in her ear and she regains some semblance of composure. However, her tearful gaze never leaves the recruit.

"*Votum meum tibi,**" he says, looking directly at the cloaked leader.

The council member nods in approval at the recruit. "*Votum tuum receptum est.***"

The rest of the young men stand at a distance in a semicircle, watching the exchange with rapt attention. I scan the crowd, searching for Ben. Once I find him, I can't stomach looking at my foster brother anymore. He can't help me now.

I keep my gaze on June as she's led back to the group of recruits.

---

* My vow to you.

** Your vow is received.

Brenda lies on the ground at the feet of the guy with the dotted mask. Her expression is blank, as though she's crawled so far into the recesses of her mind that she's not mentally present. My heart breaks all over again.

I'm so happy I stabbed that motherfucker. And that he didn't catch me.

He stands with his arms crossed, his gaze narrowed on Xavier. Then it shifts to me. And flashes with something malicious.

I return his stare. The hatred in his eyes drills into me from across the clearing, making my legs shake underneath my skirt. Even so, I don't stop glaring at him. Instead, I pull on my rising anger and shield myself with it.

The cloaked leader claps slowly, breaking our staring contest. The man gestures to the empty altar with an outstretched hand and I gulp.

"The second bride has been claimed and branded to serve as a reminder of the power that binds them," he says. "Only one remains."

Xavier's grip on my hand tightens when the leader looks in our direction. The man's face might be covered with a mask, but I can feel the anticipation rolling off of him in waves. They crash into me, weakening my resolve.

Well, fuck this guy.

Xavier leans down, his voice barely above a whisper. "It's time."

CHAPTER 29

DELILAH

Xavier releases my hand and securely wraps his arm around my waist before guiding me over to the altar. The warmth of his skin battles with the chill coating me. The second I catch sight of the link of chains ending in a manacle, my brave façade cracks.

I nearly stumble as my feet get tangled up in each other. Xavier's grip on me tightens and keeps me upright, preventing me from feeling shame. And from escape.

I didn't notice the metal restraints because they weren't used on June. But now that I have, I can't stop looking at them. Is he going to use them on me?

"Get on the altar and lie down," Xavier says. When I don't move, he leans down and lowers his voice for my ears only. "Show them your claws, little raptor."

For some reason, his nickname for me adds a layer of emotional armor. It's as though he's on my side instead of the Order's. I'm sure my thoughts are nothing more than a product of my stress, but I don't care.

"They want your fear. Don't give them the satisfaction."

Xavier's words float in my mind like a mantra, a war cry. I lift my chin and straighten my spine. I won't let them break me. They won't get my fear.

But they can have my fury.

"No." My refusal rings loud and clear.

Xavier moves quick as lightning. From one blink to the next, he grabs me by the waist and slams me onto the stone surface. The air whooshes from my lungs, making me gasp. I let instinct take over.

Like a feral animal, I attack him. My nails scrape his arms and hands, adding to the scratches that I put there earlier when he choked me. Only this time, I'm enraged.

I reach for his mask and try to rip it from his face, a message to the Order that I see beyond their games of manipulation. Xavier is as immovable as the stone underneath my spine. And just as cold.

He digs his fingers into my shoulder, pinning me down. Ignoring the pain of his grip, I swing wildly with my free arm and land a solid blow to his jaw. He grunts and leans closer, making it difficult for me to hit him again without any leverage.

"Not bad, but not good enough," he says, his gaze locked on mine.

His words are an echo of our past, the first thing he ever said to me. The silent challenge floats in the air between us. I don't answer, saving my energy for fighting him.

I shove Xavier and writhe beneath his hold as he hovers over me. He presses his body into mine to overwhelm my movements and subdue me. At the chill of metal encircling my wrist, I scream.

It's not a sound born of pain, but of rage.

The sensation of being bound is a stark reminder of his ability to overpower me. To bind me to him. I can't give in.

Between my struggles and my fist aimed at his face, he retrieves another manacle that was concealed on the other side of the altar. The moonlight glints off of the metal, creating a malevolent piece of jewelry. I renew my efforts to get free.

Xavier snaps the second manacle in place. The click reverberates in my chest, signaling my defeat. I stare up at him, unable to look away when he reaches for me.

He curls his long fingers around the neckline of my dress and tears it in one swift motion. I jolt at the fabric ripping, the sound violent to my ears. The cool night air grazes the exposed skin, beginning at my shoulder and stopping at the swell of my breast, just above my nipple.

I meet his gaze, not bothering to conceal the defiance in mine. He takes a step back, and the small action has my muscles tensing, every part of me coiled like a spring ready to snap.

I stare in disbelief at the chains and yank on them, testing their slack. There isn't much give to them. My chest rises and falls rapidly at the realization that I'm truly bound. The night air is heavy, the atmosphere filled with expectation. But not mine.

"Fuck you!" I scream at the recruits. At the Order. At Xavier.

His silver eyes remain fixed on me as he slides the signet ring from his finger. I scrunch my face in confusion, until he dons a glove and withdraws a pair of metal tongs from the brazier.

With precision, he uses the tool to clasp the piece of jewelry and lowers it into the fire. The flames lick at the metal, the reflection winking at me ominously. The face of the ring changes from gold to amber.

"No." The denial is silent as I mouth the word, my voice muted in horror.

Xavier holds the tongs away from us as he reaches down to palm my throat. He rests his forearm against my chest, keeping me still. My heart pounds so loudly I wonder if he can feel its pulse on his skin.

He strokes the side of my neck, his tender caress not visible to those around us. I stare up at him, bewildered and trembling. He leans down and whispers in my ear, his voice shaking. "Forgive me."

Before my next breath, he shifts and presses the ring into my shoulder. His face becomes a blur as the smell of burning flesh hits the air. Pain sears me, traveling along every nerve ending I possess and sparking them with agony.

I open my mouth to scream, but the pain is too great. It's like a collar on my throat, cinching it off from speech and oxygen.

Xavier removes the ring from my skin before ripping off the glove. I can't pay attention to him as the burning sensation continues. A high-pitched ringing echoes in my ears and I clench my teeth until my temples throb, refusing to cry out.

Although I can't stop my tears from falling.

He enters my line of sight, his features slowly coming into focus as he takes my face between his hands. I blink away the tears to clear my vision, unsure if I'm imagining the trembling of his fingers against my skin.

Through the mask, he stares down at me. His eyes are liquid

silver, swirling with torment and something else. Something too deep and intense for me to decipher.

"*Votum meum tibi,*" Xavier says, keeping his focus on me. His voice drifts over me like a stream of cool water, but underneath it is a raging sea, trying to pull me into its void.

The council member clears his throat and steps forward. I want nothing more than to close my eyes and escape reality for a single moment of reprieve, but I don't. I push past the pain radiating from my shoulder and glare up at the older man.

He ignores me to stare at Xavier, his eyes narrowed behind the mask. "Speak your vow to *me*, recruit."

Xavier's entire body goes rigid, and his hands briefly grip my face before he lets them fall away. Slowly, he straightens to his full height and meets the gaze of the council member, head held high. The look in his eyes almost makes me forget about my injury.

It's not an oath, but a promise of death.

The council member doesn't move. He watches Xavier, his eyes squinted in irritation. Then his gaze flits to me.

"Say the vow again," he says, his words a sneer. "And this time, do it correctly, or you can start the ritual over."

My skin prickles with fear and dread, mixing in with the ongoing pain. Is he serious? I look to Xavier, trying to gauge if he's going to brand me again. I can't go through that without giving them what they want. My fear is running rampant.

The seconds tick by, each one feeling like an eternity has passed. Finally, Xavier juts his chin, an act of defiance.

I wilt internally and fist my hands at my sides. I'm screwed.

"*Votum meum* illi,*" Xavier says.

The older man stiffens. After a moment's hesitation, he replies, "*Votum tuum receptum est.*"

I bite the inside of my cheek, unsure of what transpired through the exchange. Did Xavier subdue the man's aggression or stoke it even further? And what does that mean for me?

So many questions and fuck all answers.

---

* My vow to *her.*

CHAPTER 30

DELILAH

My shoulder pulses angrily, and my muscles tremble at the effort it takes to lie still. I don't want to draw any attention to myself while in this vulnerable position. Who knows what other fucked-up things they want to do to me?

The council member turns to face the recruits, his rigid posture easing minutely to something less hostile. The lingering tension hovering in the air is met with silence. I scan the audience, noting that no one is clapping or cheering like they did when June was branded. It tugs at my curiosity, but I ignore it when the cloaked stranger begins talking.

"Tonight's competition was a testament to your commitment to the Order over the past three years. We have responded by awarding the best of you with a bride. We value skill, power, and loyalty above all else. It is these qualities that will be tested in the upcoming Trials. Tonight, the victorious three are free from their vow of celibacy. Only them and only with their bride, each one specifically chosen to serve."

The instant the council member disappears from the clearing, the recruits' voices rise, becoming a cacophony of sound. I take several deep breaths, but my efforts are wasted. Ben rushes up to the altar at the same time Xavier unlocks the first manacle.

The look they exchange has all the air in my lungs leaving me in a rush. My mind spins as I watch them, my gaze darting back and forth. Although their masked faces reveal nothing, their eyes tell me everything.

"Delilah, are you okay?" Ben asks. He takes my hand, rattling the chain still connected to my wrist, and brings it to his chest. "Say something."

"If you don't remove your hands from my bride, I'm going to kill you." When Ben and I look at him, Xavier tilts his head. "I thought you wanted me to say something."

My foster brother rips off his mask and tosses it to the ground, his expression fierce. I gently tug on his hold and his gaze snaps to mine.

"It's okay, Ben," I say.

"No, it's not. None of this is."

Xavier leans forward, his mouth thinning with displeasure. I slap his chest and dig my fingers into the fabric of his black T-shirt. He stops and looks down at the contact before taking my hand in his.

I lie there with two men holding me, both of them ready to kill the other. All at once, the night's horrific events slam into me. I blow out a breath and scowl at them.

"I don't care about anything except getting the fuck out of here. When I'm gone, you two can whip out your dicks and slam them on this altar for a measuring contest, okay?"

Ben swallows, his Adam's apple bobbing. "Okay, Lilah." He kisses the back of my hand, earning a growl from Xavier. Then he releases me and retreats a step.

Xavier rips off his mask and stares daggers at Ben. I squeeze Xavier's fingers, and his attention immediately shifts to me. I quirk a brow and shake my fist, rattling the chains.

He's quick to remove them while Ben watches us with his arms crossed. Once I'm free, I grunt at the effort it takes to get into a sitting position. I refuse to show any weakness, but I'm physically, mentally, and emotionally exhausted. Everything takes a toll on me.

Xavier walks around the altar and slips his arms beneath my legs and around my waist. Before I can protest, he pulls me into his arms and cradles me against his chest. The movement tugs at the skin around my burn, making me whimper in pain.

"I've got you," Xavier whispers in my ear. "Just relax."

He starts walking toward the group of recruits, and Ben blocks his path. "What are you going to do with her?"

"Whatever the fuck I want," Xavier says. "With the Order's approval, I might add. You had your chance to win her, but you didn't. Now fuck off."

"I won't let you hurt her."

I roll my eyes. "Too late, Ben. That shit was brutal."

My foster brother looks down at the mark on my shoulder and winces. "I never wanted to involve you, Lilah. This is my fault."

I sigh, too tired to properly console him when I'm the one who's been traumatized. "We can argue tomorrow about who fucked up more, okay? Please don't make this a thing. Xavier already promised me he wouldn't . . ." My cheeks heat at the thought of sex with him. I hope my embarrassment isn't clearly visible in the dying light of the fire. "You know . . ." I finish lamely.

Ben shifts from one foot to the other, his unease clinging to him. "Is that true, X?"

"Oh, I'm definitely going to fuck her," he says. "But she's going to beg me for it first."

My face is on fucking fire. It burns more than the brand on my skin.

I stiffen with shock and outrage. So does Ben.

Xavier continues, ignoring both of our reactions. "If it'd make you feel better, I'll promise not to be rough with her. At least, not the first few times."

"You motherfucker," Ben says.

"Fuck you both." My voice comes out strong and firm, although still quiet. They look down at me, their expressions varying. Xavier has amusement written all over his features while a muscle flickers along Ben's jaw as he clenches his teeth.

"Either put me down," I say, "or start walking."

Xavier grins. "Yes, ma'am."

My foster brother reaches for me when Xavier takes a step. Ben cups my cheek and strokes it with his thumb. Now it's Xavier who stiffens, his body like marble against mine. A low rumble gathers in his chest, and Ben is quick to withdraw his hand from my face.

"This isn't over, X," he says.

Then he's gone.

I slump in Xavier's hold, my head falling against his shoulder. Men are stupid, and I pretty much hate all of them.

As if to challenge my sanity, another recruit walks up to us. The young stranger is lean and has a confident stride. His midnight-black hair is tousled and falling just above his shoulders, swaying with every step. His features are rugged with a strong jawline and piercing black eyes that bore into my skin, making the hairs on my arms stand at attention.

Is every man in the Order a psychotic asshole?

I shift my gaze from him to his bride. June is pressed against his side with his arm around her waist, supporting her as she leans into him. Her gaze finds mine, and tears spring to my eyes at the defeated expression covering her face.

"Are you okay, June?" I ask.

"She'll be fine," the recruit says.

"I wasn't talking to you, dick fuck." I look at my friend, the concern evident in my voice. I can't help it. "June, honey?"

"It's okay, Delilah." She sniffs and wipes the dampness from her eyes. "I'll be okay."

I run my gaze over her shoulder, finding the mark on her skin puffy and bright red. A shudder runs through me. I might have the gumption to mouth off, but when it comes to facing the reality of the permanency of the mark on my skin, I'm a coward.

Xavier adjusts me in his arms. "What do you want, Declan?"

Declan? As in June's ex? Holy fucking monkey balls.

I can't decide if this is a good or bad thing. I make a mental note to ask Xavier later, if given the chance. It's not like I don't have my own shit to worry about.

"Why did you challenge him?" Declan asks. "First you didn't recite the vow to him, and then you said it incorrectly. Are you trying to piss him the fuck off?"

The skin around Xavier's jaw tightens, and his stormy eyes flash with something violent. He doesn't respond immediately, as though choosing his words carefully. His grip on me tightens for a moment before he finally answers.

"If I didn't stand up to him now, he would use her to control me later on. You should know that."

Declan's gaze lands on me briefly, as if weighing the implications and the gravity of the hypothetical situation. His eyes widen with understanding, and he gives Xavier a curt nod. "You know him better than anyone."

Xavier blows out a breath. "Unfortunately."

CHAPTER 31

DELILAH

My fucked-up knight in black armor carries me effortlessly into the castle.

I rest my head against his chest, feeling the steady beat of his heart while mine is erratic, making my chest ache. Part of me wants to shove him away, but this is the first time someone has forced me to depend on them. It's strange . . . and comforting in an unhealthy way.

Let the Stockholm syndrome begin.

I perk up the instant he stops in front of a room on the third floor. A security panel sits to the right of the door. It's a sleek device that's been seamlessly integrated into the castle's historical ambiance.

Xavier places his hand on the flat surface, and it scans his palm through a complex pattern recognition system that's too advanced for a mere fraternity. Once his identity is confirmed, the heavy wooden door unlocks with a subtle click, and he walks inside.

The room is spacious with high ceilings and walls adorned with ancient decor and modern light fixtures. A large bed made of solid wood, draped in deep crimson and black material, dominates the center of the floor. The only light shining in the dark room is an electric candle, creating shadows that flit across the opulent furnishings.

Xavier sets me on the bed, his gaze never leaving mine. "Don't move."

"You already caught me." I lift my unscathed shoulder in a half shrug. "What the hell else am I going to do?"

"That's fair."

He leaves the room and enters what I assume is a conjoining bathroom. The sound of running water reaches me before Xavier returns. His signet ring winks at me as he makes his way across the room, and I drop my gaze. I don't remember him picking it up, but I wish he'd left it behind.

He leans over me. I lift my head and eye him warily as he grazes the unmarred skin around my branded mark. His touch is gentle for someone who threatens to kill people every five minutes.

It's difficult to breathe with him so close, his lips a few inches from mine. Our kiss in the forest fills my mind. I'm quick to shove it aside, but the damage is done. My nipples harden, and I clench my thighs to keep from squirming.

"Am I hurting you?" he asks softly. He flicks his gaze to mine and the concern there threatens to drown me in their silver depths.

I shake my head, unable to speak with his breath skimming my mouth and his fingers on my skin. He straightens and turns to the nightstand to grab a first-aid kit. Without him touching me, I collect myself.

"You had that kit ready to go, huh?" I ask. "You were pretty sure of yourself?"

He sets the box next to me, his lips a hard line. "I wasn't coming back here without you."

"But you don't even know me."

"I know you more than you think."

"And?"

He stops rummaging through the medical supplies to look at me. "And what?"

"Did you bring me here just to fuck me? Or am I a victim in the Order's agenda?"

"Depends."

"Are you always this confusing?" I ask.

"Do you always talk this much?"

"Yes, actually."

His lips twitch with amusement as he pours a clear liquid onto a cotton ball. "This is going to hurt."

I squeeze my eyes shut and give him a quick nod. The cool solution makes contact with my inflamed skin, wrenching a groan from me. However, the sting is nothing compared to the agony I experienced earlier.

Xavier works quickly, his touch efficient but gentle. Possibly even tender. After cleaning and drying the wound, he applies medicine over my raw and battered skin, causing me to stiffen until a cool relief spreads across my skin.

I sit still, hardly breathing, as he places the gauze over the wound, pressing firmly. Xavier secures the dressing with medical tape. Once he's no longer touching me, I crack open an eyelid.

"Done?"

"Yes."

"Thank goodness." With a sigh, I slowly lie down, my exhaustion overriding my vigilance. "If you're going to fuck me, do me a favor and be quiet when you do."

His laughter floats over me, giving flight to a thousand butterflies in my stomach. I sneak a glance at him, only to find Xavier already looking down at me. He crawls onto the bed to lie beside me, and my breathing thins. I stop breathing completely when he traces the seam of my lips, his gaze bright with lust.

"If you can sleep while I'm inside you, then I'm not doing it right," he says.

His words are playful but serious, sexy but shocking. Just like him, they leave me confused. And intrigued.

I turn my head to hide my face. I'm too tired to keep my feelings secret. This dangerous man already has complete access to my body; the last thing I need to do is give him a glimpse of my mind.

And certainly not my heart.

I should be screaming at him for dragging me onto the altar and branding me, but I don't have the energy right now. That's what I tell myself at least. There's something about this man that leaves me feeling high, as though on the precipice of danger. Or bliss.

Either one could wreck me.

Xavier's comment hangs in the air, a provocative statement. And a promise. It sends a rush of warmth to my cheeks. And then there's his proximity, creating an awareness within my body that brands me just as much as his ring did.

I gasp at the feel of his fingers grazing my throat. He trails them up and down, slowly and methodically, as if he has all the time in the world to touch me. As if he's pleasured by it.

A shiver snakes its way up my spine, and I can't stop it in time.

"Are you cold?" he asks.

Does it count as a lie if it's just a sound? "Mm-hmm."

He continues his gentle exploration of my body, now tracing featherlight patterns across my collarbone and along the curve of my shoulder. He's careful not to get too close to my wound, for which I'm grateful. The longer he touches me, the warmer I become.

His deep, silky voice reverberates in the dimly lit room, filling the silence with a soothing hum. "You need to get under the covers."

"Make me," I mumble, too tired to care about anything.

I can hear the laughter in his voice as his breath skims my ear. "If that's your attempt at reverse psychology, you should know it doesn't work on me."

The lopsided smile I'm fighting tugs at my lips despite the vulnerable situation I'm in. The mattress dips right before Xavier moves me so that my head rests on one of the fluffy pillows. I roll onto my side and curl into a ball, dismissing the thud of his boots landing on the floor. As well as the rustle of clothing that follows.

I'm not sleepy enough to ignore the weight of his arm when he drapes it across my waist and his fingers dig into my hip, pulling me against his chest. I blink in the darkness at the unexpected maneuver. Yes, he's still acting domineering and possessive, but now there's an intimacy accompanying it.

"You did well tonight," he says. His words are a whisper that grazes my neck and makes my skin prickle.

"I fought you and lost."

"That was inevitable."

I roll my eyes although he can't see them. "You're such a jerk-off."

"Words like that will get that ass of yours spanked, Delilah."

"Seriously?"

"Seriously," he confirms. "You carry my mark on your shoulder and that makes me fucking hard. What do you think it'd do to me to see your ass reddened by my hand?"

I suck in a breath just as he grinds into me, his cock pressing along my spine. The idea that he desires me is overwhelming. After the boys in high school avoided me like the plague, I figured no one would want me. I wonder if Xavier likes the idea of having his prize or if there's something more . . .

"One thing you'll learn soon enough, Delilah, is that I never go back on my word. If I say it, I fucking mean it."

"So when you say I did well, you meant it?"

"Yes. Everyone expected you to run and hide. To cower or beg. You didn't. You accepted the challenge, and even though you were out of your depth, you never stopped fighting me."

I consider his words, letting the weight of them sink in. Xavier doesn't seem like the type to give praise lightly. It feels good. The warmth of his body behind me is even better.

"I have another question," I say.

He sighs, and the sound is so normal, so human, it makes me smile in the dark.

"I have a feeling it's going to be one of many."

"You're not wrong." I pause, choosing my words carefully. "Are you in a relationship with someone?"

When he doesn't answer immediately, I'm certain the unspoken answer is a "yes." It's like a knife to the gut, sharp and unexpected, and has my stomach clenching.

"Why?" he asks.

"Just answer the question."

"I don't do girlfriends."

"Oh."

For some stupid reason, disappointment floods me. It doesn't make any sense. It's not like I want to be in a relationship with the man, especially not after learning he's a bigger asshole than I originally thought. However, there's something inside me that can't quite help but feel used. Or like he'll throw me away when he's done with me.

Xavier shifts before grabbing my shoulder and forcing me to lie on my back. He crawls on top of me, caging me in with both hands planted on either side of my head. He grips my chin and forces my gaze to his.

"I don't see other girls. I'm not—"

I scoff. "Xavier—"

"Don't interrupt me," he snaps. His tone has my body responding in the most inappropriate way. "I'm not interested in anyone else," he says, his eyes boring into mine. "Only you."

I study his gaze, searching their gray depths for lies and deceit. "Really?" The vulnerability in my voice shocks me, but not more than the man on top of me.

"I've already told you, Delilah. I mean what I say."

I continue staring up at him, my emotions conflicted. He caresses my jaw the tiniest bit, and it sends me further into confusion. I can't help but think of Brenda and speculate on whatever history they have.

"You're just saying that because I'm your bride," I say. "If you'd caught someone else, you'd say the same shit to them."

"If you hadn't been forced into the Bride Hunt, I wouldn't have taken a bride."

I make a face at him instead of telling him to get the fuck out of here with that bullshit. My reaction must be a little too easy to read. His expression hardens, his grip tightening.

"It's not just the truth. It's a fucking fact."

I open my mouth, but he slides his thumb over my bottom lip, dragging it across my tongue.

"Eventually, you'll learn to trust me."

"You're crazy."

He shrugs. "You're not the first person to say that, and you won't be the last. Doesn't matter because it won't change a fucking thing."

I shake my head, removing his hand, but he presses a kiss to the corner of my mouth, his lips lingering. I don't respond, and he doesn't move. When he pulls away, his eyes are glittering with lust. And something deeper.

He moves to lie on his back and pulls me toward him. He tucks my head under his chin, his fingers tangling in my hair.

"Sleep, little raptor."

The order is quiet, spoken softly, and I have the strangest urge to obey him.

CHAPTER 32

XAVIER

Delilah fucking Scott.

In my bed.

In my arms.

In my control.

For three long years, I've pictured this moment, yearned for it. Most things don't live up to my expectations, leaving me disappointed again and again. But this woman? She exceeds every fantasy I've created.

If I was a whimsical person, I'd think I was dreaming or hallucinating, at least. However, the sound of her breathing, along with the feel of her warm body pressed to mine, reminds me that this is reality. For the first time in my life, I'm hit with a sense of fulfillment and contentment that I didn't know existed.

Now that I know, I can't live without it.

Memories from the Bride Hunt race through my mind, the adrenaline-fueled chase through the forest, my unwavering determination to claim her. I fought and eliminated Eric and Benjamin to have her. Fuckers.

Not only them, but the rest of the recruits as well. I watched them during the ceremony, daring them to celebrate Delilah's suffering. I didn't have to.

They saw her fight, and their silence reflected their respect. My bride cursing at them, at my father, especially, is a memory I'll always savor. Very few people have the balls to do what she did. I admire Delilah more than I can ever say with words.

I run my fingers through her hair, marveling at the softness of it against my skin. She stirs slightly, nuzzling closer to me with a sigh. Does she feel safe with me, or is she so deep in repose that she's forgotten the things I want to do to her?

My cock instantly gets harder than stone. A-fucking-gain. I groan in the darkness and dig my fingers into her hip to stop myself from taking her. She will choose me. I said it earlier, and I still mean that shit.

Delilah will beg for my cock.

I won't accept anything less than her complete surrender. She will succumb to her need for me.

When she does . . . fuck me. I'll never be the same. Even now, I nearly lose my mind at the memory of her coming on my hand. The sound of her moaning. The feel of her body trembling. The scream of ecstasy echoing in the trees and reverberating in my soul.

I want all of that and more.

Delilah will give me everything. In return, I'm willing to do whatever it takes to keep her safe. Even if that means taking on the Order. She's worth it all.

My money.

My power.

My sanity.

I've lost my fucking mind over her. I'm beyond obsessed, beyond fucked when it comes to her. Unhinged, and willing to kill for her.

Die for her.

If she knew the depth of my dedication and loyalty, she would be the one with all the control. As I drag my gaze over her sleeping form, I repeat my vow to her: to serve her and only her.

"*Votum meum tibi,*" I whisper. "*Tibi semper sum.**"

My father's disapproval during the ceremony is going to come back and haunt me. But I couldn't bend to him. Not when it meant setting a precedent when it comes to her.

---

* I'm yours forever.

No one, not even the esteemed council members, will dictate how I deal with my bride.

That doesn't mean I won't play by their rules. To directly and openly defy the Order is the same thing as putting a pistol in your mouth. Despite their love of legacy and family ties, they'll put you six feet under before you can blink.

For better or for worse, the Bride Hunt brought Delilah to me.

Claiming her, having the right to this woman without restriction, is what I've been wanting since the day I first saw her. Although I don't prefer it this way. Originally my plan was to take her as a wife, not as a bride, but like most things in life, my plan got fucked. Now, all I can do is keep her safe since she's on the Order's radar.

How she got there is still a mystery to me. My first suspect is Eric because he's a fucking sadist. Not to mention he tried to run her down with his car. However, I can't get rid of the nagging feeling that there's something or someone else at play here.

Could Benjamin have brought Delilah to the Order's attention in hopes he could have her as his bride? I scoff in the quiet. He knows better than to expose her like that. Now she'll have eyes on her every fucking minute until she dies.

Or marries me.

There's a possibility that my father learned about my obsession concerning her. I doubt it. I've hidden her like the gem she is, deep underground in the darkness where nothing could touch her.

Until now.

I'll have to navigate this situation with all the subtlety and cunning I possess, along with my skill set. Knowing how to kill is an art form, and I've become a master. Even so, my father's influence is not to be underestimated.

In this game of shadows and savagery, I'm playing for the highest stakes. Her very life rests in my hands. So does her body.

All that's left for me to win is her heart.

CHAPTER 33

DELILAH

I moan.

The noise is low and throaty, a siren's call, an invitation to any man within hearing range. It's the sound of a woman drowning in pleasure. And pain.

There's an ache between my thighs, an insatiable need to be filled. To come. I may be innocent, but I'm not ignorant to my body's needs.

A delicious pressure surrounds my clit and I arch my back, letting my knees fall to the side, opening my legs wide. My hips lift on their own accord, and my pleasure intensifies.

"That's my good girl."

The deep, sinful voice registers. I gasp, my eyes flying open.

Xavier. Fuck.

I jerk up my head, the fog of sleep instantly disappearing. Between my thighs, Xavier's dark hair grazes my skin with every hard pull of his mouth. He circles my clit with his tongue, and my toes curl. Another moan gathers in my throat.

My body has already surrendered to his expert touch. I can't let my will do the same.

I thread my fingers in his hair and tug. He growls in protest. The vibrations against my sensitive flesh have me biting back a groan.

I yank on his hair again, forcefully this time. He doesn't budge, just sucks me harder.

"What the fuck are you doing?" I say between pants.

He flicks his gaze to mine, the silver pools swirling with mischief. He releases my clit with a soft pop and a rush of cold air replaces his mouth. A whimper slips out, and I briefly squeeze my eyes shut, embarrassed by my need.

He smirks at me from between my legs. It's a devastating sight. "What does it look like?"

"Stop."

"Why?"

"Because."

"Not good enough, Delilah."

I glare down at him, a silent demand for him to leave me alone. His gaze darkens and the gleam in his eyes is a wicked promise.

He grips the backs of my thighs and drags me down the mattress so I'm closer, my skirt bunching even more around my waist. Then he buries his face in my pussy. It flutters, begging him for things I'll never say out loud.

"I'll scream," I warn.

"Promise?" he murmurs against my skin.

Before I can respond, his tongue slips inside my pussy. A moan bursts from me, and I bite my lip to stifle the sound. He doesn't stop. The wet slide of his mouth on my flesh has my eyes rolling back.

"Oh, God."

"Either you moan my name . . ." He reaches up and wraps his fingers around my throat and squeezes, cutting off most of my air supply. "Or you don't speak at all."

"Xavier."

"That's better," he says.

I grip his hair as he fucks me with his tongue, pulling him closer instead of shoving him away. He maintains his grip on my neck, keeping me in place, reminding me with every shallow breath how dangerous he is. I can't move or speak. I can only endure the pleasure.

Then he's lifting my leg, placing it over his shoulder, spreading me wider. And he devours me. Each lick and suck is calculated. When I'm close to coming, he slows his pace until I'm ready to beg him to go faster. Harder.

He keeps me right on the edge, a prisoner to his mouth and tongue, until I'm a writhing, panting mess. And the entire time, his hand is a vise around my throat.

"You want to come?" he asks.

I nod, tears of frustration prickling my eyes.

"Words," he snaps.

"Yes." It's a wheeze, but it's all I can manage; the tiny puff of air is all that he allows me to have. At this moment, he owns me.

"Say my name."

"Xavier."

"Again."

"Xavier. *Please*."

"You're being such a good girl for me."

He loosens his grip on my throat, and air rushes into my lungs. Then he's licking me faster, harder. With purpose. His tongue dips inside me before he circles my clit. My orgasm takes hold, wringing the life out of me.

I scream.

Xavier groans.

He tightens his fingers around my throat and squeezes once more. He continues to suck and lick, extending the climax until it's unbearable. When I try to scramble away, he pins me in place with his hands, his tongue a weapon of pleasure that forces me to come again.

When he finally lifts his head, a satisfied smile twists his mouth. "You're so fucking beautiful when you come."

"I hate you," I whisper, my throat sore.

He dips his head and drags his tongue along my slit, collecting every bit of cum. Then he licks his lips, tasting me, his eyes never leaving mine. "No, you don't."

Through the haze of lust, I catch a glimpse of his face. His expression is intense, his jaw set, his eyes glittering with something dark.

It's unhinged.

My breathing is still ragged as he sits up and stares down at me, his gaze trailing the length of my body, making me shiver. When his eyes return to my face, the fire in their depths scorches me.

"Finally, you're mine," he murmurs, his tone soft but fierce. "All fucking mine."

I part my lips to respond, but a knock at the door cuts off the words.

"Who is it?" Xavier snaps, his gaze still on me.

"Open the fucking door, recruit."

I recognize the voice belonging to the council member from the ceremony, and scramble from beneath Xavier. The man on the other side of the door knocks again, harder.

Xavier jumps off the bed, and I do the same, my skirts swishing loudly. I wince when my movement pulls at my wound, but I ignore the pain, more focused on the unexpected visitor.

I sneak into the bathroom and shut the door. After waiting three seconds, I open it a crack. Xavier strides across the room and opens the door with a jerk. He's greeted by a man that's an older version of him. He has the same build, the same eyes, and the same hair color, but with a few streaks of gray peppering the sides.

The man's eyes sweep over Xavier, his gaze cold and critical. "Is she here?"

"Why do you care? The brand is on her shoulder." Xavier narrows his gaze. "She's mine."

He crosses his arms over his chest, a subtle sign of defiance. The older man's nostrils flare, and a muscle flickers along his jaw. The tension between them is like smoke, thick and toxic.

The other man lifts his hand, revealing a black envelope. "This is a summons, son."

Ah fuck, that's his dad? No wonder Xavier is a little cracked in the head.

He rips the envelope out of his father's hand and gives him a curt nod. "Anything else?"

"Yes, actually. Why did you fuck up your vow? Don't think I missed the slight change. You pledged your loyalty to *her* instead of me."

I blink in confusion. Why would Xavier do that? I get that he's attracted to me, but a public vow is something else entirely. After watching their brief exchange, I can only guess Xavier did it to provoke his father. It really has nothing to do with me.

Xavier shrugs. "So?"

"It's fucking disrespectful," his father replies. "If the other recruits weren't present, I would've resumed your training. It seems you've forgotten it already."

"Even if I managed to forget a lifetime of torture, my scars would still remind me."

My stomach drops, and my fingers tremble on the doorknob. Torture? Sympathy swells in my chest.

"Don't test my patience," his father says. "Answer the question. Why?"

"Because any oath I take doesn't mean shit when it comes to you. You made sure I understood that early on."

The man doesn't respond immediately. His eyes are fixed on Xavier, the hardness fading. "I don't expect you to understand. When you've taken my place on the council and the weight of generations is upon your shoulders, maybe you'll realize that I did you a service. If it wasn't for me, you wouldn't be strong enough to have a bride. Let alone keep her."

Xavier stiffens. It's almost imperceptible, but not to me. I've watched this man every second of every minute since he first cornered me in the forest.

"Keep her?" he repeats.

"Don't tell me you thought the Order was done testing you?" The older man shakes his head, his smile patronizing. "She will remain yours as long as you're one of the top three recruits. If your performance dwindles during the Trials, she will be given to another recruit who *is* in the top."

My pulse quickens, and the bathroom suddenly feels too small.

I'm nothing more than a toy to be shared by recruits, used to keep them motivated. In whatever way they decide.

"The Order wants results," the man continues. "Because of me and my training, you will be the best. Your bride is a reflection of you, but you are a reflection of *me*. Never forget that. If you think to embarrass me again, I'll kill her."

CHAPTER 34

DELILAH

A chill runs through me, freezing every ounce of blood in my veins. Xavier doesn't so much as twitch. Not a muscle. Obviously, this isn't the first time he's dealt with his father threatening him.

"Is that all?" Xavier asks, his tone bland.

His father stares at him for a beat longer. Then his gaze shifts, zeroing in on the bathroom door. I freeze.

Xavier moves, blocking his father's line of sight. His broad back conceals me, and I'm able to breathe easier.

"The summons," the man says, his voice hard.

"What about it?"

"Read it," his father orders.

Xavier's cool expression remains. "I already know what it says."

"Read it, son."

I press my lips together, not understanding what's happening. Without looking at his father, Xavier tears it open and pulls out a small slip of black paper. His expression remains unchanged, giving away nothing. Meanwhile, I'm standing with my mouth hanging open.

With an exhale, Xavier asks, "How long do I have?"

"Until the ceremony. It'll add another feather to your wings."

Xavier nods and places the slip of paper in his pocket. "I'll get it done. Now get the fuck out."

His father gives him a stiff nod and turns to leave, closing the door behind him. The silence is deafening. I watch through the small crack, waiting for Xavier's reaction.

When he pivots, he's calm and collected. The look in his eyes, however, is pure fire. "How much did you hear?"

I open the door, my cheeks heating. "Everything."

"Good."

I jerk back, surprised. He stalks toward me, his gaze focused, his mouth set in a hard line. His anger is a physical presence, swirling around him.

I swallow, my throat suddenly dry. "What's going on?"

"Nothing you need to worry about."

I narrow my eyes. "That's not good enough."

"Delilah."

"Xavier," I say, imitating his tone.

"Don't challenge me. Not right now."

I lift my chin, unable to stop the small act of defiance. He shakes his head and grabs my hand, tugging me forward. He walks us back into the bedroom, the mattress dipping when he sits down and drags me onto his lap.

He slides his fingers around the nape of my neck, his thumb stroking the skin there. His touch is gentle. I hate it.

Well, I'm *trying* to hate it.

"Look at me," he says, his voice quiet but firm.

I don't comply. "Tell me what's going on."

"I have to leave, Delilah."

I turn my head, my gaze colliding with his. "You're leaving?" When he nods, panic explodes in my chest, making it ache. "Someone just threatened to kill me, and you're talking about leaving me here? Am I going to have to fend for myself? Or are you going to hand me over to another recruit?"

He growls, the sound deep and dangerous. It skitters along my skin, raising the tiny hairs. "No one will fucking touch you," he says. "Especially not another recruit. I already told you: I don't share."

"But your father said—"

"I won't let that happen."

I stare at him. "How can you be so sure?"

"Because the only way that'll happen is if I'm dead."

"What does that mean?"

"Exactly what it sounds like."

"You'd die to protect me?"

He grips my neck, his finger digging into my skin. "I'd die for you, yes."

"Don't say shit like that."

He arches a brow. "Why not?"

"Because you don't even know me."

He releases my neck to grab the hem of his shirt. I lean back and he lifts the material, exposing his chest. It's the things wet dreams are made of.

There's a scar on his shoulder, along with a tattoo of a bird perched on it. I'm no bird-ologist, but I guess it to be a falcon or maybe a hawk.

"Look," he says, pointing to the scar. "This is from the knife wound you gave me three years ago."

I stare down at the pale line on his skin, my mouth going dry. Guilt churns in my stomach, and I shove it away. He shouldn't have been sneaking into the house.

But he did save me that night.

"What about it?" I ask.

"That's how long I've been watching you. Since then, I've learned everything I could. Your likes and dislikes, your dreams and fears. Every important detail of your life, I know."

I blink at him, trying to absorb his words. "Why would you do that?"

He lowers his shirt and places his hand on the back of my neck, gripping it again. The pressure is slight, but it has me leaning into him.

"Because," he says.

"Not good enough, Xavier," I say, throwing his words back in his face.

"Because I'm obsessed with you."

CHAPTER 35

DELILAH

Xavier's words echo in my head, filling the air with their significance. This is insane. He can't be serious.

I open my mouth to call bullshit, but the look in his eyes stops me. There's no humor, no teasing. Nothing except the truth.

I shift uncomfortably on his lap, and his gaze darkens. His fingers tighten around the back of my neck and he brings me in closer, his face inches from mine.

"I told you before, you're mine. The other recruits have never had the privilege of touching your body. I have. They've never tasted you. I have. And they sure as fuck haven't heard the sound of you coming. But I have. That's why I marked you. That's why I'll kill anyone who thinks they can take you from me. Do you understand, Delilah?"

I suck in a breath, his confession a jolt to my senses. "Xavier."

He presses his forehead to mine and inhales. "Fuck, I love the way you say my name."

"What am I supposed to do while you're gone?"

"Be a good girl."

"And if I'm not?"

"Then I'll punish you."

I blink at him, half turned on, the other half—the smarter one—apprehensive. "What about the other recruits? What will they do to me?"

"Nothing, if they know what's good for them. All of the recruits took a vow of celibacy for our senior year, but that doesn't mean they wouldn't try other things with you. Things I'd kill them for. You have to be careful while I'm gone."

"Xavier," I whisper.

"Yes, bride?"

"Don't leave me here alone."

"You won't be alone. June is here."

June. I forgot all about my friend, which makes me a piece-of-shit human. My only consolation is that Xavier is a force of nature, one that destroys you before you have time to protect yourself.

I shake my head, my chest heavy. "She's hurt and probably traumatized."

"But not my girl." He looks at me with pride, stroking my cheek. "I'm going to talk to Declan. He'll watch over you while I'm gone. With him having his own bride, he's the least likely to fuck you."

"Benjamin can do it. Erm, I mean, watch over me, not the other thing."

"Fuck no," Xavier says, his tone sharp.

He tightens his hold on my neck to the point of discomfort. I try to pull away, but his grip is too strong, so I glare at him. Xavier only leans in closer, his eyes narrowed.

"Never say another man's name to me in *my* fucking bed."

I swallow, my pulse pounding at the dangerous edge in his voice. "But he's family."

"I'm your family now, Delilah. It's only a matter of time until your name matches mine."

"You're fucking crazy. And you need to let go of my neck. You're hurting me."

His fingers fall away, and I rub the ache in the column of my throat.

He watches the movement, his eyes darkening. "You have no idea what I want to do to you, do you?"

"No, and I don't want to know."

"Liar."

"I don't know what your problem is, but I'm not letting go of Ben," I say, desperate to change the subject.

"Your loyalty is one of my favorite things about you, but it's misplaced. It belongs to me now."

I roll my eyes. "Get fucked."

"Careful, little raptor. That's a very tempting offer."

I scowl. "Ben—"

"Enough," he says. "I don't trust Benjamin with you."

My heart jumps, and I suck in a sharp breath. "Why? He'd never hurt me, unlike some people." I give Xavier a pointed look.

"He wants to fuck you, Delilah."

Denial is quick to rise and I sputter. "No way. He sees me as a little sister. That's it."

"He does see you as someone precious, but he also wants to fuck you. He's conflicted because you're his foster sister. All you have to do is give him the slightest provocation, and he'll fucking take it."

"Are you talking from experience?"

"You're my obsession," he says, ignoring my question. "When it comes to you, I'm the furthest from immune."

I stare at him, not sure what to make of that. He's not making any sense. But that hasn't stopped my heart from stuttering in my chest.

"I know for a fact that Ben feels the same way I do," I say.

Xavier gives me an exasperated look. "He's wanted to fuck you for three years. Maybe even longer. Trust me, he'll take any chance he can to get close to you. Why do you think he chased you in the woods? He wanted you to be his bride, not mine."

I scrutinize Xavier's face, searching for lies, but there's nothing. Nothing except a truth I'm not ready to accept.

"You're wrong, and I'll prove it to you," Xavier says. "Has Benjamin ever touched you for longer than necessary under the guise of affection?"

"I—"

"Has he ever looked at you with longing and you mistook it for platonic love?"

"Wait."

"Tell me, did he ever say something that could've held an underlying message?"

My stomach drops. I want to tell Xavier to go fuck himself, but his words have provoked my memory bank. Images from the past dance before my eyes of me and Ben.

The look in his eyes the night before he left for college. The way he said he wanted to kill Frank for me . . . I should have noticed sooner.

"No." The denial holds no power. I shake my head as though it'll clear my mind of the uncertainty plaguing me. "This isn't how things are between us."

"One final question. I know he sees you as something more, but do you see him as a brother?"

I clamp my lips, refusing to answer.

With his free hand, Xavier takes a strand of my hair and twists it around his finger. "A man who is in love with you, a man who has been a brother figure, or a man who is a member of the Order . . . which do you see?"

My chest rises and falls with every shallow breath. "Ben is my brother."

"Is he, little raptor?" Xavier's hand stills, as if he's desperate for my answer. "Don't lie to me. Not about this."

"Yes." I glare at him. "I've never looked at Ben like that."

"I love the way you look at me." He releases his hold on my neck and strokes his finger along the bottom of my lip. "Like you want to kill me, but you want to fuck me too."

I don't say anything. There are a million questions bouncing around in my head, but I can't form a single word with Xavier gazing at me with hunger in his eyes. After being ignored and rejected by guys throughout high school, his attention is unnerving and exhilarating.

I'm addicted to the feeling of being wanted, something I never felt this intensely before. Even with Ben.

"He's my brother," I whisper. It's the only bit of truth I'm willing to recognize. Everything else has major implications that'll come with change. I don't want to lose my relationship with Ben.

"He doesn't see you in the same way."

"I . . ." I close my mouth, unable to convince myself that Xavier's wrong.

He drags his lips along my jaw. "He'll fight me for you. And he'll lose. I won't hesitate to get rid of him."

"Don't hurt him." When Xavier doesn't readily agree, I lean back and squint at him. "Promise me?"

He presses his mouth to mine, stealing the rest of my plea. It's a soft kiss, meant to comfort. And to remind me I'm his.

The gesture is too tender to be from a killer. My body remains stiff with reluctance as he coaxes me with every sweep of his lips and every caress to my skin. When I don't give in, he cups the side of my face and angles my head to trace the seam of my mouth with his tongue.

I'm torn between fighting Xavier and losing myself in him.

"Promise me," I repeat against his lips.

"That's not a vow I'm willing to take, not if it keeps me from you."

"If you hurt him, I'll never forgive you."

Xavier's gaze hardens, a mixture of frustration and anger flitting across his face. He leans back as if my words have physically struck him.

"I see," he says, his voice a whisper swallowed by the tension in the room. "I promise not to hurt him . . . unless your life is at stake."

The heat of the moment dissipates as quickly as it arrived, replaced with a cold, stark reality. Xavier would kill someone I love to keep me alive. I could never choose myself over Ben, but Xavier would. Without hesitation.

"Okay," I say.

My stomach knots as my voice hits the air. Deep down, I recognize I've pushed Xavier to his limit. His compromise in this situation might be the only security I can cling to.

The complexity of our relationship, bound by a contract but initiated years ago, is something I'm struggling to navigate. However, I can move forward knowing Ben is relatively safe from Xavier's wrath.

As long as I don't provoke it.

CHAPTER 36

DELILAH

The bathroom door opens with a click, and Xavier steps out, his hair still damp. The black T-shirt fits him perfectly, the material clinging to his muscled chest and shoulders. His black cargo pants are loose and hang low on his hips, and the belt is cinched in place.

My mouth goes dry. It's unfair how effortlessly attractive he is.

"See something you like, bride?" he asks, his lips twitching.

I lift my gaze to his and my cheeks heat. "Shut up."

He stalks toward me, the amusement fading. In a blink, he's in front of me, and I have no choice but to lean back. Xavier grabs the back of my head, his fingers threading my hair.

"Careful, or I'll fuck you goodbye instead of kiss you."

"You said you wouldn't rape me."

"You can't rape the willing."

I gape at him. He chuckles and the sound vibrates through me, sending tingles up my spine. Then his mouth is on mine, his lips moving gently, as if he's savoring me.

When he pulls back, I open my eyes, expecting to find him wearing his usual smug expression. Instead, he gazes down at me, his eyes swirling with desire.

Abruptly, he turns away from me, his movements deliberate as he begins to pack his belongings scattered around the room. A set of clothes, medical supplies, and weapons. A lot of them. Guns and knives of all shapes and sizes, plus ammunition.

Each item he places in his bag feels like a brick in the wall he's building between us, a barrier made of silence and unanswered questions. As much as I want to know where he's going and what a summons means, I don't ask. Even if he did tell me, I'm not sure I could handle the truth.

Finally, he zips his bag closed and stands, his posture rigid. When he faces me, his face is covered in a mask. Not a physical one, but an emotional one void of everything except determination and focus.

"Let's go," he says. "Grab your stuff."

He jerks his chin at a table that sits in front of a window. I walk over and collect my jacket, my silver dress, and my shoes. After checking my phone, I return it to my coat pocket, resigning myself to dealing with the missed calls and texts from Raven when I'm caffeinated.

I follow Xavier into the hall. He stops just outside the door and presses several buttons before turning to look at me.

"Place your hand on the pad. It'll scan your handprint and give you access to my room. That way, you can stay here while I'm gone. No one is allowed in there except you. Do you understand?"

I nod and do as he says. The keypad lights up, going from yellow to green. Xavier looks at me and takes my hand.

"That's it?" I ask.

"Yes."

He starts walking and I follow quietly. When we arrive at another door further down the corridor, he stops. I stare at the massive piece of wood, waiting for him to open it. He doesn't. After knocking, he steps back and waits.

Declan appears a few seconds later. He rubs his eyes and says, "Why are you awake this fucking early? Shouldn't you be in bed with your bride?" He catches sight of me behind Xavier and exhales. "What do you need?"

"I've been summoned," Xavier says.

The other recruit's eyes widen. "Fuck. Already?"

Xavier nods. "Dear old dad isn't happy with me."

"The vow."

"The vow." Xavier repeats with a nod. "My bride needs a

guardian while I'm gone. I don't want the other recruits thinking she's fair game."

Declan shakes his head and grins. "Only a stupid motherfucker would go after her. I, for one, like my balls right where they are."

"That's why I'm asking you to watch after her."

"How long?"

Xavier shrugs. "I'll be back in time for the ceremony tomorrow night."

"Not bad." Declan opens the door wider. "Get the fuck out of here. I'll take care of her."

Xavier reaches for me and grips my chin, lifting my head. The warmth from his touch makes my pulse quicken. Then he brushes his lips against mine, and I can't help but lean into the kiss. It's over too quickly.

"Behave yourself, Delilah."

I roll my eyes. "Sure thing, daddy."

His gaze darkens, and a muscle ticks along his jaw. "Say it again."

Declan coughs, clearing his throat. "Jesus. Leave before you fuck her in the hallway."

Xavier ignores him, his eyes on me. "Say my name."

"Daddy Donovan."

Declan grins. "She's fucking perfect for you, man."

Xavier's lips twitch before he smiles at me. It's devastating, taking my heartbeat and repositioning it inside my pussy. It pulses with need. Damn it.

He winks at me, and then he's gone.

I wish I was completely happy to see him go.

CHAPTER 37

DELILAH

Declan gives me a once-over. "June's inside."

I nod and follow him through the door. It's another bedroom similar to Xavier's. My friend is sitting on the bed, her head resting against the wall, a vacant expression covering her face. She blinks when she sees me.

I rush to her. "June."

"Delilah." Her voice is rough and low, a harsh whisper that sends goosebumps across my skin.

"Are you okay?" I ask.

She nods, but the movement is slow, the gesture hesitant. I throw my stuff on the comforter and sit beside her. We both lean against the wall, and she studies me in silence.

June's gaze darts to Declan and returns to me, suspicion filling her eyes. "Why are you here?"

The recruit's stare drills a hole in my skull from where he stands. I catch his eye, note the subtle shake of his head, and nod in acknowledgment.

"Xavier had to leave," I say. "He thought it'd be good for us to hang out while he's gone."

June frowns. "He left you here? Just like that?"

"Yup."

"Okay," she says, elongating the word.

She makes a face at me, and I smile at her in encouragement.

This is the first time I've caught a glimpse of June's former self. I want to believe that Declan hasn't done anything traumatic to her, aside from the bride ritual, but this situation is fucked-up in ways I couldn't imagine.

I may not trust Xavier completely, but he is intent on keeping me safe. And he trusts Declan. Xavier wouldn't have left me with this guy if he were going to hurt me.

"Are you sure you're okay?" I ask.

"Yeah." She waves a hand in dismissal. "I'm just having a hard time wrapping my mind around this . . . contract." She leans over to grab a stack of papers from a nightstand. "Did you read this thing? It's ironclad. We are fucked."

I dip my head in agreement, keeping my thoughts to myself. There's no need to remind June that it doesn't matter if the contract is solid or not. The Order and its powerful members would've found a way to keep us under their thumb.

"So what do you want to do?" I ask, trying to change the subject.

"I could really use some coffee." I look down at my wedding dress, full of dirt and grass stains. "And a change of clothes. Holy shit. Raven."

"She's been blowing up your phone too?"

I nod, biting my lip.

June tilts her head. "What is it?"

"I haven't answered her 'cause I don't know what to say."

"Not a fucking word," Declan says. His voice is low, but the threat in his tone is loud.

"Of course not." I scoff. "What do you think I'm going to say? 'Hey, Raven, I know you think I signed up for some extracurricular activities to help my grades, but I'm really under a contract to be the sex slave of some guy. But don't worry, he's hot.'" I roll my eyes. "I'm not stupid."

He narrows his. "Never said you were. Just don't fuck around because you will find out the Order would replace you like that." He snaps his fingers and I flinch.

"I have no doubt," I say.

June grabs my hand and gives it a squeeze. "Come on, let's go. On the way to the dorm, we can come up with a story to tell Raven. The juicier you make it, the more likely she is to believe it."

I groan. "If I tell her I hooked up with Xavier, she'll ask for details."

"Didn't you?" June asks.

"Did you?" I jerk my chin in Declan's direction.

Her cheeks turn pink. "He's my ex. It's not the same."

I snort. "Bullshit."

Declan watches our exchange, his eyes bright with interest.

"Can we go now?" I ask.

He sighs and runs a hand through his hair. "Fine. Let's go."

"You're coming with us?"

"You aren't leaving without me."

"Okay, boss." I stand and stretch, my muscles sore. Who knew running for your life would make you so tired?

"You should probably grab some clothes too," Declan tells June. "Unless you want to stay in that dress?"

Her lips thin. "No, I'm ready to get out of this."

He jerks his head toward the door. "Come on."

Declan takes the lead and I bring up the rear. When he reaches for her hand, she lets him. I'm not sure what to think about the contact, especially when June shoots me a furtive glance and blushes. In the end, my opinion doesn't matter. I have my own problems to deal with.

I sigh. June's still the same, and yet so different around Declan. Maybe she's right about him being her ex, and things aren't weird between them. I wish I could say the same about me and Xavier. I have no idea what the fuck is going on, other than he thinks I belong to him.

"Where is everyone?" I ask as we descend the grand staircase. The empty foyer greets us with silence.

"Classes," Declan says.

I scrunch my face. "But the university doesn't have any scheduled on Saturdays."

"These classes have nothing to do with the university."

"Then what are they?"

"That's privileged information, bride."

He doesn't provide any additional details, and I refrain from probing further. It's not like he'd tell me anyway.

Once we're outside, my spirits lift. The sun is shining, and the temperature is pleasant. It almost makes me forget what a shit show my life has become. Almost.

"So, back to X," June says. "Tell me what you're going to say to Raven. And make it good."

I groan. "Why?"

"Because she knows you. You need something that'll make her understand why you aren't returning her calls. Or text messages. Or emails. She's probably lost her shit, you know?"

"Fine." I blow out a breath. "What the hell am I supposed to say?"

"I'd start by telling her that you hooked up with the guy, and he has a huge dick."

"Oh my God."

Declan snorts, and June smacks his chest. He looks down at her and lifts a brow. When she narrows her eyes, his smirk widens.

"I hate both of you," I say. They ignore me and I roll my eyes, walking faster to keep up, settling next to June. "Any other suggestions that have nothing to do with size, girth, or dicks in general?"

June hums and taps her chin. "Well, I'd also say something about getting lost in the moment, and maybe a few references to his tongue."

I choke and sputter, unable to form words. Images of Xavier's face between my thighs fill my mind. His hands on me, his mouth, his words, the way his eyes held mine as he told me to come. My body's reaction is instant. Heat rises, painting my skin in a flush, desire thrumming through my veins.

"Well, well, well," June says.

I blink, focusing on her. "Well, what?"

"Huge dick or not, X has gotten under your skirt." She tilts her head. "And definitely under your skin."

"What? No. What?"

"I was watching you just now. You looked like you were a thousand miles away. A girl doesn't get that expression on her face unless a guy is doing it for her. Big-time." June shakes her head at me. "Looks like you have your story ready to go. I can't wait to hear it."

I glare at her. "What are you planning on telling her?"

"About Declan and me?" She shrugs. "Nothing."

"Why not?"

"There's nothing to say. Besides, I'm not sure how to describe our relationship. Or whatever the fuck is happening." She bites her lip and looks at the recruit. He shakes his head, and she scowls at him.

"June," he warns.

"Whatever." She shrugs and looks at me. "I'm going to tell Raven that Declan and I are back together. It's the simplest explanation, and it's closest to the truth. The best lies are."

Somehow, I don't think I'll be lying when I tell my roommate about Xavier and how much I enjoyed what he did to me.

"You fucking slut!"

Raven's shriek has my ears ringing. She grabs me for a hug and squeezes me until I'm gasping for breath.

"Guilty," I wheeze.

"I was worried about you," she says, finally letting go. "When you didn't come home last night and didn't respond to my calls or texts—"

"Or emails," June supplies with a grin.

Raven nods. "Or emails, I thought something had happened to you."

"X happened to her," June says.

She waggles her brows, and I glare at her. It lacks any heat. Because it's all in my cheeks. Talking about Xavier and me in bed, even briefly, has caused permanent damage to my skin.

Raven's eyebrows shoot up. "How are you going to sit there and act like you're not breaking girl code by getting back with Declan? I thought you hated him?"

"Hate-fucking is the best." June shrugs. "Don't knock it 'til you try it."

"And how many times did he fuck you before you forgave him for being a dick?" Raven asks.

"Apparently, a lot," I mutter.

"Hey!"

"Where's the lie?" Raven throws up her hands. "You ran off to do something for a class and came back the next morning with a story about getting back together. Yeah, okay."

"Whatever," June says. "After I shower and change, do you want to come with us to get coffee?"

"Or alcohol," I mutter.

Raven purses her lips. "Only if we go to Brewed Awakenings. I need the good shit."

"The kind that might stop your heart?" I ask.

"Bingo."

CHAPTER 38

XAVIER

Leaving Delilah with another man, even one I trust, is one of the most difficult things I've ever done. If defying the Order's summons wouldn't put our lives in danger, I'd do it. But I can't risk my little raptor.

No matter how much it pains me to leave her.

I briefly run my fingers over the scar she gave me, as well as the tattoo I commissioned shortly after meeting her. It doesn't soothe me as much as touching Delilah, but this is the part of me that's dedicated to her. And only her.

After exiting the castle, I make my way to the garage. That's an understatement, but simple words often are. The place is more than a garage; it's a shrine to automotive excellence, guarded by the latest security tech. Around me, the air buzzes with the potential of each machine, their gleaming exteriors promising adrenaline and escape. It's a clear reminder of the Order's wealth and power.

I take a set of keys from a hook and climb into a Range Rover, tossing my bag onto the passenger's seat. The interior's scent is fresh and the leather clean, everything is in order, unlike the chaos brewing within me. As I settle behind the wheel, I can't stop my thoughts from drifting back to Delilah, to the look on her face when I kissed her goodbye.

If I didn't know any better, I'd think she didn't want me to leave. And not just to keep her safe.

I push that notion aside and pull the summons from my pocket. The paper is neatly folded, the black color representative of the crow I will become after the Trials.

Then the next step in my plan begins.

After unfolding the thick parchment, I smooth it out. The message is written in code, a series of symbols and numbers that would appear nonsensical to anyone not versed in our type of communication. It's a language taught to recruits during the first three years of training, ingrained so deeply that by the time we receive our first summons, we can read it as easily as our native tongue.

This code is a safeguard against prying eyes. Our allies are few, but our enemies are many. It's why we stick together.

As I reread the message, the reality of the task ahead crystallizes, making my objective clear. The Order has commanded me to act with secrecy and urgency, which is the standard. I know without a doubt that this mission is nothing more than my father trying to reestablish his dominion over me. Something he hasn't had since he stabbed me and I returned the favor.

The coded words provide a location, a time, the name of the target, and my objective. But between the lines is a message all of its own. The threat to me and Delilah if I choose to ignore the call. Or don't complete the task to their specifications.

I twist the key in the ignition, and the engine roars to life, breaking the silence around me. I drive out of the garage, through the iron gates, and on to the main road that leads to the highway. As the landscape blurs past my window, I find my thoughts are consumed with Delilah instead of the mission at hand.

The long drive gives me too much time to think, to brood over the complexities that have arisen from a woman with green eyes and a mouth that could drive a saint to curse. Or groan with pleasure.

I knew the moment I met her that my obsession would only grow. And it has. I didn't know that it'd consume me until the mere thought of losing her makes me want to fucking die.

Every time I touch her, a thrill shoots down my spine. Every kiss makes me fucking hard until my balls ache. I wait with anticipation for every word that comes out of her smart mouth. Rumor has it girls compare me to a narcotic, but she's my drug of choice. And I'm a junkie that's fucking desperate for my next fix.

I rid Delilah from my mind before I pull over to the side of the road and fuck myself while fantasizing about her.

With my mind clear, I focus on the upcoming task, the type of job I know well. Unlike most recruits, the Order summoned me *before* my senior year. I'm not sure if this was my father's doing or if the council saw potential in me. Either way, I've spent the last two years hunting men and taking their lives.

Before meeting Delilah, I would've been eager to carry out my assignment, to prove myself to the powerful organization. However, the prospect no longer excites me. I'm more motivated to prove myself to her—to gain her trust and the unwavering loyalty she's capable of giving—than I am to kill another spider in my father's twisted web. I'm entangled in his weapons trafficking empire more than those who answer to him. I suppose I do, too, just not in the same way.

My father's influence has loomed over me my entire life, dictating my actions and shaping my future. I live for the day when my choices aren't tied to furthering his legacy of violence and power. Maybe that day will never come, but it won't matter once he's dead.

Daylight gives way to night. My surroundings shift from the monotony of the highway to the more varied scenery of rural back roads. The target's location isn't far, but that's after nearly twelve hours of driving, going over the speed limit. My grip on the steering wheel is steady and my resolve is firmly in place.

The sooner I get this shit over with, the sooner I can return to Delilah.

As I near the dirt road leading to the abandoned steel factory, the night deepens, enveloping me in a veil of darkness that mirrors the one within me. The headlights illuminate a narrow path, but I cut them off. I can't afford to be spotted, or it'll fuck up this entire thing.

Slowing the vehicle to a crawl, I drive under the cover of night, my irritation growing. Patience has never come naturally to me, but I've learned its value, especially when dealing with high-stakes situations. It doesn't get any more critical than life or death.

When I finally catch sight of the abandoned building, I turn off the road, using the trees to conceal my vehicle. The engine of the SUV dies down to a whisper, and I'm left in the quiet, contemplating my next move. Before me, bathed in moonlight, the steel factory stands like a relic of a bygone era, its metal skeleton rusted and windows shattered.

I take a moment to survey the area, searching for any signs of movement belonging to a guard on duty. Finding no one, I retrieve my bag and unzip it, revealing my choice of firearms. One thing's for sure: being the heir to an arms trafficking empire lends itself to providing you with the best shit when it comes to weapons.

The familiar shape and weight of my favored pistol keeps my hands steady. I insert the clip, and the routine check that follows is more muscle memory than conscious thought. After that I secure my holster and place the gun there. Then I reach for another firearm that's similar in power and accuracy. A pair of knives are secured to my ankles, hidden in my boots, in case I have to engage in close combat.

Always prepare for shit to go wrong and you won't get caught with your dick out when it does.

My target is called the Broker, known for his ability to arrange massive arms deals. This man has been orchestrating one for months, but without my father's knowledge or approval. It's a clandestine operation on a monumental scale, involving the exchange of high-caliber weaponry, possibly including unmanned aerial vehicles. My father loves technology-infused weapons, but only if they're under his command. If not, they're a threat that must be eliminated.

I'm sure he's thought of me in such terms more than once.

The Broker has managed to bring together rogue states and terrorist organizations as key players in this deal, offering them access to military capabilities previously out of their reach. This deal is a bold move that signifies a shift in loyalty and power. In the underworld of arms trafficking, structure and control is everything. If this man thinks he can dictate the terms and bypass my father, then it'll weaken his position.

This Broker is either stupidly brilliant or brilliantly stupid to challenge my father.

With my weapons in place, I exit the vehicle and secure my mask. The target doesn't need to know my identity, just the identity of the one who sent me.

I make my way through the shadows, seamlessly blending in. My footsteps are muffled against the overgrown grassy field, while I strain to pick up any noises, all my senses are heightened by adrenaline. I inch closer to the side entrance, and the low murmur of masculine voices reaches me, a confirmation that my intel is solid.

A quick glance through the broken window reveals a vast space, a cathedral of industry. Rust clings to furnaces and cobwebs trail along the chains and hooks dangling lifelessly from the high ceiling. The air is thick with a metallic tang. Piles of scrap metal litter the ground, alongside tools and pieces of equipment, and possibly hazardous materials.

I head inside through a busted door, plastering myself against the wall while staying within the shadows provided by the machinery. In a control room stand three men, their heads bent over a table. Maps and documents are scattered across the wooden surface. The Broker jabs his finger at the papers, his scarred face twisting into a scowl. The two other men are of little consequence in this mission, but the guns on their hips make them important to my self-preservation.

I watch them through the grimy window, biding my time and refining my strategy. Three versus one basically guarantees a favorable outcome. Only when the number surpasses seven do I start to be concerned.

"Everything's in place," the Broker says. "The shipment will arrive by the eastern dock."

One of his men, the broad-shouldered guy with a beard, nods. "Security's tight. We've paid off the right people, but there's always a risk. What about the locals?"

The Broker waves a hand in dismissal. "Handled. They won't interfere. Our focus is the delivery. Once it's secure, we distribute as planned. This deal is bigger than anything we've done. It's going to change everything."

The other man, lean and squinty-eyed, cocks his head. "And the payment? It's supposed to be a fuck ton. How do you know we can trust these buyers?"

"The money's the least of our worries." The Broker straightens, a confident smile tilting his mouth. "They're desperate for what we're offering. Desperation makes for good business."

With the element of surprise on my side, I step into the open doorway, both pistols raised. "Don't fucking move." My voice is steady, the command in my tone easily discernible behind my mask. "Toss your guns on the floor and kick them out of reach."

The Broker and his guards reach for their weapons. Two of them remove the guns from their holsters or pockets and place them on the ground. The thicker bodyguard flicks his gaze to me a second before lifting his gun.

My warning shot echoes in the small space and my ears ring. I shake my head to clear it, my gaze never leaving the trio. The man groans and clutches his stomach, a red stain spreading quickly. His pistol clatters to the ground.

"Next time I'm aiming for your balls," I say. "Now, let's have a quick chat."

"Who the fuck are you?" the Broker asks.

"Someone in need of information. Give it to me and live." The lie flows easily from me. "If you refuse, then . . ." I shrug. "You get the idea."

The Broker studies me as though trying to see past my mask. "What do you want to know?"

"The location of the exchange."

The man scoffs. "After all these fucking months, you think I'm just going to hand it all over to some fucking stranger? You must be out of your mind."

I nod. "Sometimes, I think that's true."

I shoot the broad-shouldered man again and he crumples to the floor. The remaining pair curse and jump back.

"Ah, ah," I say, clicking my tongue. "That wasn't very helpful. Let's try this again. What's the fucking location and time? And who's the rep?"

The Broker's lips thin. "Go fuck yourself."

"You know what? I almost did on the way here," I say. "You can't threaten me with a good time."

I aim at the other guard and squeeze the trigger. His body shudders before he face-plants on the floor.

The Broker's face turns bright red, the veins in his neck bulging. "You motherfucker," he grits out. "I'm not telling you shit."

"You say that now, but after I hook you up to those chains out there," I say, jutting my chin at the hooks suspended from the ceiling, "you'll talk. I'm pretty sure I saw a couple of tools out there. It's amazing what you can do with vises, clamps, and a power tool. If you think cutting through metal is easy, then imagine how it'll tear through human bone."

CHAPTER 39

DELILAH

Earlier that evening . . .

It takes all morning and most of the afternoon to convince Raven that I'm not in a relationship with Xavier. At least, not the traditional one. I might be his bride, but that's far removed from being a girlfriend.

He'd be nice to a girlfriend. If he ever decided to date. Maybe.

Right now, he's an asshole who's making threats and demands, which pisses me off more than I care to admit. What I hate more is the thrill that zips along my skin every time I think about him touching me.

After hanging out with my roommate and June all day, under Declan's watchful eye, I grab something for dinner and head back to the dorm room. It's quiet without Raven, because she's busy with her poetry club. Or plans for world domination, knowing her.

Considering Xavier's fierce demand that Declan watch over me, I'm surprised he didn't haul me back to the fraternity. Maybe he wanted some alone time with June. He hasn't been able to take his eyes off of her to actually watch me. Not that I mind. A night alone without the Order or its minions is nice.

As the sun sets, I sprawl out on my bed with my stomach full, my body still sore from last night's activities. I'm tempted to crawl underneath the blanket and go to sleep although it's only eight, but a knock on the door has me on my feet. I was under the impression that Xavier would be gone longer than that. So why do I feel nervous and jittery at the idea of him returning so soon?

I open the door and a wave of disappointment washes over me when it's not Xavier. That emotion is quickly replaced with pain and anger, making my chest tight and my face warm. I cross my arms, as if to shield myself from the emotions churning inside me.

"What are you doing here, Ben?"

"I need to talk to you."

I glare at him. "I texted you for weeks, and nothing. Not even a fucking thumbs-up. Now you want to talk?"

He flinches. "Please, Lilah. I'll explain everything."

"Go ahead."

"Not here." He looks up and down the hallway and shakes his head. "Let's take a walk."

I study him, taking in his slumped shoulders and how his eyes are filled with regret. My heart cracks a little in my chest. This is Ben, my only family besides the girls and Gloria. But they're not here, and he is.

"Fine." I step out of the room and shut the door behind me. "But the minute I feel like you're hiding shit from me, I'm leaving."

He sighs. "I understand. Come on."

Ben guides me outside and into the cool evening air. We walk side by side, the muted sounds of our footsteps the only disturbance in the otherwise silent night. The university, usually bustling and vibrant during the day, feels abandoned now, its buildings standing like silent guardians over the empty walkways.

The path itself winds through the campus, leading us away from the main sections and into the more secluded areas where tall oaks and maples stand. Their leaves whisper above us, a hushed conversation that seems to foretell the one we're about to have. Here, removed from the rest of the world, everything feels more intimate, as if it's just Ben and me.

The way things were before I met Xavier.

Ben leans against the trunk of a large oak and faces me, arms crossed. "I don't even know where to begin."

"How about starting with the reason you never responded to my text messages? It'd better be a good one too."

"Before I answer you, I need you to promise me something." His gaze, so familiar and warm, is now cold and distant. "You can't tell anyone what I'm about to say. If you do, it'll put you in danger. Actually, just me telling you is enough to fuck us both."

I purse my lips. "Is it because of the cult you're in?"

"It's not a cult. The Obsidian Order is a secret society. By revealing its secrets, I'm breaking my vow of silence." Ben averts his gaze and blows out a breath. "It's punishable by death."

"Maybe I don't want to know."

That's a lie. I want to know everything.

Regardless of what Ben thinks, I already believe the Order is a looming threat over my life. The second I found out about their power and reach into society, I knew I couldn't run from them. The only choice left is to learn about them and find a way to survive the duration of my contract.

I won't let myself speculate about what'll happen afterward.

"I trust you," Ben says. "I always have and I always will."

"I'm not going to say anything to anyone. I just want to understand what I'm dealing with."

"It's an assassin's guild, Lilah."

My mouth falls open and no words come out. I gape at him for several seconds before snapping my jaw closed, hard enough for my teeth to click together. "Like as in . . . killing people?"

Ben gives me a wry smile. "Is there a different type of assassin?"

"No, but . . . Seriously?" When he nods, I blink several times, trying to wrap my mind around this. "Well, fuck me sideways. This is worse than I thought."

"What did you think was happening?"

I throw up my hands. "I don't know. After the bride ceremony, I thought you guys were a group of demented perverts, but I never thought you murdered people. That's just . . ."

"It's insane. I'm aware."

"Have you ever . . . you know?"

Ben's expression turns stony. "Yes. I've been summoned by the Order."

"Is that what a 'summons' means?"

"Yes."

"So right now Xavier is—"

I slap a hand over my mouth. Whatever I say about Xavier also applies to Ben, and I don't want to hurt him with my judgmental thoughts. And they're judgy as fuck. Given the way his mouth pulls into a frown, I don't think I'm successful in hiding the fact.

"Yes, he's on assignment somewhere," Ben says. "We're discouraged from contacting anyone during that time. That's why I didn't text you. I swear the Order tracks our phones and reads our messages, and I didn't want to put you at risk."

"How did you get caught in this shit?"

"I'm the bastard son of a founding family member," he says. "Apparently, my mother didn't want me, but she didn't want my father to have me either. She thought it would hurt his legacy if he couldn't find me. It's hard to say because they're both dead. Who knows why the rich do anything, unless it's to gain more power?"

"The rich include you now."

"Don't say that," he snaps. "I'm still the same person. I won't let them change me."

I don't have the heart to point out that they already have. The Ben I know only talked about killing someone, but he never would've done it. Now, he's taken a life—or more than one—and he's able to tell me without hesitation.

I walk up to Ben and place a tentative hand on his forearm. "I'm sorry."

He covers my hand with his. "It's not your fault. Sometimes I think you're in this mess because of me. Maybe if we hadn't grown up together, the Order wouldn't have targeted you."

"My contract?"

"It's legit, but the reason behind it is bullshit. From what I understand, they choose brides who have no money to fight the Order, and no family to miss them if they were to disappear."

I jerk back my hand as if he burned me. "Oh."

Ben reaches for me, grabbing my arms, keeping me still. His gaze searches mine, pleading for understanding. Something I don't know if I can give.

His grip tightens slightly, his fingers pressing into my skin with a mix of urgency and desperation. "That's not how I see you. You're the most important person in my life, Lilah."

He releases one of my arms to brush a stray lock of hair from my face, his touch gentle yet heavy with unspoken remorse. I wait for his touch to ignite the spark Xavier's does. It doesn't come. I'm not willing to admit that he was right about Ben's feelings toward me, but I know for certain that I don't reciprocate them.

"I know and I care about you too," I say. "You're my family."

I step back with a small smile, my stomach twisting at the hurt expression that flits across Ben's face. He lets his arms fall to his sides, a sigh of defeat leaving his chest.

"Family," he repeats in a whisper.

"The Order is wrong. If anything happens to me, I know you'll miss me."

"Don't say that!" His voice echoes in the air, ricocheting off the trees. "I won't let anything happen to you, before or after your contract is up."

I shrug with a nonchalance I don't feel. "I'm sure everything will be fine."

He gazes at me like I've lost my mind. Maybe I have. Finding out that there's a group of killers running around on campus kind of fucks with your brain. Especially when one of the recruits eats out your pussy like it's his last meal.

Fucking Xavier.

CHAPTER 40

DELILAH

Ben clears his throat, and the noise pulls me out of my dirty thoughts. My cheeks flush, and I duck my head, hoping he doesn't notice.

"I've been trained to fight since the first day I got here," he says. There's a hint of pride mixed in with something darker in his voice. "For the last three years, I've learned about poisons, weapons, and anything else required to carry out a summons. They've turned me into a soldier, but I'll use my skills to protect you. I just have to make it through the Trials."

"You will."

He nods, his gaze reflecting the uncertainty coursing through me. "I'm going to, or I'll die trying. It's a series of tests, designed to prove that I'm capable of whatever the Order tells me to do. They're not easy. Some people don't make it through."

"If it's dangerous, why are you doing this?"

"I wasn't given a choice," he says. "The Order sees it as my duty to serve my bloodline and the organization that's been around for centuries. It's bigger than me, and I'm powerless to stop it."

"What happens when you pass the Trials? Will they ease up on you?"

"I'll be fully inducted. I'll go from being a recruit to a crow, expected to carry out missions while running my family's tech empire."

I scrunch my face. "A crow?"

"A group of crows is called a 'murder.' It works for a league of assassins. Don't you think?" He smiles at me.

My laughter is high-pitched, bordering on hysterical. "I can't argue with that."

"There's more to it. The bird has always been synonymous with death, but it's also one of the most intelligent and highly territorial. I guess whoever came up with the symbol hundreds of years ago had a poetic side." He shrugs. "It doesn't matter. I've earned my wings."

I make a face. "What does that mean?"

He grins at me. "You'll find out during the Crow's Covenant tomorrow night. It's one of the few events the brides are allowed to attend."

"Xavier will be back by then," I say, recalling what his father said. I didn't get it at the time, but now that I do, I find that morbid curiosity rising in me like it always does.

Ben makes a noncommittal noise. "Yeah, X."

"You don't like him?"

I pose it as a question when we both know it's not. The way Ben acted around Xavier the night of the Bride Hunt was a side of him that I'd never seen before. Even now, I can't make sense of it.

My foster brother pauses, his gaze shifting before returning to mine. "It's not that I don't like him. X and I have been friends for the last three years. He saved my life on the first day of initiation."

Ben's voice takes on a tone of reluctant admiration. I can relate. Xavier is always pulling emotion from me that I wish didn't exist. Even now, finding out that he saved Ben's life does something to my heart. It softens it. Weakens it.

"I'm still pissed at him for claiming you as his bride," Ben mutters.

The brand on my skin throbs as the memories of that night race through my mind. I'm bound to Xavier for a year, but this mark on my shoulder is permanent in a way that infuriates me. Yes, I can have it removed, but it shouldn't have been put there in the first place.

"You and me both," I say. "At least you're not the one with a fucking 'D' on your body." A thought strikes, giving me pause. "Would you have branded me if you'd been the one to catch me?"

Ben runs a hand through his hair. "I would've had to. You saw the way the council member was with X. Any deviation from the norm is grounds for punishment. I'm not talking about just being reprimanded. When it comes to the Order, nothing is off limits."

A chill skitters down my arms that has nothing to do with the night air. "I get it."

He takes a step toward me. "But that doesn't mean I would've wanted to. You're not property, Delilah."

"I feel like it. I don't want to belong to Xavier."

He takes another step. "I'm going to try to take you from him."

I blink. "How?"

"By outscoring him and the other recruits during the Trials. The brides go to the top three performers." Ben cups my cheeks with both hands and tilts my head up. "I *will* be one of them."

"Why?"

"To protect you."

"Xavier said the same thing."

Ben clenches his jaw. "You belong with me. I know you better than anyone. I can make you happy."

"This is a contract, not a marriage."

"It might as well be," he snaps, his grip tightening on my face. "You have to do whatever he wants. It makes me fucking sick to think of you with him."

"I think now's a good time to take your fucking hands off of her."

The dark voice has Ben swinging around and shoving me behind him. I stumble before gaining my footing. Once I'm not about to face-plant, I lean around Ben to find Declan standing there.

He juts his chin at me. "That bride doesn't belong to you, McKenzie."

Ben stiffens, tension lining his shoulders. "She doesn't belong to you either. Mind your own fucking business."

Declan blows out a breath. "Unfortunately, that fucker X put me on bride-sitting duty. So she's coming with me."

I step from behind Ben and lift both my hands, one palm facing each man. "Both of you need to hold the fuck up. I'm going back to *my* dorm room. After that, you can have a pissing contest, or whatever guys do to establish dominance. All I know is you're not slinging your schlongs in front of me."

The pair of them look at me with wide eyes. Ben groans and massages his forehead while Declan grins. I flip them off.

"Listen, I'm already caught up in the pile of shit the Order dumped on me," I say. "I'm not interested in adding more to it by pissing them off. Leave me alone, and I promise I'll stay put."

"That's not how this works, bride," Declan says. "You're going to Xavier's room. I let you have your freedom during the day, but at night you need to be behind a locked door with security. It's the safest option."

I look at Ben, and he gives me a reluctant nod. "He's right. The rooms in the fraternity are the best choice."

"Whatever," I mumble. "Let's get this over with."

They fall into step beside me, one recruit on either side. It unnerves me. There's something about their energy that's unusual. Maybe it's because I know they're killers or that they wield power in a way that's foreign to me. I've never had money or authority, let alone inherited an empire.

I glance at Declan. "What industry does your family control?"

He flicks a narrowed gaze to Ben. "I see someone's been running his fucking mouth."

My foster brother rolls his eyes. "It's not like she's stupid. She was going to figure it out anyway."

Declan eyes Ben for a moment. "When my father passes, I'll take over his medical dynasty."

"That's not so bad," I say.

As soon as the words are out of my mouth, I recall the story June told us about Declan and his late-night visit to a clinic filled with suspicious people. And organs.

Oh, fuck.

Declan grins at me, but it's all teeth and no smile. Similar to a shark. "I save lives. Hospitals, clinics, research facilities . . . we own them, but the real market is a supply and demand that we're not going to talk about."

Ben's expression darkens, and he steps closer as if to shield me from Declan. "The Order's reach extends into gray areas."

"Gray?" Declan laughs. "It's more like pitch-black. Another reason we're called crows, man. Let's just say that my family provides specialized healthcare services and leave it at that."

"And you?" I ask Ben. "What does a tech dynasty look like?"

Declan interjects before my foster brother can answer me. "It looks like fucking everything. This bastard can hack his way into almost anything. Records, finances, satellites."

"Now who has a big fucking mouth," Ben growls.

"You broke the seal, man." Declan shrugs. "Like you said, she's not stupid. I haven't known her for long, but she's likely to get into trouble and poke her nose where it doesn't belong."

Ben nods. "You don't know the half of it."

"Hey!" I glare at one and then the other. "Do me a favor and punch each other in the dicks, yeah?"

CHAPTER 41

DELILAH

As soon as I'm alone in Xavier's room, I go through his things like a trash panda looking for food. I dig through his drawers, bathroom cabinets, and anything else that might give me a better idea of who this man is. The things I already know about him are scary.

After a while I plop onto his bed, completely exhausted and unsuccessful. Xavier remains a mystery. What drives someone like him? Wealth, status, or power? Maybe all three.

My goals are much simpler. To be loved and feel safe. These concepts are basic, yet so elusive in my life. Plus, I'm not any closer to accomplishing either. If anything, I've taken steps backward.

The situation I find myself in offers nothing good. There's a part of me that feels more afraid than when I lived in Frank's house. Although the danger here is different.

Xavier Donovan threatens to take more than my body. He could take my very soul.

Images of him dart through my mind and I release a sigh, half frustration and the other resignation. I have to find a way to navigate this dynamic, only it's like walking a tightrope and any miscalculation could send me plummeting to my literal and figurative death.

I want to strip him of the power he has over me, but I don't know how. Becoming Xavier's ally is ideal, except he's made it very clear he wants *more* than my cooperation. He said I'd beg him.

The problem is, he could be right . . .

When I think about the hunger in Xavier's gaze and the undeniable pull between us, it's terrifying. I blame it on physical attraction, but there's something more, something deeper that I refuse to acknowledge.

He has a way of looking at me as if I'm the only person that exists. That intensity is overwhelming. Despite not trusting him fully, I find myself drawn to Xavier in a way that I can't explain.

Lying on his bed, surrounded by his things, I close my eyes to block out everything. Maybe the key to surviving this ordeal with my heart intact is to simply confront my fears and desires. Both center around the man holding me captive.

A rapid succession of soft knocks on the door snaps me out of my reverie, and I sit up, my senses alert and focused. For a split second I think Xavier has returned and that I'll have to face my demons sooner than I'd planned. However, logic is quick to point out that he wouldn't hesitate to enter his room.

Maybe it's Ben?

I slide off the bed and head toward the door. A mixture of curiosity and unease slithers through me, growing stronger the closer I get. Meanwhile, the knocks persist, a clear sign that whoever's on the other side has no intention of leaving.

The monitor mounted on the wall next to the door reveals an image that's crisp and clear, displaying the hallway outside. The camera positioned above the door captures every detail with precision, from the dim lighting of the corridor to the textures of the carpet.

As well as Brenda's tear-streaked face.

The young woman stands in front of the door, her disheveled image on the monitor making my breath hitch. The screen displays the disarray of her hair, the way it falls in unkempt waves around her shoulders, and her clothes, normally pristine, are wrinkled. The stark contrast of her pale skin to the bruises dotted across her face makes my stomach churn.

However, her eyes are what gut me. She gazes at the camera with a vulnerability and desperation that makes her look like a wild animal being hunted. Stress lines her hunched shoulders, and her eyes dart back and forth in a series of nervous glances.

I open the door and the weight of her stare has my muscles going taut with wariness even as compassion floods my chest. "Brenda, what are you doing here?"

"Hey, Delilah." Her voice is low, filled with hesitation, her eyes searching mine for something I can't decipher. "I . . . I need to talk to Xavier. It's important."

Hearing her say his name does something to me. It's like a switch being flipped, releasing all of my pent-up frustration. The dark, insecure part of me wants to slam the door in her face, but the rational side says it's not her fault.

It's Xavier's.

He's the one who fooled around with her and then chose me as his bride afterward. He's the one who encouraged Brenda to seek him out for . . . whatever reason. He's the one who has the power to make us both feel tied to him and his decisions.

I pull in a deep breath, desperately trying to stifle the spread of the jealousy already running rampant. This moment isn't about Xavier. It's about a woman needing help.

"He's not here," I say. "And I have no idea when he'll be back."

She narrows her eyes, suspicion written all over her face.

"Do you want to talk about it?" I sweep my gaze along the bruises covering her jaw and her busted lip. "I'm a good listener."

Brenda drops her head, and her brow furrows with her thoughts. When her gaze finds mine, it's swirling with uncertainty. "This is . . . complicated. And you can't help me."

"What happened to you? Was it your recruit?"

"Who else?" She scoffs. "Eric's an asshole to rival all assholes." She presses her lips together and regret takes over her features. "Forget I said anything."

"I won't say a word. I know I can't help you, but what do you want Xavier to do?"

She throws up her arms and covers her face, distress and desperation in every movement. "I don't know. I thought maybe he could protect me by making me his bride instead of you."

The air around me crackles with tension as her words sink deep into my bones, making them heavy. My arms hang listlessly at my sides while I stand there with my lips slightly parted in shock.

Would Xavier trade me for Brenda? Can he?

The idea creates a maelstrom of emotions that threatens to drown me. Insecurities from my past rise like ghost ships at sea, full of corpses and other things left buried. Fear of abandonment, even by a man I hardly know, wraps around my throat and squeezes the life from me.

Not wanting to be Xavier's bride is one thing, but when it comes to another recruit, the choice is clear. I'd rather be Xavier's whore than another man's punching bag. However, that might not be up to me.

And that scares the shit out of me.

I stand there, speechless, my mind racing through different scenarios and possible outcomes. The very thought of Xavier choosing Brenda over me isn't hard to grasp. They have history. *Intimate* history.

She drops her hands and stares at me, her eyes mirroring the turmoil within me. "I'm sorry. I know this is fucked-up. I just thought that if I had Xavier's protection, things would be better. He tried to help me once, and I rejected it. Now, I'd do anything to get him back."

Her admission only fuels the flames of doubt and fear charring my insides. "Xavier chose me. Can he just give me away?"

Brenda shrugs. "I don't know. That's why I'm here. I wanted to ask him if there's any chance for us."

"Us?" I repeat, my voice a squeak.

"Yeah. I know he cares about me, or he wouldn't have tried to get me into rehab."

The word "us" echoes in my mind, the implications reverberating with unspoken and unanswered questions. Brenda's mention of rehab adds another layer to the complexity of their relationship. There's clearly a history of feelings that I wasn't aware of, but it doesn't matter.

Xavier wanted to be there for her.

"I see." I force the words from my mouth, eager to be finished with this conversation. "Like I said, Xavier's not here, but you two do have a lot to talk about."

Brenda's lips thin. "I'm not trying to screw you. I just need to get away from Eric. He . . ." She shudders. "Anyway, I'll see you around."

Her words, meant to smooth out the tension, only amplify my fear. A year is a long time to fulfill a contract.

CHAPTER 42

DELILAH

Brenda turns and walks away, dragging her feet as though heading toward an execution. Maybe she is. The recruits weren't allowed to kill one another in the Bride Hunt, but what restrictions do they have with us?

Her departure does little to ease the tight knot of anxiety in my stomach. I shut the door and lean against it with my eyes closed, attempting to draw deep breaths to steady my nerves. Feelings of helplessness wash over me.

What the fuck am I supposed to do about this? Can I do anything?

Being in this vulnerable position as Xavier's bride has my emotions shifting from uncertainty to a simmering anger. The more I reflect on the situation, the more righteous indignation heats me all over.

I pace the room, muttering to myself. I don't deserve this shit. If Ben were my recruit, he'd treat me with respect and kindness. Xavier, on the other hand, is a huge risk.

If I thought aligning myself with him would provide me with a semblance of safety, I was mistaken. Our relationship is a minefield, leaving me to navigate it while constantly worrying that my next move could be my last. Meanwhile, Xavier strolls merrily through this situation without a care in the world.

The realization halts my steps. And has me raging. If Xavier thinks he can do whatever he wants while I sit and wait for him to dictate my life, he's in for a surprise. I refuse to be a trophy. Or worse, a tool in his game of power, easily traded or discarded.

I retrieve my phone from my pocket. My fingers hover over the screen, my body humming with bitterness. I need to feel like I'm not alone, like someone gives a shit about me and isn't willing to toss me aside.

After selecting Ben's name, I type out a quick text asking him to hang out. My hands grow sweaty while I wait for his response. My foster brother might've said I was the most important person in his life, but right now, I want him to prove it.

My phone buzzes, and I open the text with trembling fingers. Relief washes over me when I read that Ben is heading over. Leaving Xavier's room against his wishes is a small step in my plans for rebellion, but any effort to regain control over my life comforts me.

Minutes later, there's a knock on the door. I check the monitor before opening the door to find Ben leaning against the wall. His presence, familiar and welcoming, immediately puts me at ease.

"I thought you were pissed at me," he says. He smiles, a genuine expression that reaches his eyes, making them bright with affection. For me. "But I'm glad you texted."

"I realized that I'm angry about this entire situation. But it feels wrong to be mad at you."

"It's so good to hear you say that, Lilah. Ready?" He offers me his arm in a gesture that's full of camaraderie, rather than authority. "I think it's time for me to introduce you to the world of video games."

I grin and weave my arm through his, allowing myself to be led away from a room that's more of a prison cell than a sanctuary.

When we reach Ben's room, I find it similar to Xavier's in appearance, but the vibe is completely different. Ben has his stuff everywhere. One look and you can get a feel for who he is as a person, even down to the candy bar wrappers lying right next to the trash can.

"So you're a slob now?" I ask with a smirk.

He chuckles. "I guess so. We didn't have enough money for junk food, so I didn't know I sucked at picking up the trash until I had the means."

I duck my head, not wanting him to feel my disconnect. I might be a part of this university and the Order in a way, but I don't have the finances like them. It's one of the reasons I'm a bride to begin with.

"You want something to drink?" he asks.

"Sure. It'd be nice to have something besides coffee for once."

Ben walks over to a mini fridge, grabs a soda, and hands it to me. I take it with a smile and settle on the edge of his mattress. "Can I ask you something?"

He frowns. "You know you can ask me anything."

I trace the rim of the can, staring down at it to avoid Ben's stare. "Can a recruit trade one bride for another?"

"Why are you asking me that?"

"Just answer the question," I snap. Belatedly realizing the severity of my tone, I lift my head, my gaze full of remorse. "I'm sorry. I just really need to know, Ben."

His expression turns serious. He takes a moment before responding, which only sets me on edge all the more. By the time he finally speaks, I'm ready to strangle him or cry.

"It has to be agreed on by both recruits, not just one," he says. "It's not encouraged. A bride is acquired through skill, so trading her would be an insult to yourself. It's saying you weren't good enough to get the bride of your choice."

I nod, barely perceptible, fear paralyzing me. Xavier does have the right to trade me. From the way he acted during the Bride Hunt, I could assume he wants to keep me, but that's not good enough. I'd be trusting a stranger with more than my safety.

I'd have to trust Xavier with my life.

Ben sits next to me, the mattress dipping under his weight. He wraps an arm around me, and I lean into his side, soaking up his presence. "Does this have something to do with X?"

I shrug. "Sort of. Brenda, Eric's bride, stopped by Xavier's room earlier looking for his help."

"She's a drug addict." A thread of disgust is woven underneath Ben's tone. "I'm not sure if she was one before she got with Eric, but I know she was definitely one afterward."

"Addict or not, the bruises on her body didn't look self-inflicted, Ben. She wants to get away from Eric and become Xavier's bride."

My words are statements of fact, nothing more, but as they sweep past my ears, my blood heats in my veins. The prospect of Xavier giving me away or replacing me with Brenda doesn't upset me only because I want to avoid abuse. It's also about the feelings of rejection stirring within me.

Fucked-up or not, during the Bride Hunt, I was someone's first choice.

For the first time in my life, I felt wanted. Valued.

It's not that I love Xavier. Our relationship, if it can even be called that, is built on ceremony and tradition. So why does the prospect of him replacing me with another woman evoke jealousy and other petty emotions?

Xavier made me feel seen. I don't want to be invisible again.

Ben sighs and hugs me tighter. "Delilah, you're not thinking clearly. X is a lot of things, but he's not someone who changes his mind. He wanted you to be his bride. I don't know why, but he did."

I pull back and frown at him. "That's not encouraging."

"I just meant that there's always a hidden agenda with the recruits." Ben runs a hand through his hair. "I didn't mean he shouldn't have picked you. Anyone would be happy to have you as their bride. Hell, most of them don't deserve you."

"Being a bride isn't a privilege. It's a prison."

He goes taut beside me. "I'm going to get you out of it. You'll see."

"I hope so."

"Until then, it's better that you're with X."

I make a face at Ben. "He's a fuck hole."

"A what?" My foster brother laughs, the tension dissipating from his body. "You come up with the weirdest shit. Like I was saying, yes, Xavier's an asshole, but he won't physically hurt you." Ben pauses, his gaze gleaming with emotion. "If he does, I'll kill him."

I bump his shoulder with mine. "Thanks for looking out for me."

"Always. You'd do the same for me."

"Always," I say.

"Now that we're done with the mushy shit, how about I beat your ass in this video game?"

I glare up at him and grin. "Bring it on, bitch nuts."

CHAPTER 43

XAVIER

Declan: You might want to hurry the fuck up and get back here.

Xavier: Is Delilah hurt?

Declan: No, but she's in trouble.

Xavier: What kind of trouble?

Declan: The kind that'll have you killing someone.

Xavier: Why didn't you stop her?

Declan: Have you met her? That woman is a pain in the ass. You should've disclosed that crucial bit of information before you dumped her on me.

Xavier: Watch your fucking mouth when you talk about her.

Declan: My bad. Maybe if you give me permission to hog-tie her, I can get her to behave. Even then, it might be too late.

Xavier: Wherever she is, get her the fuck out of there.

Declan: Dude, Ben is the face of a tech empire and his system security is top-notch. How in the fuck am I supposed to get her out of his room? You know it's basically a vault.

Xavier: I'm taking this really fucking personally. I trusted you to look after my bride, and you didn't. Now you're interrupting me in the middle of my summons to tell me that the reason you texted me can't be resolved?

Declan: Yeah, pretty much.

Xavier: You know those organs you traffic? Well, you might want to check your supply because I'm going to fucking shoot you when I get back.

Declan: Love you too.

Xavier: I'll finish up here and be back as soon as possible.

Declan: Good. Xoxo, fucker.

—

I shove my phone in my pocket and pick up the plastic gloves covered in blood. The Broker whimpers when he sees me put them back on, his eyes bulging from his skull.

"Here's the thing," I say. "My girl is back home, getting into all sorts of trouble. Which means I need to speed up this interrogation so I can get back to her."

I grab the angle grinder and turn it on. The blade whirls, a high-pitched sound that blends in with the man's cries. He jerks back, rattling the chains that are keeping him suspended in the air. The hook in his back digs deeper, and he screams.

"The faster you talk, the faster I'll put you out of your misery," I say. "A merciful death is something Edward Donovan would never offer you. Trust me, I think he's a bigger dick than you do."

"Then why are you doing this?" he sobs.

"Because my loyalty is to a woman, one who's driving me fucking crazy. And if you don't tell me what I need to know, you'll be keeping me from her. Trust me, you don't want to do that."

CHAPTER 44

DELILAH

Xavier: When I get home, you and I are going to have a chat about obedience, little raptor.

Delilah: I haven't done anything wrong. How did you have a chance to program your info into my phone?

Xavier: I've done far worse.

Delilah: Why does that not surprise me?

Xavier: Who are you with?

Delilah: None of your business.

Xavier: Answer the fucking question.

Xavier: Delilah Scott, I asked you a question.

Delilah: I'm with Ben.

Xavier: Where are you?

Delilah: In his room at the fraternity.

Xavier: Fucking Christ.

Delilah: We're just hanging out. I already told you it's not like that.

Xavier: And I already told you, Benjamin wants to fuck you. If he touches you, I'll kill him, and it'll be your fault.

Delilah: Are you serious?

Xavier: Does it sound like I'm fucking around?

Delilah: I swear if you do anything to him . . .

Xavier: You'll what, Delilah?

Delilah: 🖕

Xavier: I'll give you a moment to enjoy that, but when I get back, you're going to learn exactly what happens when you don't listen to me.

Delilah: Can't fucking wait.

—

Alcohol is my new best friend.

My blood hums merrily underneath my skin as Ben walks me back to Xavier's room. I cling to his arm after nearly tripping, and my foster brother exhales.

"You're worse than a lightweight, Lilah."

My hazy vision makes everything slightly off-kilter, like I'm in a hall of mirrors where every image is distorted. But it's amusing, not disconcerting. I think I like being drunk.

Ben scoffs. "You might like the way you feel right now, but in the morning, you're going to hate yourself. And me."

I blink up at him. "Are you a mind reader now?"

"No, you're mumbling to yourself."

"Ohhh. That makes sense."

"You're going straight to bed," he says.

"Why can't I stay with you?"

Ben shakes his head emphatically, the movement making my head spin. "X would fucking kill me if you slept in my room," he says. "I already know he's going to be pissed when he finds out that you're drunk, but I'm not stupid enough to push him off the edge."

"He doesn't care about me. Not really." I wave a hand. "He just sees me as his property."

"It seems that way, but I saw him watching you like—"

At Ben's abrupt silence, I look up at him and tap his arm. "Like what?"

My foster brother inhales deeply before blowing it back out. "He looks at you like he'll die without you."

I burst out laughing, the sound bouncing off the walls. The alcohol swirling in my veins only adds to my hilarity and my disbelief.

"That's ridiculous," I say. "Have you met Xavier? He has no fucks to give and doesn't need anyone. Maybe you're the one who's drunk."

When Ben doesn't laugh, or even crack a smile, my amusement dies. Instead, his expression hardens, seriousness etched into his features.

"I'm not joking," he says. "You might not see it, but I've known him a lot longer, and there's something going on with him when it comes to you."

"I've known him lo—"

By some miracle, I slap a hand on my mouth, muffling my drunken confession. I never told Ben that Xavier killed Frank all those years ago. And I definitely didn't disclose the fact that I had a brief conversation with Xavier—*after* stabbing him.

At first, I kept that information a secret because I was freaked out and needed time to process everything. But as the days turned into weeks and the weeks turned into months, I couldn't find the courage. If I'm honest with myself, it wasn't only that.

Xavier made me feel important.

Ben threatened to kill for me, but Xavier actually fucking *did*.

"What were you going to say?" Ben asks me.

I let my hand fall away. "I can't remember. I thought I was going to puke. Are we there yet?"

He smiles at me and shakes his head. "You act like we're hiking Mount Everest."

"Feels like it."

Ben stops in front of a door that I assume is Xavier's. I stare at it blankly. My foster brother takes my wrist and flattens my palm against the panel, and the door unlocks with a click.

"That shit is so cool," I say.

"My tech empire had a hand in designing it."

I look up at Ben and smile at the pride in his voice. "That's a-maz-za-zing."

He groans. "I don't know if I should leave you alone."

"I'm fine. I'm just busting your balls."

"Okay then. Go inside." He juts his chin at the doorway. "Promise me you won't open the door for anyone. You're protected under your bride title, but that doesn't mean one of these fuckers won't try something with Xavier gone. If he's not back by the morning, I'll come get you."

"I promise I won't open the door. Goodnight."

"Night."

Turning toward the room, I walk inside, letting the door lock behind me. Ben's words repeat themselves in my mind, a riddle that makes my head pound more than the alcohol. Xavier looks at me like he'll die without me?

Yeah, right. What do I have that he can't get from any other woman? Especially with someone like Brenda actively wanting him?

The buzz from before lessens significantly after I chug a lot of water. Then I collapse on the bed and stare at the ceiling until my thoughts quiet. The room doesn't spin as much anymore, and I sigh in relief.

A knock on the door a few minutes later has me stumbling across the room. I squint at the monitor, trying to make out the image that looks like Ben wearing a hoodie. He must've changed his mind about leaving me alone in my drunken state.

I swing open the door. "Ben, you don't have to worry about—"

The word dies in my throat when Eric's malicious gaze meets mine. His presence sends a jolt through my body, instantly sobering me. I go to slam the door in his face, and he reacts faster than my eyes can follow.

The man has his hand clamped around my upper arm and yanks me to him, causing me to grunt in pain from his fingers digging into my skin. I stumble before he slams my back against the wall, his face inches from mine, his eyes glittering with something that has my adrenaline spiking.

Panic claws at my throat, but I push past it. "Get the fuck off of me."

"Not until you deliver a message for me."

I swallow the insult gathered on my tongue. "What is it?"

"Tell that cunt Xavier that I'm coming for him. Let him know that I'm going to take everything, starting with his bride and ending with his empire."

"Why don't you tell him yourself? I don't give a fuck about any of this shit, so leave me out of it."

"I can see why he wanted you," Eric says. He slowly runs his gaze over me, his pupils contracting. My stomach churns. "You're entertaining, even if you are a mouthy bitch."

I shrug. "Thanks. 'Mouthy bitch' pretty much sums up my personality."

Eric grabs my neck. My breathing turns into wheezing, but I force myself to remain still. He won't kill me because he has a purpose for me, to deliver a message to Xavier. My body doesn't understand and trembles with the need to defend myself.

He smirks, most likely assuming I'm shaking from fear instead of rage. "Maybe I should take you now."

"If you do, I can guarantee that I won't deliver your message because I'll be too fucking busy trying to kill you."

"So delusional, but amusing." Eric tilts his head. "If he doesn't get tired of you first, I'm going to enjoy taking you from him, knowing you'll fight me either way."

His arrogance, along with the idea of him raping me, fuels my rage. I hold his gaze to avoid revealing my intentions, and smile.

The second his brows snap together in confusion, I raise my knee, aiming for his groin.

Eric grunts, and his grip on my neck loosens. Taking advantage of his momentary shock, I swing my elbow to his chest with all my strength. He staggers back, and I spin toward the doorway.

With my heart pounding in my ears, I slam the door behind me, pressing my spine to the wood. My chest heaves with breaths and spots dance before my eyes. I slide down to the floor as my vision blurs.

I lose track of time and sit there, gasping for air. The lingering taste of fear is sharp on my tongue and my instincts still scream for me to hide, to get away from this place entirely. Tremors snake through my body until nausea rises.

After racing to the bathroom, I vomit. Not only due to the alcohol consumption, but also because of the violent images running through my mind. Having Eric touch me was vastly different than when Xavier grabbed my neck in the woods during the Bride Hunt.

I thought that my arousal was because of adrenaline and heightened senses, but after tonight's near miss, I know that's not the reason. I'm disgusted by Eric and attracted to Xavier. Two men, same circumstances, with two separate reactions from me.

This entire time, I've wanted to blame Xavier for forcing sexual responses from me, making my body crave him in a way it's never done before. But now I know it's not his fault.

It's mine.

But that's a problem for sober Delilah.

CHAPTER 45

XAVIER

The instant the notification pings on my phone, my intuition flares with warning.

Keeping one hand on the steering wheel, I glance down at the screen, my heart rate accelerating along with the speed of the vehicle. The security system indicates movement outside my room. A second alert quickly follows, telling me someone has opened the door.

I tap into the live feed and dread coats my skin like gasoline, ready to ignite any second. Delilah opens the door to a hooded figure on the other side. From this angle, I can't make out their identity . . . until the man pins her against the wall.

The camera lens provides a clear picture of Eric Gage with his hands on my girl. Rage turns my blood into fire, burning me alive from the inside. I'm not sure which is stronger: my desire to kill him or my need to protect her.

"Motherfucker!" My shout is drowned out by the roar of the engine as I push the vehicle to its maximum speed. Even then, it won't be fast enough.

The violent scene unfolds before my eyes like a horror film. The steering wheel creaks under the pressure of my grip as I imagine squeezing the life from Gage when he grabs Delilah's throat. In the blink of an eye, he could snap her neck.

And my entire world would burn to ash.

The mere thought of her dying is like a physical blow. The SUV's movements reflect my internal agony, veering too far to the right before I straighten the vehicle. My hands shake uncontrollably, a manifestation of an emotion I've only experienced a few times in my life.

Fear.

I was afraid the first time my father struck me, as well as the first time he stabbed me. I was frightened when he took a whip to my flesh and when he put a bullet in my thigh. But all of that was because I didn't know the level of pain to come. It was conceivable but not confirmed.

If Delilah were to be killed, I can't even comprehend the level of devastation it would bring.

I'm going to fucking kill Gage, no matter the outcome of tonight's altercation. I'm going to torture him to the fullest extent, crush his empire, and then when I'm certain he's suffered, I'll end his life.

Although his suffering won't be a fraction of the agony he's dredged up in me with just the mere thought of Delilah's life in danger.

Fury, hot and unyielding, courses through every fiber of my being as I watch Eric engage Delilah in conversation. What the fuck is he saying to her? Is he taunting her with the intent to kill her, or is he merely toying with her to fuck with me?

It's working.

I've never been religious or given a thought to a supernatural deity, but in that moment, I pray to every god I can think of to protect Delilah until I can do it myself. Either the universe hears my pathetic attempts at prayer, or fate decides to smile on me for once instead of fucking me over like usual.

Delilah knees Eric in the balls and slams her elbow in his gut, forcing him to let go of her. I hold my breath until my lungs scream as I watch her scurry back inside my room and shut the door behind her.

I release a shaky breath, my entire body fucking trembling in relief at the close call. The tremors wrack my body to the point I lose control of my grip on the wheel, and I nearly go off the road. Again.

This girl is going to wreck me in every way possible.

Dual emotions collide inside me, a fusion of pride in her ferocity and a seething wrath aimed at Eric for thinking he could touch what belongs to me. And Delilah is mine.

I'm going to have to make that clearer.

To my enemies.

To my bride.

To the world.

The duration of the drive back to the university is the cruelest torture, each second away from Delilah adding to this bomb inside me that's ready to explode.

I constantly flick my gaze to the live feed of her in my room. Eventually, she makes her way to the bed and falls asleep. Even then, the need for violence, this level of intensity doesn't decrease. Only until I see her with my eyes and touch her with my hands and fuck her with my cock will I finally be able to think properly.

By the time I park the SUV in the garage, the sun is rising above the horizon. The urgency to see Delilah overrides any lethargy that threatens to slow me down. I don't need sleep.

I need her.

Although, I'm still fucking pissed at my girl. She's going to learn some things today. . . .

My feelings for Delilah have transcended any pretense of mere possession. She's etched herself into the very marrow of my bones, imprinted herself on my heart so that it beats for her. It *lives* for her.

When I finally reach the door, my turmoil reaches its peak. Until I step inside the dark room and my gaze lands on Delilah sleeping peacefully in my bed. After that, the agony dissipates.

I have no idea how long I stand there, simply watching the rise and fall of her chest, my eyes glued to the movement while my brain tries to reassure me she's alive. The need to touch her only grows until I'm crossing the room to feel the warmth of her skin.

After slowly lowering myself to the edge of the bed, I trace the contours of her face with my gaze, then with my fingers. I follow the curve of her lips, the angles of her cheeks, and the sweep of her jaw. She is perfection in human form.

This woman lies there in the peacefulness of repose, a stark contrast to the chaos roiling inside me. Leaning closer, so close that my breath stirs the hair at her temple, I whisper into the quiet, my words a truth I've never wanted to admit.

"A raptor is a fierce and formidable bird of prey, and the crow's natural enemy. When a crow strays from its flock, that's when it's most vulnerable, when it exposes itself to the danger of the raptor's lethal presence.

"You've ruined me, Delilah. In this world of deception and power, where I've lived among a murder of crows, you have become the one person capable of breaking through my defenses. You've made me vulnerable, isolated me from the safety of the Order and from the founding families. You are my greatest weakness."

I pause and run my fingers through her hair, watching her eyelids flutter in deep sleep. "You're also my greatest strength."

As I sit there with my confession lingering in the atmosphere, I watch Delilah breathe steadily, recalling the first time I met her. And how I commemorated it by getting a tattoo, a testament to the profound impact she had on me.

Above the scar she gave me from the stab wound is a hawk, a bird of prey that represents her. Not only for its strength and intelligence, but also to remind me that I'm weak for her. The scar marks our beginning and also serves as a tree branch for the hawk, a foundation for the very thing that makes me vulnerable. Like that tree, I will shield her and be her safety.

She's marked me in ways far deeper and more permanent than any tattoo could ever convey.

"Sleep as long as you can. When you wake up, you're going to want to unleash your claws and fight me, but only one of us will win."

CHAPTER 46

DELILAH

I can feel Xavier.

My subconscious, as well as the rest of me, recognizes his presence. I don't need a physical touch or sound to know when he's near. His scent invades my senses, his energy prickling at my awareness.

Even in my dreams, where the darkness is complete and the silence deafening, he's there. He's the voice calling to me from the abyss.

"Little raptor . . ."

His words are a low hum, coaxing me to answer. To respond. I want to, but there's something off about his energy.

"Open your eyes," he says, his tone more forceful.

My lips part on a breath, and I obey his command. My eyelids flutter, but all I see is darkness. Until I locate him sitting in a chair across the room.

I don't move. I can't. Not when I fully take in the look on his face. A man shouldn't be this beautiful. Especially since he looks like he wants to kill someone.

And he's holding a knife.

There's something almost hypnotic in the motion of his fingers as he tosses the blade from one hand to the other. Back and forth, back and forth, like a pendulum, marking each second with an unspoken threat. Then he throws it up in the air and catches it by the handle. The knife glints menacingly, a silent testament to the danger Xavier embodies. It's intimidating, reminding me of the world he comes from.

The summons he just finished.

I lie there with adrenaline flowing through me like lava, heating my veins, while his gaze holds me captive. I swallow the nerves gathering in my throat and force myself to speak, if only to break through the tension.

"When did you get back?"

Xavier doesn't answer. He rakes his eyes over me, his silver eyes bright even in the shadows.

"Did something happen?" I ask, trying again.

He remains silent and continues to look at me. His intensity, as usual, is unnerving.

"Xavier, are you okay?"

"Not even close," he says, his tone rough.

"What's wrong?"

"You."

I scramble into a sitting position and hold the comforter to my chest. Although, nothing can remove the feel of his gaze from my skin. Even from across the room, it's like a physical touch.

"What are you talking about?" I ask.

Xavier stops tossing the knife, catching it one last time. He shifts in the chair, and I stiffen, thinking he's going to come toward me. Instead, he places his forearms on his thighs and lets his hands rest in the opening between his legs, the knife hanging from his fingertips. It's a casual pose, but not with him. He's a predator ready to attack, his muscles going taut under his clothing.

He's wearing his customary black T-shirt, black cargo pants, and boots. I scan his body for signs of injury or illness but find nothing to indicate he's unwell. It only makes this conversation more bizarre.

"Your behavior is a problem, Delilah."

I purse my lips. "You're going to have to be more specific."

"You've been fraternizing with would-be crows."

His eyes flicker to the door and then my throat. Or maybe I'm just paranoid. In the dim lighting, I could've imagined the way he pointedly looked at my neck like he knows what Eric did to me. If Xavier does know, it's not because I told him.

"And if I was?" I ask, my irritation rising to the surface.

He rises from the chair like a wraith from the mist. I wait for his reprimand, but he suddenly pivots and throws the knife. It slices through the air and finds its mark in the crest above the fireplace. The blade is buried deep inside the crow's head, embedded into the wood, the handle quivering from the force of the impact.

The skill and control are impressive, but it's also a warning, a silent message of what he's capable of.

I jump at the display of violence, my eyes widening and darting between Xavier and the knife. He turns back around to face me, his expression blank, but his eyes gleam with rage.

"You deliberately went to Benjamin after I told you not to," he says.

I lift my chin. "He's family. You have nothing to worry about."

"Do you know what crows do, little raptor? They lie, steal, and kill."

"Well, maybe you should convince me that you want me as a bride instead of letting someone else do it."

Without a word, Xavier stalks toward the bed and reaches out to snatch the blanket. He rips it from my body, leaving me exposed in nothing except his T-shirt and my panties. After gripping the headboard, he straddles my hips, his chest brushing mine.

My breathing halts when he snatches my jaw and lifts my head, forcing my gaze to his. "Who's doing the convincing, Delilah?"

"Ben."

His expression darkens. "Don't lie."

"I'm not. He's the one who said you wouldn't trade me for another bride."

His gaze narrows. "Why would you think that?"

I bite my lip as my jealousy bleeds all over my heart, painting it green. Xavier's silver eyes glint with something carnal before he uses his thumb to pull my bottom lip from between my teeth.

"Stop fucking distracting me," he says. "Why would you think I'd want to trade you?"

"Brenda." Although his body is pressed to mine and his fingers are on my skin, her name is a wedge between us.

"What did she tell you?" he asks.

"That you two have history."

"And you believed her? She's an addict."

I shrug. "I saw you guys leave the library garden together. I saw the way she looked at you and heard the way she said your name. She wants to be your bride."

He scoffs and shakes his head. "If I wanted her, she'd be mine."

Profound relief sweeps through me like a cool breeze. I hate myself for it. I could lie to myself and say it's because I'm scared to be Eric's bride, but I know it's more than that.

I don't want Xavier to give me up.

He makes me feel things I've never experienced. He is like a drug, making me high on his touch and addicted to his praise. I don't know how to stop myself from wanting him.

"Well, Brenda didn't get the message," I say.

"I don't give a fuck what she wants. And you shouldn't either. Right now, you need to be concerned with what I want."

"What's that?"

"So many things . . . but you can start by telling me what happened last night." He tightens his hold on me. It's not enough to hurt me, but it gets my attention. "If you're planning on lying to me, don't."

"If you already know, then why the hell are you asking me?"

"Because I want to hear it from you."

My heart pounds furiously in my chest, drowning out my shallow breaths. I'm not sure if Xavier wants me to tell him about Eric assaulting me or that I hung out with Ben and got drunk. Both things are sure to piss him off. Well, more than he already is.

"I got drunk," I say, choosing the lesser of the two evils. "Is that what you want to hear?"

Xavier doesn't move. His breathing remains even and his gaze steady. If it weren't for the slight clenching of his jaw, I wouldn't know he's affected by what I said.

"You put yourself at risk," he says. "If anything were to happen to you . . ."

He slides his fingers from my jaw, across my cheek, and weaves them through my hair. He grips the strands until I gasp from discomfort. And arousal.

With his free hand, he traces my lips, one then the other. "What to do about your disobedience . . ."

I glare up at him. "If you want an apology, you've got another thing coming."

"Oh, I'll be coming, all right." He abruptly releases me and slides from the bed. Standing with his legs shoulder-width apart and his arms crossed, he watches me. "Get up."

The look is a silent warning that sends a shiver running through me. Xavier watches the tremor, and a slow smile spreads across his face. My throat goes dry.

"Now, Delilah."

His firm tone has heat pooling in my lower belly. I climb out of the bed, careful not to touch him. Because the minute I do, my body will take over, and it'll surrender to him.

"On your knees, bride."

I bite the inside of my cheek. "What are you going to do?"

"Fuck your mouth. Unless you prefer I take that tight pussy of yours? Given the mood I'm in, I'll wreck it."

"Xavier, wait." I fist my hands by my sides, my body trembling. I can't discern if it's from anticipation or unease. "Why are you doing this?"

"I warned you that you'd learn exactly what happens when you don't listen to me. And you said, 'can't fucking wait.'"

He takes a step forward, backing me up against the edge of the bed. His body crowds mine, and his scent wraps around me, overwhelming my senses. He lowers his head until his mouth is next to my ear.

"You still looking forward to getting fucked, Delilah?"

CHAPTER 47

DELILAH

I dig my nails into my palms, indecision warring within me. Xavier can overpower me in an instant, but does that mean I shouldn't fight him? The truth is I don't want to.

Xavier wanting me is something I can't walk away from.

When I sink to my knees, his gaze flares with lust. "That's my good girl," he says, his voice rough.

Now my eyes widen. His praise is a reward, a small dose of his affection, and the way it affects me is a weakness. It makes me crave his approval.

I swallow the nerves gathering in my throat and stare up at him, unsure of what he expects of me. Embarrassment, along with excitement, heats my face. He's aware of my innocence, but I have no idea if he knows about my inexperience when it comes to this type of thing.

He unbuckles his belt, and my eyes track the movement. After pushing his pants and briefs down, his cock juts forward. It's long, thick, and hard. The tip glistens, and my eyes widen further.

Xavier's gaze drops to my mouth. "You're going to learn to obey me."

"Or what?"

He wraps a hand around his cock and strokes the length of it from base to tip, ever so slowly. I stop breathing at the erotic sight. It makes me want to touch him, to be the one gripping him.

He smirks. "Or I'm going to fuck this mouth of yours until it says what I want to hear."

Xavier steps forward and brushes the tip of his cock against my mouth. He paints my lips with his pre-cum and then traces my cheek with his fingers.

"You're mine, Delilah. Mine to take. Mine to keep. Now, open, pretty girl."

When I open my mouth, he slides inside, a groan escaping him. "Fuck."

Xavier thrusts slowly, going deeper each time, until I gag. His hand goes to my hair, and he grips the strands to the point of pain. It only intensifies the sensations coursing through me. My pussy flutters the second I imagine his cock inside me instead of in my mouth.

"You're going to have to learn how to take me deeper."

He increases his speed, and I grip his thighs, digging my nails into his skin.

"Look at me," he rasps. "Let me see your eyes while I fuck this pretty mouth."

My gaze flicks upward, and he stares down at me, his gray eyes filled with a mixture of lust and reverence.

"So fucking beautiful."

Xavier's praise has my arousal spiking and my pulse quickening. I moan, and the sound vibrates around his length. He throws his head back, his jaw clenched.

"Do that again."

I oblige, and he fucks my mouth faster. My eyes water and I gag when he hits the back of my throat. He pauses and eases back before doing it again.

"You're doing so well," he murmurs. "Such a good girl for me."

When I whimper, his entire body tenses. His grip on my hair tightens, and his thrusts become erratic. I relax my throat, letting him go as deep as possible. Xavier fucks my mouth with a savagery that steals my breath, his control slipping as he chases his pleasure.

In this position, on my knees with him towering over me, I'm the one in control. He needs me for his pleasure. Knowing I'm the reason he's going to orgasm is a high that I've never felt before. To have this powerful man at my mercy is intoxicating. Now I understand why he made me come during the Bride Hunt.

"I'm going to come in your mouth," he growls. "But you'd better not fucking swallow."

His words are like a bolt of lightning straight to my clit. My nipples tighten and I moan, wanting more. I need to come almost as much as he does.

Xavier pumps his hips, his cock pulsing as he empties into my mouth. It's hot and salty. When he pulls out, the cum dribbles out of the corner of my mouth.

He slides his finger underneath the collar of my shirt, the movement silencing me. He studies my mouth with an intensity and a hunger that makes my body tremble, but I remain still. The air is charged with electricity, and my body vibrates with awareness.

"Take your shirt off," he says.

I hesitate because I have nothing on underneath. By the time I remove his shirt and cover my breasts, he's put his cock back in his pants. I don't have time to be disappointed because he yanks me to my feet. When he speaks, his voice is rough with lust. With dominance.

"Open."

He slides his thumb along the seam of my mouth and presses it to my tongue. Xavier's eyes flicker as he watches me. I can only stare up at him.

He sweeps his thumb through the cum pooling in my mouth before going to stand behind me. He takes my hair and places it over one shoulder. Then he drags his thumb over the skin of my back just under my neck.

I don't move, and I can't talk because I have his cum in my mouth. He occasionally dips his finger inside to coat it before drawing on my back again. The cum begins to dry by the time he's standing in front of me.

"Now you can swallow."

I do. "What did you—"

He tweaks my nipple, and I groan. Xavier grins, and his eyes sparkle with something dark and wicked.

"You'll find out soon enough."

CHAPTER 48

DELILAH

That evening . . .

"Once we're inside the chapel, don't say a word unless I give you permission to speak."

Xavier's sharp tone has me frowning at him. "Why?"

"Every recruit and leader of the founding families will be at this ceremony. These men are the most dangerous in the world. If you piss them off, you'll get us both killed."

"Both of us?"

He stops in the stairwell and looks down at me. With him wearing his mask, I can't see anything except his eyes, but they glitter with emotion.

"Yes, both of us," he says. "If anyone threatens you, I'll kill them, and we'll be outnumbered. I'm not easy to kill, but I'm not invincible either."

The seriousness of his tone and the gravity of his words leave me speechless. My reaction isn't purely based on the danger that lies at the top of the tower. It's because of Xavier's promise to protect me, even to his detriment.

His dedication to me and preserving my life leaves me awestruck. A warmth gathers in my chest and encases my heart, making it beat a little faster. For him.

I nod to show my understanding, and we resume our ascent of the granite steps. The hem of my skirt drags behind me, the fabric whispering against the cold stone. The dress is a masterpiece of design and craftsmanship, a combination of elegance and sensuality. Its shade is a midnight blue, almost black like Xavier's clothing in the dim light of the stairwell.

The bodice is fitted, adorned with intricate black lace that snakes across the neckline, outlining the mounds of my breasts. The gown is sleeveless and leaves my arms bare, as well as my upper back. Xavier demanded that I style my hair in an updo to keep it off my shoulders.

His dried cum remains scrawled across my skin, a secret between us. I assume it's part of his "lesson" from this morning, and I can't find the energy to care. Not when every time I think of his cock in my mouth, I become aroused.

Beneath the expensive fabric cascading in a flood of silk and shadow, my legs tremble from the steep climb and my sensual thoughts. The material of the skirt brushes against my thighs and calves with every step, the heat trapped underneath in direct contrast with the cool air of the castle. Xavier left me with the need to come, my body stimulated, and my mind full of him all day.

His warning to remain silent is enough to calm my arousal but not erase it completely.

I sneak a glance at him, drinking in the man beside me. He's dressed entirely in black per his usual, the color accentuating the mystery and elusiveness that I've come to associate with him. His mask hides his expression, making it impossible for me to gauge his thoughts, but his hand gripping mine tells me of his desire to keep me close.

His stride is confident and steady the entire way. Once the door comes into view, he stops and turns to face me. I wait, the hairs on my arms lifting with apprehension.

"Don't look anyone directly in the eyes," he says. "They'll see it as defiance or an invitation. Keep your head bowed and your gaze on me."

"Okay."

He reaches out to grab the nape of my neck. He pulls me closer, his breath skimming my lips. "I mean it, Delilah. I won't hesitate to punish you again, but this time I'll fuck your sweet cunt."

"Jesus fucking Christ," I hiss.

"Considering we're about to walk inside a chapel, I think that's the right mindset."

Without letting me go, he opens the door and leads me through. At our arrival, a hush falls over the assembled crowd. All eyes lock on us, scrutinizing and evaluating. The weight of their gazes has me bowing my head.

Xavier squeezes the back of my neck in response and I school my features, keeping my smile from forming. His praise never fails to stir something in me. I crave his approval with an intensity that scares me.

The atmosphere around me is thick with anticipation. It feels at odds with a place designed for humility and faith. The chapel, in its restored glory, is a testament to the reverence of the past. History and art can be found everywhere I look.

The windows, tall and narrow, have been fitted with panes of stained glass that filter the moonlight into a kaleidoscope of colors. These have been strategically placed to tell a biblical tale, bathing the interior with color, the hues dancing across the stone floor. Statues line the walls like guardians of doctrine, and the wooden pews have been polished to a soft sheen. Each row of seating is adorned with plush velvet cushions in a deep green.

This is where the recruits sit. I catch sight of June and Brenda among them, their formal wear similar to mine. June has her hair pulled up in a sleek bun and wears a dress of soft ivory that clings to her stiff frame. Her rigid posture softens the tiniest bit when our gazes meet.

With Xavier's order to remain silent firmly planted in my brain, I can only offer my friend a brief smile. A silent communication passes between us and I relax at knowing she's all right. At least for the time being.

Brenda, on the other hand, stares at me with open envy. Her dress, a shimmering red, flows around her like spilled wine. Her hair is loose, and her body language is just as unrestrained as she leans toward Xavier. Her eyes hold a fragility that makes me grow cold. But not more than Eric's gaze when it lands on me.

Well, he can get fucked. Not exactly the most pious of thoughts, but certainly the most honest.

I ignore Eric's stare as my recruit leads me to our designated seats directly in front of June and Declan, the masked recruit next to her. We settle on the cushion, and I take a deep breath while hardening my resolve to keep my wits about me. Even with Xavier's mask in place, I can sense his tension. It clings to his shoulders just as tightly as he grips my neck.

At this moment, I'm acutely aware of the delicate balance of power and danger that defines Xavier's world. As I stand by his side, facing the gathered assembly of assassins and leaders, I realize the depth of my trust in him. Despite the danger, despite the overwhelming odds, I know he'll protect me.

I relax in his hold, and he flicks his eyes to me, his gaze questioning. Before I can convey a silent message, a masked individual makes his way to the front of the room. The pews face the heart of the chapel where an altar stands. It's made of wood and decorated with a single tapestry that showcases a crow, its vibrant threads bringing the creature to life.

The man situates himself behind the altar. In the light of the numerous electrical sconces lining the walls, his black robe seems to absorb the brightness, rather than reflect it as he raises a hand. The gesture demands our attention more than a shout would. The quiet around me drops to a deafening silence, and I find myself holding my breath.

"Welcome, esteemed members of the council, leaders of the founding families, and recruits of the Obsidian Order," he says. His voice echoes through the chapel, rich and full of authority. "We gather here tonight under the watchful eyes of our forebears, in the hallowed grounds of our ancestors, to celebrate the Crow's Covenant."

He pauses, letting his words sink in, his gaze sweeping across the room, locking briefly with every pair of masked eyes. "This ceremony is not merely a tradition. It is a rite of passage, evidence of the strength, loyalty, and unwavering commitment of those who stand ready to embrace the mantle of the crow."

Another pause, this time filled with the noise of movement as the attendees shift in the pews, the weight of his words pressing down on all of us. "To be a crow is to accept the burden of shadows, to operate within the veil of secrecy that protects our world. It is a life dedicated not to glory or honor, but to the silent safeguarding of balance and order. And absolute power."

He turns slightly, gesturing toward a row of tables beside the altar where an array of tools lie in wait, along with nine wooden chairs.

"Tonight, our newest recruits will receive their feathers, each one a symbol of a summons completed to the Order's exacting specifications. These are not mere decorations, but marks of achievement, of sacrifices made, and dangers braved in the service of our cause. Rise and reveal your wings."

With that, the man steps back, nodding to Xavier and the other recruits, a silent invitation to come forward and accept their new marks of honor. All at once, the young men remove their black T-shirts and a collective gasp ripples through the chapel.

It's drowned out by the sound of my heart breaking in two.

My eyes are drawn to Xavier, to the tapestry of scars and mutilated skin that covers his back. Each one tells a story of torture and abuse, every mark physical evidence of his past suffering. The urge to reach out, to somehow erase those years of pain, is overwhelming. Instead, I do what he told me to.

I keep my gaze solely focused on him.

Xavier takes his place among the others, his stance unyielding, a silent display of his inner fortitude. After they take their seats with their spines facing the audience, the lights dim, plunging the room into darkness. Then the UV lights lining the rafters flicker on, and that's when I see them—the outline of wings on my recruit's back.

The UV tattoo spans the entirety of his back as though he's able to take flight. The feathers are empty spaces, but their shapes are precise, giving them a realistic appearance. Under the proper lighting, this artwork is breathtaking.

The sound of buzzing soon fills the air as the tattoo artists are summoned from the pews and take up their position, along with their tools. I watch in fascination as the empty spaces within the feathers on Xavier's back start to get filled in. Under the glow of the UV lights, each stroke adds depth and dimension to the wings, transforming them from mere outlines into something alive, something pulsing with an unseen energy. It's a slow, meticulous process, but with each feather that gains its texture and color, the more magnificent the wings become.

A tap on my shoulder nearly makes me shriek. I whirl around, my heart in my throat, to find June. She has both arms propped on the pew and leans toward me. I squint in the dim lighting, barely able to make out the look of concern on her face.

"Hey," she whispers, her voice barely audible over the continuous noise of the tattoo guns. I stare at her, unable to believe she's risking conversation after the warning Xavier gave me. "There's something on your back. It's glowing under the UV lights."

My fingers flutter over the skin of my back, but my mind already knows what she's seeing.

It's Xavier's cum.

CHAPTER 49

DELILAH

Embarrassment slams into me, causing my face to burn with shame. It pairs with a sense of vulnerability and exposure that I hadn't anticipated experiencing tonight. I want to jump out the nearest window.

I glance around, catching glimpses of curious stares directed our way. "What . . . What is it?" I finally manage, my voice shaking. Fuck Xavier and his command for silence. If I make it out of here without screaming, it'll be a miracle.

June hesitates, her expression full of sympathy. "It's just one word. 'Mine.'"

I'm going to fucking kill Xavier.

It's a good thing he told me not to look at any other recruit because if I see a look of disappointment—or even worse, disgust—on Ben's face when he returns to his seat, I'm going to cry. Not to mention the fact that my foster brother is currently getting tattoos that signify he's killed people. If I don't look at him, I won't have confirmation of the number of lives he's taken.

As the ceremony progresses, my agitation grows. Along with my level of self-consciousness. One by one, the recruits return to their seats, their newly tattooed feathers flowing under the UV lights. I don't have to see them to hear their snickers or feel their gazes on my back.

Throughout my humiliation, Xavier remains at the front, the recruit with the most marks. I count them, and the heat of embarrassment leaves my cheeks, leaving me pale. He's been summoned ten times.

Xavier has killed at least ten people, if not more.

This part of the ritual is a validation of his skills, something he can show off with pride. I'm beginning to think he was right about being the best person to protect me from the Order.

Despite my admiration and fear of Xavier's exploits, my anger continues to rise. The word "Mine" written on my skin is a claim of possession, similar but dirtier than the brand on my shoulder. I know without a doubt this was a deliberate act meant to mark me as his in front of this assembly of the world's most dangerous individuals.

The real question is why? Did he do it to embarrass me? To put me in my place? Or is he so deranged that he believes marking me with his cum is what it takes to keep other men away from me?

My intuition says it's all of them.

As the final feather is filled in and Xavier rises from the chair and makes his way back to his seat, the complexity of my feelings for him is overwhelming. My skin is buzzing with energy, and my limbs are twitching. I'm torn between attacking and kissing the man beside me.

Xavier has driven me insane.

Admitting to myself that he's right for the second time in one evening really chaps my ass. When he said that I look at him like I want to kill and fuck him, he wasn't wrong. And still isn't.

When the regular lights flicker back to life, I smother a sigh of relief that the cum is no longer visible and glowing. Keeping my head bowed, I fold my hands in my lap to keep from strangling the man beside me.

Xavier, either uncaring or oblivious to my fury, grabs the back of my neck again. I stiffen under his touch. The pressure of his hold doesn't increase like I expect. Instead, he massages the side of my neck and the curve where it meets my shoulder.

The word "Mine" sits just under his tender ministrations, a declaration that ignites both anger and arousal.

The robed member, his presence as commanding as ever, returns to the altar, drawing the room's attention back to the front. And away from me. Thank God. If He's even listening to this cum-stained girl's prayer . . .

"The Crow's Covenant is complete," the man says.

His voice irritates me with its familiarity. Xavier's father. It took me the entire ceremony to figure it out, but now that I have, I want to get out of here even more.

"We have witnessed the embodiment of skill, dedication, and determination. Our recruits have not only accepted the marks of their accomplishments but have also embraced the weight of the responsibility those marks represent."

I try to tune him out, but with nothing else to concentrate on, I find myself absorbing his words. And the unspoken ramifications behind them.

"The Trials that lie ahead," the council member continues, his tone growing more solemn, "will be full of danger and the utmost challenge. They are designed to test not just your physical strength and skill, but your mental resilience, your loyalty, and your ability to adapt and overcome.

"You are the future of this Order, the guardians of our way of life. Rise to the challenge and may you emerge victorious."

With the ceremony officially over, the assembly gets to their feet. Xavier stands and pulls me up with him, his fingers still clasping the back of my neck. It's a possessive gesture that isn't necessary given the cum across the top of my spine.

I glare up at him and part my lips. He squeezes my neck with a shake of his head. "Not here," he says, so low I barely hear him.

We exit the chapel together, leaving behind the vaulted ceilings painted with angels and saints, while the word "Mine" burns invisibly on my skin. The silent claim leaves me with mixed emotions because I've never been more humiliated.

But I've also never felt more wanted.

After we leave the chapel, we walk down the tower stairwell and head outside. Xavier guides me deep into the forest instead of the side entrance leading to the main foyer. I remain quiet the entire time. Although it's been several minutes and we're alone, I'm not confident I can talk without yelling.

The cool night air nips at my skin, but the heat of my anger keeps me warm. Xavier eventually stops and turns to face me, his gaze searching mine in the moonlight that filters through the branches. I bite the inside of my cheek, trying not to stare at his torso.

His back might be scarred, but the rest of his body is perfect. His chest, abdomen, and biceps are toned, his muscles flexing as he removes his mask. The man is a masterpiece.

And there's his tattoos.

Xavier has several, most of them encircling his arms like sleeves, the black ink designs, intricate and detailed. I want to touch them, to trace their patterns, and to explore their meaning. Especially the single bird perched on a branch. No, it's a scar, the one I gave him.

"Delilah, I know you're pissed. I also know you like asking a million fucking questions. So, go ahead. Ask them."

His voice has me snapping to attention, bringing my gaze to his and my anger to the forefront of my mind like a shield. "Fine. Why did you write that word on my back?"

He steps forward and grabs my chin. His lips are inches from mine, his silver gaze piercing. "I don't want you to ever forget who you belong to. Not even for a second." He points in the direction of the castle off in the distance. "And those motherfuckers are the kind that would try to steal you from me. It was a message to you and to them."

Xavier knows about Eric threatening me. I've admitted everything else, so it's the only logical explanation for his behavior.

"Did you like humiliating me?" I whisper.

He tightens his grip on my chin, tipping my head back until I can't look away. "I'll tell the truth if you do."

"About what?"

"I want to know what Gage said to you. Word for fucking word."

"It doesn't matter if you end up trading me for Brenda."

He leans closer until the tip of his nose grazes mine and his fingers dig into my skin. "If you wanted my attention, then you fucking have it. Listen, because I'm only going to say this once. I'll *never* give you up. And I'll destroy anyone who tries to take you from me. If you look to another man for something I can give you, I'll show you just how possessive I can fucking be."

Xavier's expression darkens, but his eyes glint with something fierce. "Don't try to change the subject again. What did Gage say to you? Give me a reason to rip his fucking tongue out."

My heart is pounding so hard and fast that I'm starting to feel lightheaded. The way he says those words is so final, so sure, it scares the hell out of me. He did it once before to Frank, but I'm not worried about myself.

I don't want anything to happen to Xavier because of me.

"I'm going to tell you the truth, but I need to know something first," I say.

Xavier studies me, his gaze intense. Then he nods once. I take a step back and he lets his arm fall to his side.

"Okay." I pause as my thoughts collide with one another, all of them demanding to receive answers. I settle on the most important one, the very question that started this entire thing. "Why were you at the house three years ago?"

"My father sent me to watch over Benjamin. Without any uncles or cousins, he's the only heir to the McKenzie family."

"So it had nothing to do with me?"

Xavier slowly shakes his head. "No."

"Makes sense."

Something inside me dies. I can't explain why, but it shrivels, leaving me withering inside. Of course, Xavier didn't really want me. He killed Frank to protect Ben. I'm positive Xavier chose me as his bride just to piss off Eric. It was never about me.

He might want me now, but he didn't in the beginning.

"Eric said he's going to take what belongs to you, starting with me and ending with your empire," I say. "I don't know why you two have this rivalry going on, but from now on, leave me out of it."

I turn around to walk away, needing to be alone and sort my thoughts into something that makes sense. Xavier moves quickly, snatching my wrist and halting my steps. He pulls me toward him until the tips of our shoes are touching.

"Where are you going?" he asks.

"I'm leaving, so I won't punch you in the face."

He scoffs. "If you hit me, you'd better fucking run. Because when I catch you, I'm going to fuck that attitude right out of you."

"Are you serious?"

"Do it and find out."

I stare at him, his beauty an illusion to his viciousness. A contradiction of hard and soft, gentle and rough. This is a game of power, his dominance over my submission.

My heart pounds, adrenaline coursing through me. Xavier doesn't move. He merely lifts an eyebrow. That cocky expression is what sets me off.

I hit him so hard in the chin, I knock myself off-balance and my knuckles crack. Or is that the sound of my bones breaking?

Holy fuck balls, that hurt.

He massages his jaw, working out the ache. His eyes narrow in warning, but I'm already sprinting, his words trailing behind me.

"Run, little raptor."

CHAPTER 50

DELILAH

The forest becomes a blur as I dart between trees, their gnarled roots and low-hanging branches are mere obstacles in a game that's suddenly all too real. My breath comes in ragged gasps, the cool night air sharp in my lungs, but I push myself harder, driven by apprehension and anticipation.

Behind me, the night is quiet except for the sound of air rushing past my ears. I strain to hear any signs of Xavier moving through the darkness. He's not just following me.

He's hunting me.

The occasional rustle of leaves or the snap of a twig heightens the tension streaming through me.

This isn't like the Bride Hunt. This time, I *want* to be caught. Well, my body does. My mind isn't sure that submitting to Xavier is the wisest decision. And my heart . . . is confused by what he makes me feel. By the things he makes me yearn for.

I weave through the trees, my heart beating unsteadily, the pain in my knuckles forgotten. Every shadow that moves causes adrenaline to flood me until every sense is heightened and my skin tingles with the sensation of being watched.

I swear I can almost feel him closing in, his steps are measured and silent, like a ghost in the night. Until he catches me. Then he'll be completely flesh and blood.

Suddenly, he's there, staring at me through his mask. He emerges from the trees with a grace that belies his size. He doesn't grab me, doesn't try to stop me. Instead, he matches my pace, running alongside me.

I give him the middle finger and take off, pushing my body to the breaking point. My breaths are short, sharp bursts, and each one has pain streaking through my chest. Dots appear in my vision, and I rapidly blink them away.

Unsure if I'm successful in my getaway, I chance a look over my shoulder. The absence of his presence throws me off-kilter. I slow to a jog, glancing around, wondering if I've lost him or if he's given up the chase.

Until he wraps his arms around me from behind. My scream bounces off the trees, getting lost in the night. The thrill and surprise of being caught are quick to wear off when he drags me backward.

This is a test of wills between predator and prey, where the lines are blurred and the outcome is uncertain. Does he really plan on fucking me or was that an empty threat to scare me into obedience?

I dig my heels into the ground, losing one shoe and then the other. My struggle doesn't deter Xavier in the slightest. He continues taking me to an unknown destination.

Until the ceremonial altar comes into view.

I fight him with everything I have, my movements fueled by a panic brought on by my past experience in this place . . . and the arousal building at his domineering touch.

Xavier tightens his grip, and I thrash harder. He growls and flips me around to face him, his hand gripping my wrist. Still, I struggle.

"Let go."

When he doesn't answer me, I try to hit him again. My fist connects with his shoulder, but he doesn't loosen his hold. He grabs the back of my neck and pulls me close, his body pressing into mine.

"You played the game and lost," he says. "Now be a good girl and let me fuck you."

Xavier pushes me until the backs of my thighs hit the altar. He grabs my waist and lifts me up to set me on the stone, his gaze hot and hungry. My heart is a violent thunderstorm, the blood pounding through my veins. I'm both frightened and turned on by the intensity in his gaze, by the way his breathing has deepened.

Faster than I can blink, he grabs my throat and slams my back onto the flat surface, the air whooshing from my lungs. Before I can draw breath, he crawls on top of me and straddles me, his knees on either side of my hips, his face inches above mine. I have no idea what to expect, and he gives me no time to contemplate the possibilities.

He snaps a manacle in place.

My breath hisses between my teeth, and I tug against the restraint. "Take this off."

He answers me by securing my other wrist. I lie on the cold stone, staring up at the man responsible for my current situation.

Xavier leans over me. "This is supposed to be a consequence, but I don't think you'll feel that way by the end."

He removes a knife from his pocket, the blade glinting in the moonlight. My muscles clench as he trails the tip along my lace bodice, his gaze locked on mine, his other hand still on my throat. With a flick of his wrist, the blade slices through the delicate material.

He uses the knife's edge to peel back the fabric, and I gasp as the cold air hits my newly exposed skin. My nipples harden under his gaze, and I squeeze my thighs together to ease the ache building inside me. He continues running the knife over my dress, slicing through the layers until I'm in nothing except my bra and panties.

"Those are pretty," he says.

I hold my breath as Xavier traces patterns on my skin with the tip of the knife. But he never breaks the skin. He's playing with me, using my fear to heighten my arousal.

It's working.

Finally, he cuts through the remaining scraps of lace covering me and tosses them onto the ground. He sets the knife down next to me and runs his hand over my bare skin, his eyes on mine, his pupils contracting with lust.

I can't breathe. My breasts are heavy, aching for his attention. My pussy flutters, wanting to be stroked, to be filled. He's got me craving things I never imagined.

He drags his fingers down my stomach, over my clit, and along my pussy. I can picture him smiling behind his mask when he finds the dampness between my legs.

"You're so fucking wet for me."

He eases down my body, and I spread my thighs in invitation. It's not begging, but it's close.

"If I don't stretch you, you won't be able to take me," he says.

Xavier slides his finger inside, up to the first knuckle. I stiffen at the new sensation. He doesn't stop, just continues forward, until the heel of his palm is flush with my pussy.

"Fuck," he says. "You're going to kill me."

I can't get the words out to ask why because he starts moving his finger in and out, caressing the inside of me. I close my eyes and arch my back, my hips following the rhythm of his hand.

He adds a second finger and scissors them, stretching me further than before. He continues adding more force and power with every thrust. The chains on my wrists rattle in time to his movements.

"You like that?" he asks.

I open my eyes to look up at him and nod.

"Use your words, Delilah."

"Yes."

I moan when he hits a particularly sensitive spot inside me. My orgasm builds quickly, jolts of pleasure skittering through my body. The sensation becomes more intense with each passing moment, as does my desperation for relief.

"Xavier, faster."

"Not yet, pretty girl. We're just getting started."

His words are the only warning I receive before he inserts a third finger. I freeze until he starts fucking me with them. Of their own accord, my hips buck. His fingers are relentless, but he never increases his pace like I want.

"I need . . ." I say between pants. "More."

He lifts his head and withdraws his fingers from me. I stifle a groan of frustration. He's the one who has my body under his control, leaving me helpless to do anything except follow his orders. He's unraveling me, destroying my will with every touch and every kiss.

"Are you ready to beg, little raptor?"

CHAPTER 51

XAVIER

I stare down at Delilah, knowing I'll never see anything as beautiful as her wet and ready to take my cock. Fingering that fucking tight cunt of hers nearly pushed me over the edge, into a realm of madness that can only be relieved by fucking her until I pass out.

She might be the one who's chained, but I'm a slave to her.

My cock is so hard that one touch from her could be it. I can't allow her to ruin this for me, not when I've waited so long for this moment. If she hadn't sucked my dick earlier, I might not be able to hold back. Even now, if I don't get inside her soon, I'll lose my fucking mind.

"Tell me what I want to hear," I say.

She gazes up at me, her green eyes like grass, dewy with tears of frustration. Something I'm very familiar with. I've fucked my hand more than she'll ever know.

"What?" she asks.

"Beg me to fuck you." I briefly glance at the chains. "Those aren't coming off until you do."

She narrows her gaze in challenge, and I groan. My girl is feisty, and it makes pre-cum gather on the tip of my cock. It twitches, needing relief.

I'm quick to remove the rest of my clothing before straddling her once more. I stroke myself, watching her eyes follow my hand up and down. "You have no idea how many times I've thought about this. You, spread for me, your pussy dripping."

Her eyes widen when I lean forward and drag my cock along her slit and line it up with her pussy. Her wetness and my pre-cum mix together, making me grit my teeth with satisfaction. She's pushing me to my limits, so it's time to return the favor.

I tease her, using the tip of my cock to draw circles on her clit. Delilah moans and shifts underneath me, trying to find relief, but there won't be any. I need her to break so I can put her back together in a design of my choosing.

"Either fuck me or don't," she hisses.

I click my tongue at her. "That's not begging."

"I won't."

"You *will.* I've waited three fucking years for this. Do you think I won't prolong it for another hour or two?"

She licks her lips. "What?"

"I haven't fucked anyone since the night I met you, and nothing is going to stop me from hearing you choose me."

"I have."

"Then fucking say it."

When she shakes her head, I stop gripping my dick to wrap my fingers around her throat. I squeeze until her lips part, the sound of her ragged breathing making my balls tighten.

"The next fucking word out of your mouth better be 'please.'"

"Please," she gasps.

I tilt my head. "What was that?"

She struggles in earnest, her skin changing color. "Please, Xavier."

I release her neck to line up my cock with her cunt and drive it as deep as I can when she sucks in a breath. Her gasp fills my ears, but I'm still waiting for her scream. I'm not even halfway in.

Delilah is so fucking tight. Her pussy clenches around me, the walls of her cunt gripping me like a fist. It feels so fucking good, her heat and wetness enveloping my cock. It's like heaven and hell all at once.

She's going to fucking kill me.

I slide my hand around the nape of her neck to anchor her to me as I thrust my hips forward, claiming another inch of her pussy. And then another. She groans, the sound vibrating through her body and straight to my cock. It pulses, ready to fuck her raw.

But I won't. Not yet. I want to savor every part of her.

I keep pressing deeper until I'm filling her, until she claws my back, drawing blood as I take her virginity, drawing hers. No one has ever been inside her, and no one else ever fucking will. The moment is so intense that I pause, wanting to commit every single detail to memory. But it doesn't last long because my need to fuck her takes over.

I pull out almost completely before ramming back into her, forcing her body to accept me. My pace becomes rough and demanding, my grip bruising. I don't stop, not when her nails rake down my back, over my tattooed feathers. I don't stop when she whimpers into my shoulder right before her teeth sink into my flesh.

I want to claim her. And I am. Her body is mine.

"Look at me," I say.

It takes a moment, but her eyes find mine, the green glittering like emeralds. The sight of her looking up at me, full of my cock with my cum on her back, makes me thrust harder, faster, deeper.

"You feel this?" I ask, slamming into her again, the chains rattling loudly. "This is real. This is what I've protected for three years, what I've waited for. What I'll never fucking share."

I punctuate the statement with another hard thrust, the force causing her body to slide up, her hair spilling over the edges of the altar. Delilah moans and lifts her hips, her eyes glazed with lust.

The sight is almost too much. My possessive nature and her acceptance of it is my undoing.

I grab the chain connected to the manacle and yank her toward me, the movement forcing me deeper inside her, tearing a cry from her lips. I can't take my eyes off of her, the way she responds to me, her skin flushed and glistening with sweat.

Her moans increase in volume and frequency as her pussy gets wetter. I drive as deep as I can go, wanting this to last but knowing she needs relief. As long as it's when *I* say, my girl always gets to come first.

I reach out and grab her throat. "I just need a little bit more."

Her cunt squeezes me as if to give me what I want. Every minute spent inside Delilah is fucking perfection. She takes me so beautifully, even though she's gasping for air.

"Come for me," I say, releasing her throat.

My command is all she needs. Her pussy contracts, and her body jerks. She screams my name. The sound of it sets off my orgasm, and I fill her with my cum, the force of it making my vision blur.

When I blink, she comes into focus. She's the most beautiful woman I've ever seen. And she's all mine.

CHAPTER 52

DELILAH

The morning sun shines through the purple curtains, casting a violet shadow across the floor. I tug at the hem of my skirt, trying to decide if it's too short for me.

"It's not going to get any longer, no matter how much you pull on it," Raven says. She watches me from her bed with a textbook propped open in her lap, her mouth twisted in amusement. "But your legs are banging."

"Thanks."

"Is that skirt for X? Better access and all that?"

I meet her gaze and a flush spreads over my cheeks. "No, it's for me. I'm feeling sexy today."

When I look at myself in the mirror, I see the same face, but underneath I'm a completely different person. The woman who stares back at me has a sparkle in her eyes, a sensual smile, and her shoulders squared with confidence. Xavier put those there.

"You know, you never confirmed if he's as hung as people say." When I shoot her a look, she shrugs. "You can't blame Sherlock for gathering clues."

My flush spreads, crawling down my neck. "I'm going to confirm, and then we're never going to speak about it again. Yes, he's huge."

I feel the aftereffects of him fucking me every time I take a step. It reminds me of what happened between us, and then my pussy flutters, making everything worse. I'm going to have to take painkillers all day.

"I fucking knew it," Raven says with a salacious grin. "I'm happy for you. Insanely jealous but happy."

I duck my head. "Thanks. Are you sure this skirt isn't too short?"

Raven waves a hand. "Nah, you look amazing."

"I'll see you in the library this afternoon?"

"Yeah," she says. "As long as you don't ditch me for your boyfriend."

I'm of half a mind to tell her that Xavier and I aren't together like that, but the truth doesn't matter. June said that the best lies are steeped in truth, and I'm going to run with that.

"I won't. See you in a bit."

I grab my backpack and sling my purse over my shoulder before walking out of the door. As I make my way down the hallway and outside, I retrieve my cell phone. My eyes widen at the number of texts waiting for me. Seeing Xavier's name on the screen has my heart beating faster.

Xavier: That skirt is too short.

Xavier: Take it off or I will.

Xavier: I mean it, little raptor.

Xavier: Answer me.

I look at the time on my phone and bite my lip. If I go back upstairs and change, then I'll be late for class. Xavier is going to have to be pissed.

Xavier: Stop biting your lip. Unless you're trying to get me to fuck myself. I don't think the professor would appreciate that.

Delilah: How do you know what I'm wearing and what I'm doing? Stalker much?

Xavier: It's not stalking when I own you.

Delilah: *Rolls eyes*

Xavier: Your legs and that pussy between them are mine.

Delilah: What about the rest of me?

Xavier: Every. Single. Inch.

I hurriedly text him back as I walk through the doors of my first class. The way he talks to me makes me angry but also turns me on. I don't understand him or myself.

Delilah*:* I can't change until after my second class. I don't have the time.

Xavier: If you don't change, I'll punish you.

Delilah: You want me to suck your dick again? Maybe I'll like it.

Xavier: If that's the case, then you'll love what comes next.

Delilah: Don't you know what a joke is?

He doesn't reply to my text, and I'm left wondering if his words are a promise or a threat.

I'm quick to dismiss all thoughts of Xavier as I take my seat and retrieve my laptop.

Luckily for me, my first class goes by quickly after taking notes for an hour straight. When I get up to leave, I find that the painkillers have done their job, and I haul ass to Professor Ames's class.

Dread coats the inside of my stomach, making me queasy. I haven't seen him in class since I became Xavier's bride. I'm sure he was there for the Crow's Covenant ceremony, but he was wearing a mask like everyone else, hiding his identity. Meanwhile, I was sitting there with Xavier's cum on my back.

My face burns as I walk into the lecture hall. I settle in the chair at the very back of the room, putting as much distance between us as possible. After triple-checking that my phone is on silent, I wait for class to begin.

The second Professor Ames strides into the room, my embarrassment morphs into irritation. This man falsely accused me of cheating and forced me into signing a contract that gave Xavier the right to control me. Righteous indignation rises in me, and I grit my teeth while keeping my eyes on my computer screen.

Another student drops into the chair next to me. I ignore him, but he doesn't do the same. His gaze slides over me, pausing on my legs before traveling back up to my breasts. When his eyes meet mine, he grins.

"You look familiar," he says. "Have we met?"

I shake my head.

"Maybe we should. I'm Victor."

"I'm not interested," I whisper, giving him a pointed stare.

"Too bad. You look like you'd be fun."

I silently fume the entire lecture. By the time class ends, I'm more than ready to get the hell out of here. I shove my personal belongings into my backpack and head toward the door.

Victor falls into step beside me, his long legs easily keeping up with my fast pace. I glare up at him.

"Can I help you?"

"Yeah, I was hoping you'd let me take you out on a date."

"My boyfriend wouldn't like that," I say.

It's not a lie exactly. Xavier may not be my boyfriend, but he definitely wouldn't like me dating someone else. Even having this type of conversation with another man is enough to piss him off.

As if conjured by my thoughts, my phone pings, notifying me about a text from Xavier.

Xavier: Tell him to fuck off, or I will.

Delilah: Seriously, how do you know what's happening?

Xavier: It doesn't matter. Get rid of him.

Victor glances at my phone and shrugs. "I'm not worried about your boyfriend."

"You should be."

"Why? What's the worst he'll do? Fight me?"

I snort. "No." *More like kill you.* "Listen, I'm not going to tell you again; I'm not interested."

He exhales, a mixture of frustration and resignation. "Whatever. You know where to find me if you change your mind."

"I won't," I mutter.

I make my way across campus to the library, eager to get away from stupid men and their presumptions about me. Another text notification lights up my phone, and I check it with a sigh.

Xavier: Is he gone?

Delilah: As my stalker, shouldn't you know the answer to that?

Xavier: Don't push me.

With a grin, I step inside the library. The atmosphere relieves me of my tension, and I relax a little. After a few minutes, I locate Raven sitting at one of the many tables in the center of the large room, a coffee next to her notebook.

"Ready to study?" I ask.

"Meh."

I almost laugh. "I don't want to either, but it's part of the college experience, right?"

"I'd rather shove a pine cone up my ass."

We settle into our study session, flipping through textbooks and jotting down notes. It's a comfortable silence, punctuated by the occasional whisper from nearby students and the shuffle of turning pages. I'm so absorbed in my task that the rest of the world falls away.

Until the energy in the air shifts.

It starts with a glance, then another, until it feels like the entire library is looking at me. My skin prickles with anxiety and a knot forms in my stomach. I try to shake off the sensation of being watched, telling myself that I'm paranoid and imagining things.

Raven snaps up her head, her gaze scanning the room. "What the fuck is everyone staring at?"

I shrug.

"The fire alarm isn't going off, but everyone looks like their asshole is burning."

She scrunches her face in confusion, her brows knitting together. Her cell phone makes a buzzing sound, and she unlocks the screen, her eyes darting back and forth.

"Blimey!"

"Everything okay?" I ask.

"Well, my dear Watson, it looks as though we have a case on our hands."

I frown. "What?"

"Xavier just updated his relationship status."

"Huh?"

"He made it official. You two are 'in a relationship.'" She glances around the room before returning her attention back to me. "Apparently, everyone is freaking the fuck out. It's the first time he's ever done that, and I've known him since middle school."

She shoves her phone in my face. The display is on the social media site, and she taps the profile picture. Sure enough, a status update is the first thing I see.

Xavier Donovan: Obsessed with Delilah Scott.

Relationship: Taken.

Comment: Delilah is mine. Everyone else can fuck off.

"Bloody hell," I mumble, my accent horrible compared to Raven's.

She laughs and throws her arm around me, pulling me close. I want to disappear when she clears her throat.

"Listen up, everyone, my roomie here has the magic pussy that *snatched* X. Pun intended. Now, be good boys and girls and mind your fucking business. Please and thank you."

My cheeks burn, and I stare down at her phone, blinking in disbelief. The post has only been up for two minutes, but it already has hundreds of likes and shares. Raven drops her arm and turns to me.

"So, are you going to move in with him now?"

I shake my head. "No, I need my own space."

"You're always welcome in the den of poetic chaos."

"Thank you. Do you think we can go back to studying?"

"Erm . . . I don't think so, Watson."

She angles her head, and I follow the unspoken direction to find Xavier standing a few feet away.

CHAPTER 53

DELILAH

Xavier walks over to the table and plants his hands on the flat surface, leaning toward me until I can see his gray eyes swirling with possessiveness.

"You didn't change your clothes," he says quietly.

My gaze widens, and my heart leaps. Straight into my pussy. It starts pulsing at the sight of him.

"I was busy," I say. "Class, remember?"

Raven gets to her feet and grabs her books. "I think this is my cue to go. If you need me, roomie, I'll be in the dorm room."

"Okay, bye," I say, keeping my gaze on Xavier.

As soon as she's gone, he snatches my wrist and pulls me to my feet. I gaze up at him, unsure of what he wants.

"Follow me," he says.

He tightens his grip as I trail behind him, his pace so fast I have to jog to keep up. The students we pass watch us, their expressions ranging from shocked to curious. A few even smirk.

I yank against his hold, but Xavier only increases his speed. "Where are we going?" I ask.

He turns down another row of books, leading me deeper into the stacks. "We need to talk."

"Can't we do that in the middle of the library?"

He shakes his head and rounds the corner, finally coming to a stop at the end of the aisle. I look around, finding us completely alone and surrounded by shelves of books.

Xavier releases me and steps forward, trapping me between a short bookcase and his body. "Do you know how dangerous it is for you to disobey me?" he asks, his tone low and threatening.

"I have a feeling you're about to tell me."

"You've pushed me all day," he says. "It's like you want me to fuck that attitude right out of you."

"I'm pretty sure you tried to last night."

He smirks at me. "Obviously it wasn't hard enough."

His eyes flash with intent, right before he spins me around. He places a hand between my shoulder blades and shoves me forward, forcing me to bend over and grab the low shelf. I have a moment to react, to process what's happening. But then he leans into me, his erection digging into my ass.

Arousal hits me hard, and I close my eyes. "Are you serious?"

"Absolutely," he whispers.

"If anyone comes back here, they'll see us."

"You'll have to be quiet then, won't you?"

"Xavier—"

He silences my protest by slipping his hands underneath my skirt and dragging it up, exposing me. Cool air caresses my thighs, followed by his warm touch. It burns me.

Xavier cups my pussy with a groan. "You're soaked. Is it because you like the idea that someone else might see how wet you get for me? How desperate you are to come?"

I can't answer because he rips my panties, leaving me gasping. He runs his fingers along my slit and then spreads the dampness all over my clit. I bite back a moan as he works my body, making me delirious with lust.

He removes his hand and I whimper. The rustle of clothing is followed by skin-to-skin contact, making me sigh. He presses against me, his cock settling against the seam of my ass. I shift, lifting my hips, wanting him inside me.

"Is this what you want?" he asks.

I bite my lip, waiting for him to push forward.

"Say it, Delilah. Use your words."

"Please."

He lines up his cock and slams into me. I groan at the fullness, as well as the soreness that returns. My pain makes my pleasure all the better.

"Fuck," he says, his breath skimming the back of my neck.

He grips my hips and drives into me, pushing me against the bookshelf. The wood digs into my palms and bruises my flesh, but I barely register the discomfort. It's nothing compared to the feeling of Xavier inside me.

"You feel so fucking good," he says.

He increases his pace, the sound of our bodies slapping together echoing off the shelves around us. I press my lips together, trying to keep quiet, but the way he's fucking me makes it impossible. A moan slips from me when he angles his cock and it hits deeper than before.

"Be quiet, little raptor." He reaches around and slaps my panties against my lips. "Open."

When I do, he shoves the underwear inside my mouth. He drives his cock into me even harder than before. It's almost like he wants someone to see us. His thrusts are so deep and powerful that I'm forced onto my tiptoes. My breasts rub against the rough surface of the shelf, sending tingles across my skin.

My pleasure builds quickly, the tension in my lower belly growing. It's a delicious sensation, but not enough. Xavier doesn't let me get too close, denying me the release I crave. Instead, he keeps his pace steady and rough, his fingers digging into my hips, his grip bruising. The heat of his body envelops me, his chest pressed against my back, his mouth on my neck, his breath tickling my skin.

"I love the way you fuck," he says. "The way you take my cock."

I whimper again, his words causing my pussy to spasm.

"That's it," he says. "Take what I give you."

The words aren't just a command. They're a demand and a promise.

And I'm gone.

Pleasure rips through me, stealing the breath from my lungs and the strength from my legs. My vision goes white, and my ears fill with a ringing sound. Xavier fucks me through it, his pace never slowing.

"That's a good girl," he says. "Give it to me. Every breath, every moan."

After a few more thrusts, his body tenses. He drives his cock deep, burying himself inside me, his fingers leaving imprints in my flesh. Then he stills, his breathing labored and his body slick with sweat.

Xavier rests his head on my back, his arms wrapped around me, our bodies joined. It's only when I begin to tremble from the effort of holding this position that he eases out of me and adjusts his clothing.

He helps me to stand, his hands moving to fix my skirt and remove the panties from my mouth. His gaze locks onto mine. "Next time I tell you not to wear that skirt, you'd better listen."

"Yes, sir," I mutter, putting my underwear back on.

His lips twitch. "Good girl."

Xavier wraps an arm around my waist and pulls me closer. My knees are wobbly, and I sag against him. His eyes roam over my face, and he presses his lips to mine, kissing me softly. I return the kiss, wrapping my arms around his neck.

He pulls back with a groan. "We have to stop, or I'll fuck you again."

I nod, still reeling from the intensity of the moment and the tenderness that followed. Xavier's protective demeanor doesn't wane as he guides me back to the tables where my personal belongings lie unattended. The juxtaposition of his earlier dominance with his current gentleness creates a whirlwind of emotions inside me.

As we exit the library, I lean into him, finding an unexpected comfort in his nearness. The fear and adrenaline that surged through me when we first met began to dissipate more and more with every interaction between us. Now, because of his protectiveness and affection, my perception of him is starting to change. For the first time in my life, I feel safe.

And it's with an assassin.

CHAPTER 54

XAVIER

Delilah sighs in my arms, her body relaxed with sleep, her skin warm against mine. I can't imagine anything better. I think this emotion is . . . happiness.

It's strange. New. Unknown to me.

She's brought me to life after being dead inside.

The atmosphere around us is peaceful, yet there's a restlessness within me. Anticipation sweeps through my blood and heats my veins. It's only a matter of time until the Trials begin. My only concern is getting through them with enough points to keep Delilah.

She hums, the tiny sound dragging me out of my churning thoughts. I brush back her hair, and she instinctively snuggles closer to me, grinding her ass against my cock. I love the way she fights me with her words, but her body is mine to control. It obeys me like a good soldier, following my every command.

I slip my hand between her thighs and lightly grab her cunt. It's soft and warm, teasing me without even trying. But it's still dry. I lift my head, placing my mouth next to her ear, my breath grazing the side of her neck.

"Delilah," I murmur, drawing out every syllable of her name like a prayer. There's no redemption for me, but I'll still worship her until I die.

The change in her is immediate. She shifts and mumbles in her sleep, gently grinding against my hand. A streak of dampness now covers my palm.

I smile in the darkness. It only took one fucking word to make her wet for me. Even while asleep, her subconscious recognizes my voice and shows me what she wants. The only thing left to do is give it to her.

I glide my fingers through her slit, and her arousal coats them, drenches them. Against my chest, I can feel her heart rate increasing, her chest rising and falling faster, her skin growing warmer. I play with her clit slowly, not wanting her to wake up just yet.

A moan leaves her lush mouth, and Delilah tilts her hips, begging me without words. I slip a finger inside her. Her hips jerk at the penetration, forcing her to arch her back, her perfect tits jutting forward. I slide my other arm underneath her waist and drag her back to me, adding another finger and shoving them deep.

The groan that hits the air is sultry, needy, and fucking sexy.

I grit my teeth and force myself to withdraw my hand from her pussy in favor of replacing it with my cock. I grip her leg and lift it so that it's draped over mine. In this position I have complete access to her.

Delilah grunts when I slam my cock home. She's so fucking tight. Even after I've taken her cunt over and over. It still grips me, her pussy fluttering with pleasure, the sensation so intense my eyes roll back.

"Xavier?"

I pull out and ram back inside her.

The next time she says my name, it's a moan, not a question. The third time, it's not a word, but pure sound, full of desperation and desire.

The urge to move becomes overwhelming, so I fuck her. My thrusts are rough and demanding. She shifts to accommodate them and grabs my forearm against her stomach, digging her nails into my skin.

She grunts when I push deep inside and moans when I withdraw, the sounds growing louder and more frequent. Those noises have me teetering on the edge of sanity. It doesn't matter how many times I've had her. It'll never be enough.

Her pussy tightens around me, getting wetter with every thrust, making my dick twitch. Her hips follow the rhythm of mine, submitting to my demands and my pacing. And her nails draw my blood before clawing at the sheets.

My girl is close.

I reach up to grip her throat, resting my thumb on her pulse. It flickers wildly at my touch. She always responds, even in the barest of ways, and it drives me fucking crazy.

"Give me your mouth," I say, barely able to get the words out.

She turns her head, and I crash my lips against hers, devouring her moans. I drive my tongue into her mouth, taking possession of it, just like I'm owning her pussy. I drive my hips forward, the force of the movement shoving her up the mattress, but I bring her right back.

I want her closer.

Need her close.

Her skin is so hot I swear it's melting into mine. I break the kiss, and her breath comes out in a rush, the sound punctuated by a whimper. Then she leans into me, trying to take me deeper. Her cunt is greedy. Just how I want it.

The pressure inside me builds, my balls tightening and my cock throbbing. But she *has* to come first. I won't accept anything else.

"You have three seconds to come," I say, squeezing her throat. "I'm not going to last with your tight pussy gripping me like this."

"Three."

I dig my fingers into her belly and pull her onto my cock.

"Two."

I drive deep and hard.

"One."

I release her throat. "Now, Delilah."

She stiffens, her entire body tense. Then she screams. Her intense reaction sets me off.

"That's right." I rake my teeth over her earlobe. "Take it. Take what's yours."

I don't stop fucking her. I can't. My need for her is too great, and her body is giving me exactly what I want. Complete surrender.

I wish her heart would do the same.

I keep driving into her, wanting her pleasure to last. The tremors wracking her cunt squeeze me so tightly that I have no choice but to come. I release inside her, filling her with my cum, wishing I could fill her with my baby. Not yet, but one day. For now, it's good she's on birth control.

Our ragged breathing hits the air while our hearts pound in our chests. I can feel hers working hard against my fingers on her throat.

"Xavier?"

I brush my lips along her shoulder, leaving a trail of kisses. "Hm?"

"Can I go back to sleep now?"

I smile before nipping at her skin. "Yeah, you can."

She releases a sigh, full of contentment. Satisfaction washes over me, a bliss I've never experienced until I fucked her for the first time. If I could make her body my home, I would.

The world doesn't exist when I'm with Delilah. The people in it don't matter. And time is irrelevant unless I spend it with her.

I lie there, awake and still buried deep inside her, long after Delilah has gone back to sleep. My thoughts, once peaceful, slowly compound until I'm clenching my jaw. The sense of foreboding returns.

The room is silent except for Delilah's soft breathing, a gentle sound that contrasts sharply with the turmoil inside me. I lift my head to look down at her, needing to see her face. A smile tugs at my lips. I love the sight of her in my bed, her long limbs tangled in the sheets.

My gaze runs over her smooth skin, lingering on the swell of her breasts and the curve of her hip. I trace the same path with my fingers, memorizing the shape and feel of her body. I savor the warmth and softness of her, the way she fits perfectly against me.

Every inch of her was made for me.

She is the picture of innocence in the moonlight filtering in through the curtains. But the life I've been forced into won't allow her to stay that way unless I protect her from its violence. She's already gotten a taste despite my best efforts.

The knock on the door is barely discernible, but to my senses it might as well be a gunshot. It sends a jolt through me, and my entire body stiffens with alarm. It's nearly 4 a.m., but the Order operates on its own timelines.

I hesitate. And it's because of the woman in my arms. The idea of leaving her fucks with my head, but I don't have a choice.

Not wanting to wake her for a second time, I slip from the bed. However, I can't stop myself from placing a kiss on the side of her neck, flicking my tongue over her pulse, loving how it jumps at my touch. She stirs, a slight frown crossing her face before she settles again, and my chest tightens at the sight.

This fucking girl . . .

If the Order doesn't kill me, she'll be the death of me.

CHAPTER 55

XAVIER

I dress quickly. Each piece of clothing feels like armor, a barrier against the uncertainty of what's to come. The Order calls, you answer. You just don't know what you've agreed to.

After checking the monitor next to the door, I open it. The crow waiting for me on the other side nods once. "It's time."

I resist the urge to look back at Delilah one more time. I can't risk it. No one can know what she means to me, and a single glance could give me away.

I step into the hallway and shut the door. It locks with a soft click, and I take solace in the fact that Delilah's safe. As we walk through the quiet halls of the castle, my thoughts are of her. I make myself suppress the memories of her, along with the feelings she evokes.

If I'm to pass whatever test lies before me, I can't be distracted.

The chill of the early morning air pricks my skin as we ascend the winding staircase to the roof of the castle. The stone beneath is smooth, its texture refined by countless soldiers climbing these very steps in preparation for battle. We emerge at the top, and the expanse of the night sky greets me, the moon hanging overhead like a silent witness, providing the only light available.

The roof itself is a large, flat space, designed with functionality in mind instead of aesthetics. Battlements rise like teeth against the skyline, offering protection and a panoramic view of the surrounding area. This high up, the air is crisp, carrying the scent of pine and oak. Below, the castle walls stretch out like a maze of stone and shadow, a fortress guarding its secrets.

And the Obsidian Order.

In a straight line are the ten leaders. They wear their ceremonial black robes and masks, as well as silence. Like their clothing, it's meant to create mystery and unease.

I catch my father's eye, but it's only for a moment. He said they'd be watching, and he was right. The atmosphere is thick with tension, the quiet only disturbed by my arrival and the occasional shuffle of feet or the soft rustle of fabric.

Everyone's attention is on the platform in the middle of the rooftop. My adrenaline kicks up a notch at the sight. It's reminiscent of a gallows, constructed from wood, now weathered and aged. It rises a few feet from the ground, supported by sturdy beams that ensure its stability.

It's a fucking stage.

An ominous presence lingers in the air, combining with the anticipation of the men nearby. In the center of this platform is a wooden board. It's fashioned from tight-grain wood, mounted to a stand, and positioned at an optimal height for knife-throwing practice.

Then there's the blood, fresh and wet, still traveling along the wood in rivulets that look black in the night.

I scan the area, my veins icing over at the tarp-covered bodies scattered about. Three of them, to be exact. My guess is they're recruits who failed to pass the test.

That won't be me.

One of the leaders, Leonard Gage, ruler of the drug empire, raises his hand. My father goes taut beside him, but I keep my gaze on my rival's predecessor.

"Xavier Donovan," he says, "you stand before us at the threshold of your first Trial. This is not merely a test of skill, but a measure of your resolve, your dedication to the principles that bind this Order together."

The group of them nod, their minute movements reflecting the solemnity of this event. Gage gestures toward the wooden target. "This right of passage will transform you from recruit to crow, from soldier to leader. You are granted but a single attempt. The knife you throw must not only reach the target, but it must embed itself in the wood, a symbol of your deep commitment to this brotherhood. Miss and you fail. If the knife doesn't remain secure in the wood, and falls to the ground, you fail. Succeed, and you affirm your spot in the remaining Trials."

He retrieves a knife from his cloak and hands it to me. I take it, familiarizing the weight of it before I run out of time. My focus narrows, but he interrupts my concentration with a simple wave of the hand.

"Hold. Your target arrives."

I look from the wooden target to the woman being dragged onto the rooftop. Delilah's blindfolded, her movements hindered by restraints, and a gag stifles any protest she might have. The moon bathes her in an ethereal glow, her bridal gown bright in the darkness.

Inside, I'm an accumulation of fury, rage, and wrath all combined into one tempest threatening to combust. Outside, I remain stoic, my expression bored. The leaders watch me, their gazes scrutinizing behind their masks.

This isn't merely a test of skill. It's one of loyalty.

The sick and twisted pieces connect to form a clear picture of what's expected of me. They're searching for a reaction from me at seeing her vulnerable. And harmed.

The wooden platform is now something sinister, a stage that's become an altar. One I must sacrifice her on. Even at a distance, her confusion and fear are heavy, her body tense.

A crow shoves her against the board, wetting her skin with blood and staining her dress with red. They rip the blindfold from her eyes and the gag from her mouth.

"Xavier!"

Hearing the longing in her voice nearly fucking breaks me. The visceral reaction within me has my skin vibrating. My hands shake as I fiddle with the knife, disguising my fury by tossing the weapon casually.

"Don't move, bride," I say.

Delilah freezes, but her gaze zips back and forth, her pupils expanding with fear. The instant her eyes land on the bodies nearby, she straightens, her spine so rigid it might snap.

I stand there, my gaze fixed on her with a detached expression completely at odds with the emotions inside me. The ones brought to life because of her. She's my weakness. My little raptor.

"Stand up straight," I say. "Hold completely still."

Her inner fire warms the coldness of her fear, the sparks flaring in her eyes. "Why?"

"Because I fucking said so, bride."

Without moving, I flick my gaze to the body nearest to her. Now I wonder if they're targets who tried to flee instead of dead recruits. Delilah tracks my eye movement and returns her attention to me with the barest of nods. Pride washes over me at the sight of her lifting her chin and pressing her back flush to the wood behind her. She balls her fists at her sides, keeping her arms straight.

Delilah stares at me and nowhere else, as if tethered to me body, mind, and soul. Her absolute trust nearly brings me to my knees.

After this, I'm going to lose it. And any hope of her loving me.

I raise the knife, knowing I only have one chance to get this right. The years of practice flood my memory and strengthen my grip. I focus on her abdomen, specifically the area void of vital organs, near the outer edge. There's less risk of permanent damage.

And death.

I can't hesitate or I won't put enough power behind the throw and immediately fail. I'm confident in my skill, but, fuck, am I reluctant.

If I don't hurt her, they'll know I love her.

And she'll be killed.

Breathe. Aim. Release.

Delilah's scream rings out, along with the thud of the knife striking wood. I fist my hands to refrain from going to her as blood spreads from the wound, covering her dress. She lifts a hand, her fingers fluttering over the knife's handle as she stares at it with disbelief.

Then she whispers my name.

It's a broken sob, one that guts me where I stand.

After a lifetime of torture, nothing has ever wounded me more than the look of betrayal in Delilah's eyes.